THE
WHITECHAPEL
MURDERS
&
MARY JANE
KELLY

Peter Caldwell

New Generation **Publishing**

Contents

Foreword

Over the years, many books have been published claiming to identify that most elusive of killers, Jack the Ripper, and this has always seemed rather suspicious. There appeared to be just too many theories, too many suspects. It was almost as if someone wanted it to be that way, to muddy the waters, to prevent the truth from being discovered.

Then the books, Jack the Ripper: The Final Solution, by Stephen Knight (1976), and The Ripper & The Royals, by Melvyn Fairclough (1991), were published, and these finally dragged the killer from the seemingly inaccessible sanctuary into which he had been placed by others for security - and should have destroyed the long-accepted myth of Jack the Ripper once and for all, since the books demonstrated that the 1888 killings were not the work of a solitary killer who murdered at random, but were in fact organized killings, their motive being directly connected with the British Monarchy.

Through further research we now discover additional details about the victims and their families, and why each successful murder did not, as they expected it should, lead the killers back to their main target, the woman whom they knew by name, the woman who had to be tracked down and killed at all costs - Mary Jane Kelly.

In this book we see how four of the five murders were carried out in a coach, and the most likely modus operandi of the Miller's-court murder.

Evidence is shown that Stride *did* have grapes in one of her hands. New light is shed on the significance of the brass rings and coins, and on the piece of muslin and the comb which were laid out beside Chapman; on the cachous in Stride's other hand; and on the subtle clues which Walter Sickert inserted into several of his paintings.

The date of the Mary Jane Kelly murder is examined for the first time. Although desperate to kill her, her home was kept under surveillance for several weeks. Why was this? Was Kelly's a ritual murder, the timing being specifically selected? Could the day chosen by the killer to complete his grisly work have been of such significance to him that it was almost essential that the murder of the most important target of all be carried out then?

This book not only produces *proof* of the involvement of the heir to the Crown, Prince Albert Victor, with the low-born Annie Elizabeth Crook, which resulted in the birth of a daughter, but also furnishes evidence that the Whitechapel murders were sanctioned and orchestrated by powerful men, men such as the Commissioner of the Metropolitan Police, Sir Charles Warren, who were self-motivated to protect the status quo of the British Establishment.

Also introduced are fresh revelations about the murders, and finally uncovered are the hitherto unknown origins and personal details of the woman who has until now been shrouded in mystery - *Mary Jane Kelly.*

And, was she really a Police Agent as Inspector Frederick Abberline implied in his diary, and did she actually die in Miller's-court? Were the entries in the Abberline diary as straightforward as they seemed to be - *or was the diary itself part of the elaborate cover-up?*

In the aftermath of the Whitechapel murders, also revealed is how the attempt by the Victorian Royal Family to protect Prince Albert Victor from being further implicated in the Cleveland Street male brothel scandal of 1889 rebounded, leading to more accusations and a further cover-up over the birth in 1890 of another child - this time a son.

Also brought to light by the declaration in 1892 that the Duke of Clarence (Prince Albert Victor's new title) had died at Sandringham, is the unreliability of Royal death pronouncements, and the most likely place of his death is disclosed.

Chapter 1

Illuminating the Darkness

The number of victims of many serial killers far exceed those of the Jack the Ripper murders in the Whitechapel district of London's East End in 1888, but it is the name bestowed on the murderer, the ferocity of the method of killing, the terror associated with the murders, and the killer's astonishing ability to seemingly vanish like a phantom into the night after completing his grisly work, which has seared the murders indelibly into the human psyche.

Various individuals have been theorised as being the killer. Amongst those put forward have been Aaron Kosminski, Neil Cream, James Maybrick, James Kenneth Stephen, Alexander Pedachenko, Thomas Cutbush, Montague Druitt, the Duke of Clarence, Michael Ostrog, Joseph Isenschmid, and Severin Klosowski. It has even been suggested that the Ripper was a woman. No lack of conjecture, for sure, as to possible suspects, but a motive for the murders has always been conspicuous by its absence. The murders have always been classed as murder by person unknown, random killings by some madman with a hatred of prostitutes.

Then, in 1973, an artist named Joseph Sickert, son of the famous Victorian painter Walter Sickert, said that he was prepared to reveal the mystery of Jack the Ripper and 'name everyone involved in the blackmail conspiracy and cover-up.'

Joseph Sickert's account appeared in the East London Advertiser, where he stated that there was indeed a motive behind the Jack the Ripper murders, and that this motive was directly involved with his own family:

'My grandmother was a poor shop girl working in Cleveland Street (near Tottenham Court Road in London's West End). My father lived opposite. My father had been asked by Princess Alexandra to take her son Prince Albert Victor under his wing, out of the confining circles of the court.' [Princess Alexandra was married to the Prince of Wales, so Prince Albert Victor - later made Duke of Clarence - was Queen Victoria's grandson, and heir presumptive to the throne. This request from a member of the Royal family to an artist may seem odd, but Princess Alexandra was Danish, the daughter of King Christian IX of Denmark. Both Walter Sickert's grandfather Johann, and his father Oswald, had been employed by the Danish Royal Family. Alexandra would almost certainly have known Johann and his artist son, Oswald. She felt a bit of an outsider with the British Royals - rather like Princess Diana in modern times - and wanted her son to experience life outside the stifling British Royal Court. So, turning to Walter Sickert, grandson and son of the artists she had known in her homeland, was not as surprising as it might at first seem. And, like herself, Walter had been born abroad (Munich).]

Walter Sickert did this, and introduced Clarence to the artistic people who lived in that area. Clarence posed as Sickert's younger brother (Walter Sickert was born in 1860, Prince Albert Victor in 1864).

'In Cleveland Street he met the woman who turned out to be my grandmother. She was a poor Catholic girl called Anne Elizabeth Crook. Clarence fell in love with the girl, and despite stern disapproval from his family, refused to give her up.

Anne became pregnant, and a child was born in 1885. It was a girl. He (Prince Albert Victor) later married her (Anne) in secret. This was terrible. Not only had the heir presumptive associated with a Catholic girl, he had given her a child and had also married her! And she was a commoner!

The reaction at court and from Salisbury, the Prime Minister, was violent in the extreme. Salisbury was convinced that if news of such a match leaked out the security of the throne would be in grave danger. He strongly opposed the marriage some years later of Clarence to a Catholic princess because the Irish problem was then even more of a powder keg than it is now (1970's).

Imagine his horror on learning of Clarence's recklessness. The truth must not leak out at any cost. A nurse was needed to look after the child in secret, and a young girl was brought in from a convent.

Her name was Mary Kelly. All went well until the police raided my father's house in Cleveland Street. During the raid Clarence and Anne were parted.

Under the instructions of those in power, the Royal Physician, Sir William Gull, certified Anne as insane. She was incarcerated for more than 30 years until her death in 1920.

Mary Kelly escaped with the child, first to a nearby convent and later to another convent in the East End. The child was looked after by Walter Sickert with the help of friends. To protect her he passed her off as his own daughter. But later on, when she grew up, he fell in love with her and she had two children by him. The first, a son, disappeared shortly after his birth. I am the second son.

The escape of Mary Kelly was the touch-paper of the bomb that was to explode into the Jack the Ripper atrocities. Her subsequent actions were to provide the match with which to light it.

Simply, she knew too much. News trickled back to those in power that Kelly had confided her forbidden knowledge to others. She had to be silenced.

Gin and poverty had taken their toll on Mary Kelly. She had degenerated into a prostitute in the streets and hovels close to Spitalfields Market. But among the thousands of prostitutes in the area she was hard to find. That she had to be found became clear to those at the top when they heard that she and three associates were using their knowledge for the purposes of blackmail.

In their plans to silence Kelly and her three friends it seems unlikely that Salisbury and the cabinet wanted her murdered. More likely they had in mind kidnapping, deportation, bribery, or, most likely of all, certification as insane.

Sir William Gull had done such an effective job of silencing Anne Crook by placing her in an asylum that he was put in charge of the operation. What was not taken into account was that Sir William, one of the greatest doctors of his day, was a very complex character himself.

With the help of a coachman, John Netley, Sir William tracked down the three women involved with Mary Kelly - Polly Nicholls, Annie Chapman and Elizabeth Stride. Having disposed of the three of them and also made it appear that the killings were the random work of a madman, Sir William turned his attentions to Mary Kelly. Here he made a mistake. Poor Catherine Eddowes had lived with a man called John Kelly and she often called herself Kate Kelly. She was killed in the belief that she was Mary Kelly. Mary Kelly finally met her end on November 9 and Jack the Ripper was never heard of again.

I have personal knowledge and involvement in this case, said Joseph Sickert. All previous writers and investigators have worked from the outside and none has even scratched the surface. The identity of Jack the Ripper is two names. The Ripper was two men: Sir William Gull and John Netley.'

Joseph Sickert stated that three of the murders were carried out by Gull in a moving carriage driven by Netley, and said that grapes laced with either a drug or poison were first given to the victims in the carriage, thereby removing the possibility of screams because the women were unconscious when killed. The bodies were placed at a chosen spot when the coast was clear, and this would explain why there was such a lack of blood at the places where the bodies were actually discovered.

However, far from being an interested outsider as Joseph seemed to believe, Walter Sickert had such intimate knowledge of the Ripper murders that he must have been a member of the group of individuals who were privy to the truth. Walter Sickert knew Mary Jane Kelly personally - *he was the only man involved who could identify Kelly, the main target of the Ripper. He had to have been more than an innocent bystander.*

Tracing the four women was a task which could only have been undertaken by people who could blend in with the working class of London's East End, public houses being the most likely places to find their intended quarry, and once their victim's 'local' had been tracked down the woman's fate was effectively sealed.

The two most likely members of the Ripper clique to visit East End pubs were John Netley and Walter Sickert. Netley was working class and fitted in easily. Sickert could also come and go in the East End without arousing any suspicions. He could play many parts, being an ex-actor. He had played at Sadler's Wells, and had once been a member of the famous Sir Henry Irving's company. For example, while touring with George Rignould's company who were performing Henry V, Sickert played five different parts. He gave up his acting career in 1881 in order to concentrate on his painting. Playing and dressing the part in order to blend in with East End pub clientèle would have presented no problem at all for Walter Sickert. He could 'be' anyone he needed to be.

The account by Joseph Sickert was indeed a revelation. It certainly provided a motive at long last for the murders. And what a motive it was! The heir presumptive to the British Crown had not only married a Roman Catholic, he had fathered a child by her. This would have been explosive if the knowledge became public. The monarchy would almost certainly have fallen.

By the Act of Settlement of 1701, future monarchs had to be communicant [regular takers of communion] members of the Church of England. *By this Act, even today an heir to the throne would have to forfeit the right to succeed if he or she became, or even married, a Catholic.*

But, might Queen Victoria have survived if such explosive information had become public knowledge? After all, the history books tell us that she was very popular. But was she in fact the popular monarch of the history books?

A prince of the realm marrying a member of the working-class. An heir to the throne marrying a Roman Catholic, thereby placing his succession to the crown in jeopardy. Although it might seem rather far-fetched, Prince Albert Victor was not the first heir to the Crown to have performed the above-mentioned acts. Precedents, in fact, exist for both. But, is there any other source to back up Joseph Sickert's account of the Jack the Ripper murders? Amazingly, there is.

Clandestine Royal Marriages:

Hannah Lightfoot

A rumour that the present Royal Family are not the rightful occupants of, but 'pretenders' to, the British throne, has persisted for over two hundred years. Hannah Lightfoot was born into a Quaker family on 12th October 1730, in Wapping. After her father's death, Hannah and her mother Mary went to live with Mary's brother, Henry Wheeler, when she was 3 years old. Henry is said to have had a draper shop in St James' Market, near the old Opera House.

The Royal Family used to pass through St James' Market on their way to the Opera House, and on one of these visits in 1753, George, Prince of Wales, saw Hannah, known as the 'Fair Quaker'. She was very beautiful, with long golden hair, and young George, age 15, was smitten. An introduction was arranged by Miss Chudleigh, Lady in Waiting to the Queen.

Hannah could not possibly assent to a casual affair because she had been brought up as a strict Quaker. To her, only marriage would suffice. What their son was contemplating soon reached the ears of his parents, so the Prince of Wales hurriedly arranged a 'marriage' for Hannah. If she was married, the concerns of the king and queen would be removed. After all, their son could hardly marry someone who was already married.

Hannah was betrothed to a man named Isaac Axford, and on 11th December, 1753, they were married in St George's, Hanover Square. As soon as Hannah emerged from the church, a coach driven by agents of the Prince of Wales drew up. She entered the carriage and was driven off at high speed.

Her mother organised a search by the Society of Friends for Hannah, but after a year they gave up their search as it was fruitless, and cast her off from Quakerism because she had 'entered into a state of marriage by a priest not of our Society which is repugnant amongst us. We endeavoured to find where she was, but to no purpose. Nor could we obtain any intelligence as to where she is. We therefore disown Hannah Lightfoot.' Neither Hanna's mother nor Isaac Axford ever saw her again.

Tradition states that on 17th April 1759, George, Prince of Wales, and Hannah Lightfoot were married by Anglican ceremony at Kew Chapel, the service being carried out by the Rev. James Wilmot. Some

17

days later, a ceremony took place in their 'secret house' in London.

George and Hannah were said to have had two sons and a daughter, the eldest son being George Rex. [Coincidentally, Isaac Axford also married in 1759. On 3rd December that year he married Mary Bartlett at Erlestoke, Wiltshire. He could scarcely have married if his first marriage was still valid. A marriage could be legally annulled for non-consummation of the marriage. Also, if one of the parties has been missing, thought to be dead, the other party would be free to marry again. In Hannah's case, both would be applicable. It is interesting to note that when Isaac Axford married Mary Bartlett he listed himself as 'widower'.]

In 1760, George II died, and the Prince became King George III. In 1761 he 'married' Charlotte of Mecklenburg-Strelitz, a German princess. They produced 15 children.

During the night of 22nd February 1845, the marriage records at Kew Chapel vanished when the wooden chest containing all Parish registers since 1714 was mysteriously stolen from the church. Three weeks later the empty chest was found in the river Thames below Kew Bridge. The registers which had been in the chest were never seen again.

In 1866 however, documents were produced in the Court of Chancery (the Lord Chancellor's Court) in London by a Mrs Lavinia Ryves. Amongst these documents were two which claimed to be the two marriage certificates of George, Prince of Wales, and Hannah Lightfoot. One document read:

'May 27, 1759. This is to certify that the marriage of these parties, George, Prince

of Wales, and Hannah Lightfoot, was
duly solemnised this day according to the
rites and ceremonies of the Church of
England.
J. Wilmot'

The certificate was signed by George Guelph and Hannah Lightfoot, and witnessed by William Pitt, the former, and future, Prime Minister of Great Britain. [Guelph: the surname of the royal family, i.e. George's surname.]

The Attorney-General stated, "I do not disguise from myself that this is nothing less than a claim to the British Throne."

The Lord Chancellor declared, "It really is a great indecency to inquire into matters like these, affecting our Royal family."

The Attorney-General brought in the most renowned handwriting expert in the land on behalf of the Crown, Frederick George Netherclift, confident that he would repudiate the signatures on the document. He studied the signatures very carefully - then, to the utter dismay of the Attorney-General and the Lord Chancellor, pronounced them, without any doubt, genuine.

The Lord Chancellor then interrogated Mr Netherclift, but the Establishment's own expert would not be bullied, and he refused to back down. He again stated that the signatures on the document were completely genuine.

The second document produced in the Court of Chancery read:

'This is to solemnly certify that I married
George Prince of Wales to Princess Hannah

his First Consort, April 17 1759 and that
the true princes and a princess were the
issue of that marriage.
J. Wilmot '

Also produced in this civil court case was the Last
Will and Testament of Hannah Lightfoot:

'Hampstad, July 7th 1762

I commend my two sons to the kind protection
of their Royal father, my husband, His Majesty
George III, Bequeathing whatever property I die
possessed of to such dear offspring of my ill-fated
marriage. Amen.
Hannah Regina '

The will was witnessed by a Mrs J. Dunning and by
William Pitt.
The Court ruled that the documents were to be
seized and impounded, and this was done.
[Even for most of the 20th century these documents
were still locked away. They can now be viewed in The
National Archives at Kew.]
It is not known for sure when or where Hannah
Lightfoot died, but tradition has it that she is buried in
the graveyard of Islington Church under an assumed
name.

St Peter's Church, Carmarthen, Wales

The historic tiled floor of St Peter's Church,
Carmarthen, had subsided. During restoration work in
September 2000, the following discovery was made:

'Also buried in the chancel is Charlotte Augusta
Catherine Dalton (died 1832 aged 27 years), grand-
daughter of King George III and his first wife Hannah
Lightfoot (married in 1759).

Sharing her tomb is her niece Margaret Augusta
Prytherch (died 1838 aged 8 years), great grand-
daughter of the king.'
(St Peter's Church web site)

The bodies were in a large vaulted tomb with a
domed roof situated right in front of the altar. The tomb
was marked with a stone slab giving names and dates.
No record of the burials existed.

'The then Prince of Wales had fallen in love with
Hannah Lightfoot, a London Quaker girl and daughter
of a London linen-draper, and married her in complete
secrecy at Kew on the outskirts of London on 17th April
1759. They went on to have three children.
Catherine Augusta [Hannah and George's
daughter] married James Dalton of Carmarthen, a
doctor and an officer of the East India Company. They
had two sons and two daughters - Charlotte Augusta
Catherine and Caroline (who was mother of Margaret
Augusta).
Between the Chancel and the Consistory is the
eighteenth century piped organ built by George Pike
England on the orders of King George III. The king had
originally planned that the organ should go to the
Chapel Royal, Windsor. However, he changed his
mind, and it found its way to St Peter's.'
(St Peter's Church web site)

[Charlotte Augusta Catherine Dalton was born 13 July 1806, Tamil Nadu, India.

Father: James Dalton

Mother: Catherine Augusta ------

Margaret Augusta Dalton Prytherch was born 20 May 1830, Carmarthen.

Father: Daniel Prytherch

Mother: Caroline Georgina Catherine (Dalton)]

Catherine Augusta - George III's daughter.

Charlotte Augusta - George III's granddaughter.

Margaret Augusta - George III's great granddaughter.

George III's mother was Princess Augusta.

George Rex

It was said, and many believed, and indeed still believe, that the person known as George Rex was the eldest *legitimate* son of King George III and Hannah Lightfoot. Legend states that he was summoned to his royal father's presence in 1797, and was told:

'We have arranged for you to go to the Cape of Good Hope. You must never return to England. You must never marry. There must be no legitimate heirs. And you must never speak of our relationship.'

The probable reason for the 'exile' of George Rex was that the British Royal Family was very unpopular because of their immoral behaviour. Their incompetence had resulted in the loss of the American Colonies. There had been the Gordon Riots of 1780 in London during which 12,000 troops - summoned by King George III - had fired on the people. Around 700 had been killed and 450 were arrested, 25 of whom were then executed.

Crucially, the French Revolution was well under way. The monarchy there had been overthrown, the king and queen having had their heads cut off. In other words, what the Establishment here really feared was the *British Revolution.*

Any new royal scandal could be the fuse which would light the powder-keg. If it became known that King George had married twice - the first ceremony being a secret marriage to a commoner which had resulted in a *legitimate* heir - this would be potentially explosive. Perhaps it was best - for the Establishment - that the 'problem' be removed to a far-away land.

In October 1797, George Rex sailed into Cape Town. He arrived with a Royal Warrant given to him by King George III.

'George III, by the Grace of God, of Great Britain, France, and Ireland, King, Defender of the Faith, have granted unto George Rex the office of Marshal, and Serjeant of Mace of our Vice-Admiralty of the Cape of Good Hope.'

George Rex, in a carriage pulled by eight horses, later moved farther eastwards along the coast from Cape Town, to a place named Knysna. (pron. Nysena)

With him went skilled manual workers such as blacksmiths, carpenters, etc, together with life's necessities. These were carried in sixteen wagons pulled by oxen. On his 22,000 acre estate at Knysna he even had his own church built.

George Rex had nine children by a South African woman whose name was said to be Johanna van der Caap - but he refused to marry her. An insight into his knowledge of the latest events in the outside world appears in a letter written by him:

'I had accounts of the death of George IV for some time, but the governor over at Cape Town has not yet received his official despatch.'

To say the least, he was certainly kept up to date. Even although he was living in a detached spot such as Knysna - over 300 miles farther eastward than Cape Town, and a few miles from the coast - George Rex had received information about the death of King George IV in 1830, long before the British Governor. Why should this be?

On 3rd April 1839, George Rex suffered a massive stroke, and as he lay dying he made two unconditional requests:

'The royal insignia that appears on our cutlery and elsewhere must be obliterated.'

'I must be buried at Knysna on my estate. Under no circumstances must my bones be removed and buried in England.'

It is said that on his deathbed, the mother of his nine children told him that she wished to be married to him before he died. George Rex is said to have replied that he could not break his oath.

His will decreed that his estate be shared amongst Johanna and his children. However, he publicly declared his children as being illegitimate:

'I, George Rex, residing at the Knysna,
and not having submitted myself to
the matrimonial laws of this colony.'

Soon after his death, the house at Knysna burnt to the ground. Knysna has been visited by several British royals over the years, including Princess Victoria, Queen Victoria's daughter Princess Alice, and the Duke of Windsor when Prince of Wales.

As the house at Knysna was burning, someone managed to save a couple of items from the building. In Cape Town Castle are two black ebony chairs from Knysna. Each chair has the insignia of the Prince of Wales' feathers in silver on its back-rest.

*   *   *

Marshal, and Serjeant of Mace -   a Marshal was an officer of a law court. The Serjeant of Mace was an officer with only Ceremonial duties. He carried the mace – staff of office of the court - and laid it on the table in front of the judge. This meant that the court was officially now in session.

The Vice-Admiralty Court was a branch of the British High Court of the Admiralty which in time of war was set up for convenience in various British colonies with power to adjudicate in Admiralty Causes (legal actions) such as Piracy and Prize - particularly in cases of Condemnation (goods declared forfeited) which provided the Lord High Admiral, one of the great officers of state, with the majority of his income.

During war years, cases of Prize (ships and property captured in naval warfare, i.e. booty) totalling more than 1,000 per year, sometimes more than 2,000, were brought before the court.

The badge of the Admiralty Court was a mace in the shape of a silver oar which was carried in and laid on a table before the presiding judge whenever a case was to be heard. The posts of 'Marshal, and Serjeant of Mace,' were highly sought-after positions in the colony.

Maria Fitzherbert

Mary Anne Smythe was born in 1756, very probably in Acton Burnell, Shropshire, the eldest daughter of Roman Catholic parents, Walter Smythe and Mary Errington.

The family moved to Brambridge, Hampshire, around 1762, because, on the death of his cousin Henry Welles in August 1762, the hamlet of Brambridge passed to Walter Smythe in Henry's will.

Mary Anne Smythe and Edward Weld, a middle-aged property owner, were married by William Walmesley of the Order of St Benedict on 13 July 1775, at Brambridge.

Only three months later, on 23rd October, Edward Weld died, his death being caused, it is said, from injuries sustained after falling from his horse.

After the death of her husband, Mary moved to London where she moved in fashionable society, meeting wealthy Thomas Fitzherbert. On 24th June 1778, they were married in St George's Hanover Square - the same church in which the marriage of Hannah Lightfoot and Isaac Axford had taken place some twenty-five years previously.

Just under three years later, Mary - now called Maria - at only 24 years of age, was a widow for a second time. It would seem that Thomas Fitzherbert had contracted a disease of the lungs, and he died on 7th May 1781.

Sometime in 1784, George, Prince of Wales, met Maria Fitzherbert, fell in love with her, and begged her to become his mistress. Maria, a Roman Catholic, refused.

It is said that George attempted suicide - whether real or pretended, is unknown - Maria being called to his side in time to 'save' him.

George considered asking her to marry him, but *Maria was not only a commoner, she was a Roman Catholic.*

By the Royal Marriages Act of 1772, a marriage by a member of the royal family under 25 (George was 23) required royal permission. If he married without his parents' consent, his right to the throne was seriously threatened.

Even more of an obstacle to his marriage to Maria was the Act of Settlement of 1701. By this, no Catholic, or anyone married to a Catholic, could become king.

George went ahead anyway. A secret marriage was arranged, and on 15th December 1785, George Augustus Frederick, Prince of Wales, married Maria Anne Fitzherbert at her house in Park Lane, Mayfair.

The marriage ceremony was carried out by an Anglican clergyman, the Reverend Robert Butt. He was, until then, confined in the Fleet Prison for being a debtor, i.e. he was in a debtors' prison. The Rev. Robert Butt was said to have agreed to perform the marriage ceremony in exchange for promotion to bishop when George became king - and presumably his debts being paid to get him out of the Fleet Prison.

The marriage was to be kept concealed, so George and Maria Fitzherbert lived in separate houses. However, though 'secret', the subject of the marriage was raised in Parliament - *where it was, of course, denied that such an event had taken place.*

Although the marriage contravened the Act of Settlement and the Royal Marriages Act, *it was totally valid in the eyes of the Roman Catholic Church.* Pope Pius VI assured Maria that her marriage was perfectly legal.

By 1787, George, Prince of Wales, was deep in debt, and could no longer afford the upkeep of his house, Carlton House, in Pall Mall, and he withdrew to a place of refuge - a farmhouse near Brighton.

Then, in 1795, in return for Parliament paying off his debts (said to be over £300,000) the Prince of Wales agreed to marry his cousin, Caroline of Brunswick.

The 'marriage' took place that year, and on 7th January 1786, a daughter, Charlotte, was born.

After her birth George and Caroline lived separate lives. Their daughter would be their only child.

Two days after Charlotte's birth, George made a will bequeathing a shilling to Queen Caroline and everything else to Maria Fitzherbert.

Mistresses came and went, but George always returned to Maria. It is said that when he - as King

George IV - died in 1830, he was wearing a miniature of Maria round his neck. After his death, Maria was still the beneficiary of George's last Will and Testament. The government came to an 'agreement' with her that she give up her claim to George's property in exchange for a yearly allowance of £10,000 (£500,000 - £700,000 nowadays).

In the judgement of the Roman Catholic Church, the marriage between the Prince of Wales and Maria Fitzherbert had been completely legitimate. The marriage being considered technically invalid in legal terms by the Establishment would have meant nothing if it had become known publicly that the heir to the crown had married a Roman Catholic commoner. The government and monarchy would almost certainly have fallen.

What the public reaction would have been if it was generally known that the heir to the throne had fathered a child by his Roman Catholic wife can well be imagined.

A boy was said to have been born to George and Maria on 1st December 1786. The birth was denied by the government, who had also denied the marriage. The child was named Henry Augustus Frederick Hervey. (Hervey was the family name of the Earl of Bristol, a close friend of the Prince of Wales.)

The Establishment, of course, has made a thorough effort to erase all trace of the child's connection with the heir to the throne. However, during George's self-imposed residence in his Brighton farmhouse, an anonymous cartoon appeared. The cartoon, called Loves Last Shift, was published by S.W. Fores on 26th February 1787.

29

George and Maria sit either side of a fireside. A sheep's head (cheap meat) is cooking in the fire. George is sitting without his breeches, while Maria is mending them.

A string is attached to one of George's fingers, the other end of the string being attached to a cradle in which a baby lies. George's task is to rock the cradle in order to get the baby to sleep [the last shift of the day].

On the wall above the fireplace is a sheet of music named 'A Begging We Will Go.'

Kneeling at the back of George's chair is an attendant in livery - said to be the Clerk of the Kitchen - who is placing a basket of oysters (food of the poor) onto the floor.

Another liveried servant is walking towards George's back carrying a tankard, a vessel used especially for the drinking of ale (drink of the poor) than brandy or port, which would be his normal choice.

Later, an 'adopted' niece who lived with Maria was also strongly believed to actually be the child of George and Maria.

Charlotte, only child of George, Prince of Wales, and Caroline of Brunswick, died 6th November 1817, age 22, after giving birth to a still-born son in their home, Claremont House, Esher, Surrey.

So, two generations of heirs had died in the one day. Now an heir to the throne was required.

George's brother, Edward, Duke of Kent, was the first to produce one - Alexandrina Victoria, born 1819 - and she was crowned Queen Victoria in 1837.

Henry Augustus Frederick Hervey married in 1810, and fathered four children. The 'adopted niece' also married and had a family.

On 27th March 1837, Maria Fitzherbert - Mary Anne Smythe - died in Brighton. She was buried in St John The Baptist R.C. Church, Brighton. Founded in 1779, Maria had contributed financially to ensure that it was built.

Chapter 2

Victoria's Mythical Popularity

Queen Victoria, British monarch beloved by her subjects, was not quite the universal view of the general public. She was not so popular as the history books would have us believe. There were several political movements during her reign, amongst which was the Chartist Movement which campaigned for more political power for the working classes, the Socialist Movement which demanded greater distribution of wealth, and the Nationalist Movement which demanded Irish Home Rule. Victoria regarded all of these as being led by rabble-rousers who were trying to stir up her people against her. She became Queen in 1837, and early in her reign became unpopular with the British public.

Lady Flora Hastings

Victoria had an intense dislike of a man named Sir John Conroy. He was the private secretary and comptroller (he ran the household) of the Duchess of Kent, who was Victoria's mother. Victoria believed that he exerted too much influence over her mother, and also suspected that there was something going on between them. When she became queen she determined to get rid of him.

Lady Flora Hastings, was one of her ladies-in-waiting, and was unmarried. In 1839, age 32, Flora's stomach began to swell. Victoria accused her of being pregnant with the child of Sir John Conroy. This caused a national scandal.

Flora protested her innocence, stating that she was a virgin. Victoria forced her to have an embarrassing and humiliating medical examination, and this proved that Flora had told the truth.

Victoria refused to accept this verdict and banished Sir John Conroy and Lady Flora Hastings from Court in disgrace.

In July 1839, Lady Flora Hastings died of the liver cancer which had caused her stomach to swell.

Victoria expressed no regret, and gave the family of Lady Flora Hastings no apology. *She sent them a bracelet.*

The public were outraged. She was heckled when she attended Ascot races. When she appeared in public she was jeered by crowds who derided her with calls of 'Mrs Melbourne!' (Viscount Melbourne was Prime Minister), and eggs were thrown at her carriage.

Threats and Assassination Attempts

10 June 1840 - She was shot at twice by 17 year old Edward Oxford, an unemployed pub servant-boy, who had a pistol in each hand. Oxford was obviously not much of a shot, because, only a few yards from his target, he missed.

This attempted assassination took place at Constitution Hill, next to Buckingham Palace. Edward

Oxford was declared insane and put into an asylum. He was set free in 1867 - on condition that he left the country. He sailed in December that year for Australia.

29 May 1842 - John Francis fired a pistol at her. This attempt took place in front of Buckingham Palace.

John Francis was condemned to death. Then declared insane, the sentence being changed to 'transportation for life and subjected to hard labour in the most penal settlement in Australia.'

3 July 1842 - A shot was fired at her by John Bean. This attempt took place as she was being driven from Buckingham Palace to the Chapel Royal, St James' Palace.

John Bean was sentenced to death. Then declared insane, his sentence being commuted to 18 months in prison.

John Wardle

John Wardle, aged 24, had worked as a coal miner in the colliery of the Earl of Dartmouth at West Bromwich. On the 19th March 1849, he was charged with sending threatening letters to the queen:

'That unless he and his family obtain their rights, she would die by his hands.'

[John Wardle's grandfather had been a soldier, and had served in the British Army in North America. He was persuaded to marry a servant girl who had had a child by Edward, Duke of Kent, the king's son, in return for a promise that, at his death, the duke would leave £10,000 to the Wardle family in gratitude. This promise was not kept. The family received no money.]

34

The following extract is from the Times, 27 March 1849:

'These facts, the prisoner said, were communicated to him when he was 13 years old by his grandfather on his deathbed, and he was determined to have his rights. After minutely examining into the particulars of the case, the magistrate sentenced the prisoner to three months' confinement in Stafford Gaol in default of his finding bail to keep the peace, which expired in the early part of May last. In the following month the prisoner found his way to London, and underwent several examinations before the Lord Mayor of London and Mr. D.W. Harvey, the City Police Commissioner, which resulted in his being sent back to West Bromwich and placed under the surveillance of the police.

On 18th of December last, the prisoner wrote a letter to Mr. Abbott the Superintendent of the North Staffordshire Police, stating that he was determined to have " his rights" if he "swung for it", and he also addressed a similar letter to Sir G. Grey, the Home Secretary, under date of December 21. No notice was, however, taken of these letters beyond their being forwarded to the solicitor for the Treasury. About a month or six weeks since, a communication was received at the Home-office stating that the prisoner had left West Bromwich, as it was supposed, for Windsor, he having expressed his determination to proceed to that place to "obtain his rights".

Nothing further was heard of the prisoner's movements until Thursday, the 8th inst, when he presented himself at the residence of the Dean of Windsor, and, having been relieved with refreshments, he told his tale to Mr Wise, the butler of the Dean, stating that he was determined to see the Queen and get his due, even if his neck was stretched for it.

In consequence of this threat, Mr Wise deemed it was his duty to give the prisoner into the custody of Mr Eager, the Superintendent of the Windsor Police, as a vagrant; but he having repeated his threat to the Superintendent, when the prisoner was brought before the magistrates, the charge against him assumed a more serious character.

The case was postponed till Monday, the 17th instant, when Mr Hayward of the office of the Solicitor to the Treasury attended to watch the case, and was about to ask the magistrates to hold the prisoner to bail for using threatening language, when Mr Pearl, a surgeon of Windsor, who had examined him, expressed doubts of the prisoner's sanity. Upon this, Mr Hayward asked for a remand to obtain further evidence on that point.

Accordingly, the prisoner was again brought up yesterday, when, the above facts having been deposed to, and Inspector Walker, who does duty at Her Majesty's palaces in London and Windsor, having expressed his belief that the letters were in the hand-writing of the prisoner, he was examined by Dr Monroe relative to his sanity.

The doctor stated that he had had an interview of over an hour's duration with the prisoner, and he was clearly of opinion that he was a dangerous lunatic, whom it was not safe to trust at large for a single hour. Upon this evidence being given, Mr Hayward applied to have the prisoner committed to the County Lunatic Asylum under the provisions of the act 1st of Victoria, cap. 14, which provides that if "a person shall be discovered and apprehended under circumstances that denote a derangement of mind and a purpose of committing some crime" any two justices may, upon the evidence of a "physician, surgeon, or apothecary" showing him to be insane, commit him.

The Mayor having asked the prisoner if he had any explanation to give of his conduct, he replied that it would be useless, as he was like a lamb in a den of wolves.' [On the 'evidence' of one doctor, surgeon, or even apothecary (pharmacist), a person could be confined in an asylum.]

One thing stands out in this story, and that is John Wardle's absolute determination to obtain what he was convinced to be his family's right. He had told his story to the Earl of Dartmouth - that his mother was the daughter of the Duke of Kent - and asked for his help, but was mocked instead. Wardle, formerly employed as a coal miner, must have received a fairly good education, because he wrote letters to the Queen, the Home Secretary, and the Staffordshire Police. It must surely have been extremely unusual for a member of the working-class to be able to compose entire letters in his own hand in the 1840s - Annie Crook could not sign her name, and had to make her mark thus, X, on her daughter's birth certificate in 1885.

John Wardle was imprisoned in the Littlemore Lunatic Asylum near Oxford. He was incarcerated only eight days after he was charged with 'sending threatening letters'.

Littlemore Asylum had been recently opened (1846) to care for pauper lunatics of the county of Oxfordshire. Being neither a pauper - employed as a waiter in a tavern, having seemingly lost his job in the colliery after calling into question the conditions of the colliery workers - nor living in Oxfordshire, it seems rather odd that John Wardle was incarcerated in this asylum.

Prince Edward Augustus, Duke of Kent, was the fourth son of King George III. He became Colonel of the 7th Royal Fusiliers, who were sent to Canada in 1791 (Prince Edward Island is named after him.) He had several mistresses, and at least one (Adelaide Dubois), it was rumoured, had given birth. The Duke of Kent died, age 52, in 1820, so, presumably, this is when the Wardle family would have expected to receive the promised £10,000.

In 1818, Edward Augustus had married Princess Viktoria of Saxe-Coburg-Saalfeld, and they had one child, a daughter, Alexandrina Victoria of Kent - the future Queen Victoria.

John Wardle was admitted to Littlemore Asylum 'under circumstances that denote a derangement of mind, and a purpose of committing some crime, *to wit* assaulting our Most Gracious Majesty the Queen and committing a breach of the Peace'.

Wardle showed no sign of insanity other than the committing himself, evidently having persuaded himself of the truth of his story, to an outrageous course of conduct.

Having 'recovered' from his 'derangement of mind' after 9 months incarceration, he was released from Littlemore in December 1849. It seems reasonable to suppose that John Wardle eventually retracted his demand for his rights in order to get out of the asylum.

19 May 1849 - A pistol was fired at her by William Hamilton. Victoria was in no danger - Hamilton had forgotten to load the bullet. This attempt took place on

Constitution Hill. William Hamilton was sentenced to transportation to Australia for 7 years.

27 May 1850 - As she left Cambridge House, Piccadilly, Robert Pate, ex-lieutenant of the 10th Hussars, stuck her on the head with the knob of his brass-handled cane, knocking her out. Robert Pate was sentenced to transportation to Australia for 7 years.

29 Feb 1872 - Arthur O'Connor pointed an unloaded pistol at her head as she stepped out of her carriage in front of Buckingham Palace. John Brown leapt on him before he could 'fire'.

O'Connor had a petition in his other hand which he wanted Victoria to take. This demanded the release of the Irishmen known as the 'Fenian prisoners'.

Arthur O'Connor was sentenced to 1 year's imprisonment with hard labour plus 20 strokes of the birch rod. In 1874, he was then put into an asylum.

2 Mar 1882 - As she was being driven from Windsor railway station in her carriage, Roderick MacLean stepped out of the waiting throng and fired a pistol at her. He was overpowered by the crowd before he could fire another shot.

Tried for high treason, Roderick MacLean was found 'not guilty' on the grounds that he was insane. Sentenced to be detained in an asylum 'during her Majesty's pleasure'.

26 May 1882 - Albert Young was found guilty of sending letters threatening to kill her. He was sentenced to 10 years penal servitude.

Irish Republicanism

After the death of her husband, Prince Albert, in 1861, Queen Victoria withdrew almost totally from public life for over ten years. On several occasions she refused to attend the State Opening of Parliament. The story circulated that she was having an affair with her servant, John Brown. There was even a strong rumour that a child had been born - on her death, her son, Edward VII, personally shattered every miniature statue of John Brown he could find in Victoria's rooms. The fact that there actually *were* miniature statues of Brown is extremely suggestive.

Support for republicanism in Britain grew. Reformers and revolutionaries were even demanding the abolition of the monarchy. In 1864, a placard was fixed to the gates of Buckingham Palace which read:

*'These premises will be let or sold due to
the decline in the late occupant's business.'*

In the decade of the Ripper murders, as well as two riots in Trafalgar Square, one of which became known as Bloody Sunday, the campaign of violence by Irish Catholic republicans seeking the overthrow of the British government in Ireland increased. Attacks on London in the 1880s:

15 Mar 1883 - A bomb exploded in a building in Charles Street, Whitehall. The target was the Home Office. Soon after this incident, the Special Irish Branch, controlled by the Home Office, was formed at Scotland Yard under Inspector Williamson. Williamson

regularly analysed information with his contact at the Home Office - Robert Anderson. [This was the work of a group called the United Irishmen.]

13 Oct 1883 - Bombs detonated at Praed Street (Paddington) and Westminster Bridge underground stations. More than seventy people were seriously injured. [The work of an organisation named the Clan-na-Gael.]

26 Feb 1884 - Bombs were discovered at three railway stations, Charing Cross, Ludgate Hill, and Paddington, but a fourth bomb went off in Victoria Station. [Clan-na-Gael]

30 May 1884 - Two bombs exploded just off Pall Mall. A third bomb went off at Whitehall - the office of the Special Irish Branch was destroyed. [Clan-na-Gael]

2 Jan 1885 - A bomb went off in the railway tunnel between King's Cross and Gower Street stations. Several people injured. [Clan-na-Gael]

24 Jan 1885 - There was public outrage when bombs exploded at the Tower of London and the House of Commons. [Clan-na-Gael]

Government Intrigues:

The machinations of the 1887 Jubilee Plot were not dissimilar to three other historical conspiracies which were government-controlled: the Gunpowder Plot of 1605, the Titus Oates Plot of 1678, and the Cato Street Conspiracy of 1820.

Remember, Remember, the Fifth of November,
Gunpowder, Treason, and Plot.

I see no reason why Gunpowder Treason
Should ever be forgot.

The Gunpowder Plot

The purpose of the gunpowder plot was to blow up the British Establishment, to remove the ruling elite at one fell swoop. The plotters were Roman Catholic.

The main participants were the leader, Thomas Catesby, Thomas Percy, Guy Fawkes, Thomas Wintour, Robert Wintour, John Wright, Christopher Wright, Francis Tresham, Robert Keyes, John Grant, Ambrose Rokewood, Sir Everard Digby, and Thomas Bates.

Being a soldier, Guy Fawkes was the practical member of the group. (He had fought as a mercenary on the Continent, and had started to call himself Guido after a trip to Spain.) Fawkes was the gunpowder expert. A house was rented in Westminster by Thomas Percy, and Guy Fawkes moved in.

The war with Spain had finished, and there would now have been a surplus of gunpowder, but it could not be bought just anywhere. The government had a monopoly on it. It was manufactured by royal license in powder-mills. It must surely have been unusual for an individual citizen to purchase a barrel of gunpowder, yet Fawkes managed to buy 36 barrels of the substance, possibly from Rotherhithe powder mill, south of the river, and convey the barrels to his lodgings in Westminster, north of the river. The purchase of such a quantity would have been highly suspicious, to say the least, and must have been reported. If the powder was purchased from abroad, the transportation and time involved would surely have made discovery even more likely.

The plan was to dig a tunnel from the house in which Guy Fawkes was ensconced to the Palace of Westminster, but this proved much more difficult and prolonged than was anticipated. At this point, when it looked like the plot might have to be postponed or perhaps even cancelled, *the large cellar right under Parliament suddenly becomes available for lease* - what a slice of good luck for the conspirators.

During the summer of 1605, the 36 barrels of gunpowder (about 2½ tons in weight) were then transferred from the rented house to the cellar beneath the Palace of Westminster. A huge pile of firewood was placed over the barrels to conceal them.

On the night of 26th October, Lord Monteagle, Francis Tresham's brother in law, received a letter.

Official Version: Lord Monteagle received a letter, handed to him by his servant. When asked who had delivered the letter, the servant said that he had been accosted by a masked stranger who had handed the said letter to him. The letter - unsigned - warned Monteagle not to attend the State Opening of Parliament, because - 'they shall receive a terrible blow, this Parliament.'

Not able to grasp the meaning of this, Monteagle immediately rode to Whitehall where he handed the letter to the Secretary of State, the notoriously anti-Catholic, Robert Cecil. Cecil was King James' spymaster (like MI5 and MI6 combined in one person).

Cecil, also unable to understand the message contained in the letter, took it to King James. He immediately focused on the words 'terrible blow', and said that to him this suggested gunpowder. He then suggested a search of the cellars. *Robert Cecil waited until the evening of November 4th.* The search came upon a bearded man by a pile of firewood which seemed rather too large. On further investigation it was discovered that the lodgings were leased to a Catholic. Baffled, they took their information to King James, who immediately ordered a second search to be made of the cellar, and there they arrested the bearded stranger. Under the firewood were found the barrels of gunpowder.

The conspirators are able to purchase thirty-six barrels of government-controlled gunpowder and then transport it - gunpowder may have been plentiful, but one man buying 36 barrels! It is then carted to a rented house. *The perfect site becomes available for rent, right under the intended target (a bit like al-Qaeda renting the White House basement).* How lucky can you get! *The gunpowder is moved to the Parliament building itself,* where the barrels are stored in the cellar below. None of this arouses any suspicion. Lord Monteagle's servant is accosted by a Zorro-like figure who hands him an anonymous letter. Monteagle, unable to put two and two together, hotfoots it to Robert Cecil. Cecil, head of the Intelligence network in England, is also unable to see the blindingly obvious, so he takes the letter to the king. *Only the king is wise enough to understand the letter.* Even although ordered to organise a search, *Cecil waits until the eve of the State Opening of Parliament.*

The conspirators found out that Lord Monteagle had received the warning letter and had taken it to spymaster Cecil, but, incredibly, Catesby decided that it changed nothing. The plotters' names were not known (i.e. they believed their names were not known). This was the point where they could have - *should have* - cut and run. The leader, Robert Catesby, decided that the plot should carry on regardless. This almost beggars belief - and is very suspicious.

When the search of the cellar is eventually made, again those in charge of state security are bewildered. They see a bearded stranger wearing a black hat and cloak, riding-boots and spurs, with a lantern, standing beside an enormous pile of firewood situated directly under Parliament. Nothing suspicious here. They leave, but decide to 'investigate' who has leased the premises.

They 'discover' that Thomas Percy, a Catholic, has rented the cellar. Still baffled, the king is again consulted. *Only the king is wise enough to interpret the facts. Only the king is wise enough to make the connection.*

Within a few weeks of the arrest of Guy Fawkes, it is hardly surprising that the theory circulated *that Robert Cecil had known of the plot for some time.*

The warning letter has been attributed to Francis Tresham since he was Monteagle's brother-in-law. Surely this made it *less likely* for Tresham to have been the writer. Why would he write an anonymous letter. Being a relative, Tresham could simply have had a word with Monteagle, making up some pretext for him not to attend Parliament - some family matter perhaps.

The letter is highly suspicious. Being anonymous, anyone could have written it, but its most likely writer is surely *Robert Cecil* - if all the conspirators are killed, or in the unlikely event that those surviving don't talk, the letter provides hard evidence of a plot against the king.

Cecil could have had the letter delivered to Monteagle, then waited to see what would happen. Monteagle was Catholic, but attended Protestant services - he was looking after his own prospects. If Cecil knew exactly who the conspirators were, he knew Tresham was one of them, so he was also testing Monteagle. Monteagle played it safe. Although he must have had a damn good idea what the letter meant, he took it to Cecil, not only to show *his allegiance to the king, but also to ingratiate himself with Robert Cecil*, who, after the king, was the most powerful person in the kingdom (for his loyalty, Monteagle received a pension of £500 per year for life (£60,000 - £80,000 nowadays).

Robert Cecil did not have the cellar searched right away. *He let the plot simmer and ripen. He waited until the eleventh hour to bring it to its theatrical climax.*

[Guy Fawkes intended to blow those assembled in the Palace of Westminster on November 5th, 1605, to kingdom come. But the Palace of Westminster which he intended to blow sky-high was nothing like the present Palace of Westminster.

As the name suggests, the original building was actually a royal palace. It was said to date from the time of Edward the Confessor (11th century), and consisted of more than one building. The palace was damaged by a fire in 1512, and, although most of it survived, it was no longer used as a royal residence.

Both the House of Lords and the House of Commons sat in the surviving part of the old palace.

The history we are taught has conjured up an image of Guy Fawkes underground in a dungeon-like cellar below the Houses of Parliament building (i.e. the building where both 'houses' of Parliament met).

It was not like that at all. The parliament building was just under 70 ft. long and 30 ft. wide, and consisted of two chambers - a ground floor and an upper floor,

46

that is all. The Houses met in the upper chamber, which was accessed via a small stairway leading to a door on the side of the building. The so-called cellar was an undercroft, a ground floor storeroom. The 'cellar' of Guy Fawkes was in fact the ground floor of the building!

This, of course, meant that the 36 barrels of gunpowder, each barrel containing 70 lbs. of powder, (a total of 1 ton of gunpowder) had to be taken into the building at street-level. Although this task would, presumably, have been undertaken at night, anyone passing by would have witnessed barrels of gunpowder being carried into the space directly below that in which the State Opening of Parliament was shortly to take place. Those in attendance would be King James I, all the Protestant (and Roman Catholic) aristocracy, and all high-ranking clergymen, including the Archbishop of Canterbury. Obviously, no suspicions were aroused, since the whole plot was said to have been foiled because of a letter conjectured to have been written by one of the actual conspirators to a Catholic peer.]

Robert Catesby, Thomas Percy, John Wright, and Christopher Wright, were killed when running out of Holbeech House, Staffordshire, à la the finale of the film 'Butch Cassidy and the Sundance Kid'. (It was said that the sheriff's men arrived at Holbeech House almost as quickly as the conspirators.)

Thomas Wintour and Ambrose Rokewood were taken to London. The rest of the group were captured and joined Guy Fawkes, Wintour, and Rokewood in the Tower.

The trial, which was half an hour in duration, with no defence, took place in January. On 31st January 1606, all (except for Guy Fawkes who, wisely, jumped from the scaffold and broke his neck) were hanged, drawn, and quartered in Old Palace Yard - *except one man* - and their heads stuck on poles on London bridge.

The exception was Francis Tresham (the 13th recruit to the conspiracy). When arrested, he was immediately locked up in a cell. There, he was found dead (23rd Dec 1605) due to the administration of poison. Was Francis Tresham a double-agent? Almost certainly. But, now that the conspirators were dead or imprisoned, he would have been a liability. It would have been far too risky to free him in case he talked.

Robert Catesby insisted that the plot was not compromised when the letter was delivered to Monteagle warning him of the 'terrible blow' which was about to befall the king. The plot should have been abandoned forthwith - *it was the blatantly obvious thing to do*. But Catesby convinced the rest of the conspirators that their plan of action should carry on, that the letter didn't make any difference, that the plot could still succeed. He seemed very keen for the plot to continue until it reached its conclusion. Was Catesby a religious fanatic, his judgement clouded by Catholic zeal, or was he Robert Cecil's man? It is said that John Street, the musketeer marksman responsible for shooting dead Robert Catesby, was later granted a government pension of 2/- per day (roughly £15-£17 nowadays) for life as a reward. Were the deaths of Robert Catesby and Francis Tresham the result of loose ends being tidied up by Robert Cecil? To celebrate the saving of the king, bonfires were lit throughout Westminster and London, the normally pitch-black streets becoming ablaze with light.

[Robert Cecil hated Roman Catholics, and considered that the king's attitude towards them was too lenient. Cecil, created 1st Earl of Salisbury in 1605 by King James, had a huge spy network. He, more than any other man, knew what was going on.

Did Robert Cecil encourage, perhaps even instigate, the Gunpowder Plot, in order to force the king to take a more severe stance towards Roman Catholics? Very probably.

Catholics were not allowed to study at university in England - if they wished to go to university they had to enrol in one on the Continent. After the Gunpowder Plot, laws were also introduced which banned English Catholics from practising law, from practising medicine, from voting in elections, and from becoming officers in the army or the navy.]

The Titus Oates Plot

King Charles II made a secret deal with the French King, Louis XIV, that, in return for a French pension (he was short of money) he would restore the rights of English Catholics. Information about this 'secret' pact leaked out and Charles denied any such deal had been made. In spite of this, in 1674 he was called to take an oath before Parliament that there had been no such agreement - this he swore.

Charles' marriage had produced no children, so his brother James, Duke of York, was the legitimate heir, and James, unlike Charles, did not hide the fact that he was a Catholic.

Titus Oates was an Anglican priest. In 1677 he joined the Catholic Church. Soon after, he claimed that he had discovered a Catholic plot to kill the king and place his brother James on the throne.

6 Sept 1678 - In London, Oates swore an affidavit before a well-known Anglican magistrate, Sir Edmund Godfrey, detailing his accusations against certain Catholics, including Catholic nobles.

12 Oct 1678 - The magistrate Godfrey disappeared. Five days later his body was found in a ditch on Primrose Hill. He had been 'run through with his own sword'. Oates stated publicly that Godfrey had been investigating a Catholic plot to kill the king when he was murdered, and accused the Jesuits (a staunch Roman Catholic order) of killing him. The body of Sir Edmund Godfrey was put on display. Panic swept through London, and this led to the prosecution of more than 1,200 Catholics and the execution of 24 men and women.

King Charles interrogated Titus Oates personally and found several discrepancies in his story. He ordered Oates' arrest. A couple of days later, Parliament forced his release.

When James came to the throne in 1685, Titus Oates was tried and convicted of perjury, having concocted the plot and caused a reign of terror. He was again imprisoned, but when James was deposed in 1688, Oates was released and awarded a pension by Parliament. The killer, or killers, of the magistrate, Sir Edmund Godfrey, were never brought to justice. The case remained unsolved.

The Cato Street Conspiracy

The Cato Street conspiracy was a plot to assassinate the British cabinet. Led by Arthur Thistlewood, there were some twenty-odd men involved, one of whom was

George Edwards. *Edwards was a government agent.* About six agents were involved, spying on the conspirators. George Edwards actually came up with the means to carry out their desired purpose. Edwards pointed out to the group a newspaper article which stated that several members of the government were going to attend a dinner at the house of the Earl of Harrowby at 39 Grosvenor Square.

Arthur Thistlewood took the bait, and decided that they would enter 39 Grosvenor Square and assassinate the cabinet ministers who were there.

A two-storey building, comprising a stable with hay-loft above, was rented in Cato Street, which was only about a mile from Grosvenor Square. The plotters would gather at their rendezvous, then make their way to No 39.

The authorities, of course, knew every detail of their plan, and Bow Street Runners watched the conspirators arrive at their meeting-place in Cato Street. When they were all inside, they raided the building to arrest them. Amazingly, Arthur Thistlewood, after killing one of the Bow Street Runners, escaped with three others out of a back window. The authorities, of course, already knew the names of every man involved, and the four escapees were captured the next day.

The government did not dare to use the evidence of George Edwards in the trial, because the defence would have accused him of being an agent provocateur, so two of the conspirators were offered their lives to turn King's Evidence and they gave evidence for the prosecution against their former accomplices and friends.

Arthur Thistlewood and four others were found guilty of high treason, and were hanged at Newgate

Prison. Five others were also condemned to be hanged, but their executions were commuted to transportation for life. (Cato Street is an alley leading from Crawford Place, off the Edgware Road.)

The Jubilee Plot

The Golden Jubilee of Queen Victoria was celebrated on the 21st of June, 1887. Plain-clothes detectives mingled with the crowds as the royal procession made its way from Buckingham Palace to Westminster Abbey for the thanksgiving ceremony. The day's festivities passed off without incident.

Four months later, in October, the Assistant Commissioner of the Metropolitan Police, James Monro, revealed that the day of Victoria's Golden Jubilee had not been quite so care-free, that there had in fact been a bomb plot by Irish Catholics to blow up Westminster Abbey and assassinate Queen Victoria, together with the leading British aristocracy. The Press named it the Jubilee Plot.

It was claimed that preventing a national catastrophe was a triumph for the Secret Service (headed by James Monro and Robert Anderson) and the Metropolitan Police (headed by Sir Charles Warren).

The leader of the bomb plot was Francis Frederick Millen. Like the previous conspiracies, double-agents were involved, and the principal agent in the Jubilee Plot was the said *Francis Frederick Millen* - agent provocateur. Irish-born, he had fought in Mexico for Benito Juarez against the forces of Emperor Maximilian in the 1860s. In 1866, Millen was recruited as an informer by the British government, and the next year he joined the Clan-na-Gael, an Irish-American revolutionary organisation. Its aim was to overthrow the British Government in Ireland, and achieve Home Rule.

Millen became Chairman of the Military Council of the Clan-na-Gael - and from this organisation the Jubilee Plot originated.

In the lead up to the Golden Jubilee celebrations, newspapers predicted an Irish terrorist attack on Queen Victoria. The terror plot was secret - *yet newspapers published warnings of a forthcoming bombing outrage.* There is only one way in which the Press could have obtained this information, and that is a leak from a source involved in the actual plot. This source would not have been the Clan-na-Gael, for obvious reasons, so the leak to the newspapers must have had a police or government origin.

Of course, the day was peaceful. No bombs exploded. As was later claimed - *the Jubilee Plot had been stopped in its tracks.*

James Monro named Francis Frederick Millen as being head of the plot by the Clan-na-Gael to assassinate Queen Victoria, the British aristocracy, the Prime Minister and his Cabinet, etc, on the day of Victoria's Golden Jubilee. It was admitted that Mr Millen [a British agent whose payments came from the Foreign Office under the authority of the Prime Minister and Foreign Secretary, the Marquess of Salisbury (Robert Cecil) - direct descendant of the Robert Cecil (Gunpowder Plot), spymaster of King James] had managed to evade capture, and had escaped back to New York, 'despite the huge police hunt for him.'

Two plotters, Clan-na-Gael members Michael Harkins and Thomas Callan, were arrested in November, and at the Old Bailey in February 1888 they were sentenced to 15 years with hard labour. [The Jubilee Plot was created by the British Establishment - a government conspiracy whose motive was to discredit the Irish Catholic revolutionary organisations, and to destroy their aim of Home Rule for Ireland. *The mastermind of the plot was the Prime Minister, the Marquess of Salisbury. Major participants behind the scenes were James Monro, Robert Anderson (who ran his own agent within the Clan-na-Gael), and Sir Charles Warren.*]

In early 1889, The Times became involved in negotiations with Millen in New York. They offered him a total of £10,000 (£600,000 - £800,000 nowadays) to return to Britain and disclose the government's knowledge of the Jubilee Plot.

Millen liked to work alone in his study during the night, and on the morning of April 10th 1889, Francis Frederick Millen was found dead, sitting in his chair, by one of his daughters.

It was concluded that he had died from natural causes, that his heart had simply stopped. He was 57. Did Francis Frederick Millen actually die from natural causes, or was he silenced by British Intelligence? One thing is for sure - *the death of the Prime Minister's agent certainly occurred at a very convenient time for the British Government.*

Bloody Sunday

On the 22nd of October 1887, Sir Charles Warren, Commissioner of the Metropolitan Police, asked for 20,000 special constables to deal with socialist meetings in London: "We have in the last month been in greater danger from the disorganised attacks on property by the rough and criminal elements than we have been in London for many years past. The language used by the speakers at the various meetings has been more frank and open in recommending the poorer classes to help themselves from the wealth of the affluent."

A march was organised by the Social Democratic Federation for Sunday 13 November, culminating in Trafalgar Square, where a meeting would take place, demonstrating against the Coercion Act in Ireland, and to demand the release from prison of the M.P. William O'Brien. The Coercion Act gave the authorities the power to impose curfews, to hold trials without jury, allowed suspects to be detained for a time without trial, and introduced 'incitement' as an offence - the socialists and radicals no doubt feared the introduction of a similar act in mainland Britain.

William O'Brien M.P. had organised a rent strike on the estate of Lady Kingston, near the town of Mitchelstown, Co. Cork. Three tenants on this estate had been shot dead and others wounded on 9th September at the courthouse where William O'Brien was on trial at the time for 'incitement'. His imprisonment provoked protests and riots - such as Bloody Sunday, in London.

The march took place to a backdrop of extensive unemployment, social unrest, and Irish nationalist agitation against the British Government. The demonstrators were composed of socialists, republicans, left-wing radicals, and the unemployed. Among the marchers were people such as women's rights activist and brilliant orator, Annie Besant, the trade unionist John Burns, the socialist and champion of the workers, Liberal M.P. Robert Cunninghame-Graham, the artist and designer, William Morris, Eleanor Marx, widow of Karl Marx (all members of the Social Democratic Federation), and George Bernard Shaw.

The government, led by the Prime Minister, the Marquess of Salisbury, banned the meeting and took steps to prevent it taking place. Sir Charles Warren had posters put up at all street entrances to Trafalgar Square banning marchers from entering the square on Sunday 13th. When the marchers, numbering about 10,000 (The figure given out by the police. The number was actually estimated at 100,000), arrived at Trafalgar Square, they were confronted by 2,000 police under the control of Sir Charles Warren. There were also police on horseback. Many of the police had long truncheons and cutlasses. Warren also had hundreds of Grenadier Guards with loaded muskets and fixed bayonets, and the Life Guards (Household Cavalry) at his disposal.

In the violence that followed, two people died and almost two hundred marchers were injured. The demonstrators were beaten with truncheons and driven into side streets. Those who tried to get into the centre of Trafalgar Square were charged down by police horses. Charing Cross Hospital was filled with the badly-injured. Among the many arrests were those of

John Burns and Robert Cunninghame-Graham who were sent to Pentonville Prison.

Edward Carpenter, one of the demonstrators at Trafalgar Square on Bloody Sunday, described how events began to unfold: 'I was in the square at the time. The crowd was a most good-humoured, easy going, smiling crowd, but presently it was transformed. A regiment of mounted police came cantering up. The order had gone forth that we were to be kept moving. To keep a crowd moving is, I believe, a technical term for the process of riding roughshod in all directions, scattering, frightening, and batoning the people. I saw my friend Robert Muirhead seized by the collar by a mounted man and dragged along, while a bobby on foot aided in the arrest. I jumped to the rescue and slanged the two constables, for which I got a whack on the cheek-bone from a baton, but Muirhead was released. Later, in court, I was asked whether I had seen any rioting, and I replied in a very pointed way, "Not on the part of the people." '

A witness to the arrest of the workers' champion, Cunninghame-Graham, gave the following account: 'After Mr Graham's arrest was complete, one policeman after another, two certainly, stepped up and struck him on the head from behind with a violence and brutality which were shocking to behold. Even after this, when some five or six police were dragging him into the square, another from behind seized him most needlessly by the hair and dragged his head back, and in that condition he was forced many yards.' Presumably, Robert Cunninghame-Graham was amongst the injured admitted to Charing Cross Hospital.

In the 1880s, socialists, reformers, and revolutionaries, were on the march. There was working-class unrest over widespread unemployment, insanitary living conditions, and oppressive laws. There was also Irish Nationalism. In Victorian Britain, anti-Catholicism was deep-rooted. Less than forty years before, violent demonstrations had taken place in London, with Catholic churches and priests being attacked. As recent as 1886, when the Prime Minister, William Gladstone, tried to introduce Irish Home Rule, the Bill was defeated, and Gladstone had to resign. (To this day, by law, Catholics are barred from ascending the throne or from marrying the monarch - there are no plans to repeal the law.) And, of course, terror had been brought to the streets of London for several years by an Irish bombing campaign.

The underclass was a cauldron of discontent. All that was needed for the cauldron to boil over was a final ingredient, an event to take place which would galvanise the poorest classes - an event such as the heir to the throne marrying a Roman Catholic.

Chapter 3

Annie Elizabeth Crook

Census records (1891) list Annie Elizabeth Crook as born in the Parish of St Pancras, London. According to the ages listed for her in censuses, her birth took place sometime between April 1862 and April 1864. She was the daughter of William Crook and Sarah Annie Dryden. [Annie's mother is mostly listed as Sarah Annie Crook or Sarah A. Crook on censuses and birth registrations, but is also listed as Annie Crook. The ages given for her mean that she should have been born 1838-1839.]

Annie Elizabeth Crook was said by Joseph Sickert to have been the only child in the Crook family who was a Roman Catholic.

William Crook, son of William Crook and Sarah Quarterman, was Anglican. He was christened 24 October 1830, in the Church of St Mary the Virgin, Eton. [C of E]

So, if Annie was a Roman Catholic, it must have been through her mother, who is listed on the 1881 census as having been born in Scotland, and on the 1871 census as having been born in Berwick on Tweed - right on the Scottish border.

There is no record of the birth of Sarah Annie Dryden, or Annie Dryden, for Berwick on Tweed, Northumberland - or for the County of Berwick, Scotland. Or even for North Berwick, East Lothian.

William and Sarah Annie Crook had the following children:

Annie Elizabeth
Sarah Mary born 30 Apr 1866 Marylebone
    bap. 29 Jun 1867 All Souls Church
        [C of E]
Alice born 10 May 1868 Marylebone
    bap. 13 Jul 1870 St Andrew's Church
        [C of E]
Catherine born   1 Sep 1870 Marylebone
    bap. 24 Oct 1870 St Andrew's Church
        [C of E]

The glaringly obvious facts are that Annie Elizabeth Crook's birth registration and baptism are missing.

If Annie Elizabeth Crook was baptised a Roman Catholic, it is certain that her parents were married in a Roman Catholic church, and no record can be found of the marriage of William Crook and Sarah Annie Dryden.

If parents had only one of their children christened, it would be the first-born, yet, of William and Sarah Crook's four children, *the baptism details of their first-born are the only ones missing.*

With the question of Annie's religion being so important, it is *extremely suspicious,* to say the least. The fact that her records are the only ones missing points the finger at skulduggery.

For someone in authority, making Annie Elizabeth Crook's birth details disappear would have presented no problem at all. The following method would ensure this:

Her birth certificate is physically removed from the Record Office. The page containing the entry of her birth is taken out of the Birth Indexes book. This page is then rewritten without her birth entry, and replaced in the book. The book is then sent for rebinding.

For an individual with power and influence, removing Annie Elizabeth Crook's earliest details would have been so easy. For the British Establishment nothing would have been simpler.

Very few people would have had a transcript of their own birth certificate. Having personal possession of a copy of one's own birth certificate was not important in the 19th century for a working class person, unlike the obsession nowadays (even *before* the threat of terrorism) when proof of identity is necessary in order to obtain common modern-day items such as driving licences, bank or building society accounts, medical cards, passports, pensions, etc.

Annie Crook's life

Annie could not have had much of an education, because she could not sign her daughter's birth certificate when she was age 22-23, marking her X instead. In her teens, she worked as a domestic servant until she got the job as a shop assistant in Cleveland Street. She moved into a room in the same street, close to her place of work, while her parents lived in Rose Street, Soho, less than three quarters of a mile away. She met Prince Albert Victor, son of the Prince of Wales and Princess Alexandra, in Walter Sickert's studio in Cleveland Street in 1884 when she was modelling for the artist. Annie lived at 6 Cleveland Street and worked in James Currier's confectionery shop at 22 Cleveland Street, where she first met Sickert, whose studio was at No 15.

The couple fell in love, Annie became pregnant, and a daughter, Alice Margaret, was born on the 18th April 1885. The couple married in a Roman Catholic ceremony in the chapel of St Saviour's Hospital, Osnaburgh Street. [Oddly, there has been some dispute as to whether Annie actually lived at 6 Cleveland Street. On the birth certificate of Alice Margaret, the residence of Annie Elizabeth Crook is clearly stated as being 6 Cleveland Street. The name of the father is of course missing from the certificate.]

Details of the marriage and child eventually reached the Prime Minister, the Marquess of Salisbury. A raid was carried out in Cleveland Street, and Prince Albert Victor and Annie Crook were separated forever. He was taken back to court. She was held in Guy's Hospital where she was operated on and certified insane by Sir William Gull. Annie spent the rest of her life going in and out of different workhouses and hospitals. In between these periods of incarceration she more than likely lived on handouts from the civil parish or worked in low-paid jobs. For instance, in 1891 she is listed as a jam maker - possibly working in some menial capacity in a jam factory.

Annie Elizabeth Crook died in the Lunacy Ward of St George's Union Infirmary at 367 Fulham Road on 23 February, 1920.

The cause of her death is stated to be: (1) Myocardial degeneration. (2) Dementia. She was 56.

Annie is listed as normally living at 5 Pancras Street, St Pancras. She is stated, of course, to be 'Spinster'. The certificate is signed by her daughter, Alice Gorman.

St Saviour's Hospital

St Saviour's Home was opened at 10 Osnaburgh Street in September 1852 by the Rev. Edward Bouverie Pusey. It stood less than 100 yards from the north end of Cleveland Street, and was run by the Sisters of the Holy Cross, who had been founded by Pusey in 1845. The Sisters worked with Florence Nightingale at the hospital in Scutari during the Crimean War (1854-1856) tending wounded and diseased soldiers.

St Saviour's Hospital, 10 Osnaburgh Street

St Saviour's was a place of refuge, a home for 'Orphans and Distressed Women', and contained both an infirmary and a chapel which was situated at the east end of the building.

The Rev. Edward Bouverie Pusey was Regius Professor of Hebrew at Christ Church, Oxford, and he founded the Oxford Movement which was dedicated to returning the Church of England to its pre-Reformation state. Pusey advocated the use of Roman Catholic-style rituals in Anglican services.

So pro-Catholic was the Oxford Movement that John Kensit, a London bookseller, founded the Protestant Truth Society in opposition to the Oxford Movement (Also known as the Puseyites. Pusey House, an Anglican-Catholic house of devotion and learning, opened in Oxford in 1884.)

Pusey's friend, Edward Palmer, took over St Saviour's in 1877, and the 'Home' became a hospital - St Saviour's Cancer Hospital. In the chapel, Palmer installed a baroque altar-piece, and stalls (seats enclosed at the back and sides) which had once resided in the church in the Monastery at Buxheim in Bavaria, the former residence of Carthusian monks.

On the back and sides of the stalls various religious figures were carved. Amongst these were the twelve Apostles, St Benedict (founder of Roman Catholic monastic communities for monks and nuns), St Celestine (Pope Celestine V), St Dominic (founder of the Roman Catholic religious order, the Dominicans), St Ignatius of Loyola (founder of the Jesuits, a Roman Catholic order of priests who take a special oath of obedience to the Pope), and the Virgin Mary.

Roman Catholic baptisms and marriages would certainly have taken place in St Saviour's Chapel.

The Ornate Carving behind the Altar in St Saviour's Chapel

Evidence of Annie Crook's marriage in St Saviour's could have been removed from official sources even easier than her birth details, which had been registered for over 20 years before they became a problem. If the government had knowledge of the marriage within a year to eighteen months - which they would have had - it would simply be a case of withdrawing the certificate. Entries in the Marriage Indexes book took time to compile, as marriages from all over the country had to be gathered and collated. If a marriage took place in the autumn of say, 1885, it could be late 1886, or even early 1887, before the entry was ready for insertion into the indexes. The problem for the

Establishment was Annie's copy of the marriage certificate.

In 1897, St Saviour's Cancer Hospital became St Saviour's Hospital for Ladies of Limited Means, and the only surviving records are administrative records (1897-1941) for this hospital. The hospital was in use throughout World War I and World War II, but in 1963 a new St Saviour's was opened in Hythe, Kent.

The old hospital in Osnaburgh Street was demolished in 1964 to allow the widening of Euston Road.

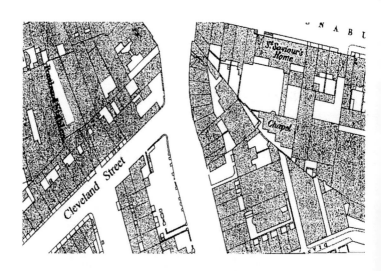

Map of 1873

Shows the proximity of St Saviour's and its Chapel to Cleveland Street.

Chapter 4

The Whitechapel Murders

Mary Ann Nichols

Mary Ann Walker was born 26 August 1845 at 1 Daws Court, Gunpowder Alley, off Shoe Lane, near Fleet Street. She was the daughter of Edward Walker and Caroline Webb. She had a brother, Edward, who was two years older than her. Mary Ann Walker's mother died before she was 6 years old, leaving Edward Walker to bring up his children alone.

Mary Ann Walker - married William Nichols 16 January 1864, St Bride's Parish Church, City of London.

William Nichols was born in Oxford, and was a machine printer. At the time of her marriage, Mary Ann's father, a locksmith, was working as a blacksmith. William and Mary Ann Nichols lived in Bouverie Street, off Fleet Street. They latterly lived in Peabody Buildings, Stamford Street, Lambeth. Their children were:

Edward John - born 1866, Camberwell
Percy George - born 1868, Newington
Alice Esther - born 1870, Bermondsey
Eliza Sarah - born 1877, Lambeth
Henry Alfred - born 1879, Lambeth

In 1880, the couple separated, she leaving Peabody Buildings and 'taking to the drink'. She began to spend her nights in different workhouses and ended up in the East End. At the time of her murder she was living at 56 Flower and Dean Street, Spitalfields, Whitechapel.

Killed: 31 August 1888. Body found at 3.40 am, in Buck's Row, Whitechapel, by P.C. Neil (probably Thomas Neal). He said that when he passed through at 3.15 am the body was not there. Neal obtained the assistance of P.C. Jonas Mizen and P.C. John Thain. P.C. Thain then sent for Dr Rees Llewellyn. Mary Ann Nichols last seen alive at 2.30 am.

Injuries: Lying on her back next to gates leading into a stable yard. Throat cut, left to right, from ear to ear, the windpipe, gullet, and spinal cord being cut right through. Abdomen cut open from the ribs on the right side down, under the pelvis. Jagged cut from there up to the left of the stomach. The intestines exposed. No unusual noise heard by anyone living nearby.

Blood: Very little blood at the spot where the body was found.

If she had been cut open where her corpse was found, the spot would have been very bloody. It was not.

East London Advertiser, 8th Sept 1888: 'The woman was found with her throat cut from ear to ear, and her body ripped open from the groin to almost the breast-bone. The whole affair is mysterious. The place where the body was found was evidently not that where the murder was committed. There were stains and pools of blood at intervals for a considerable distance from the spot where the corpse lay, and at this spot no screams or sounds of any kind were heard by the inhabitants of the street, though a night watchman in a warehouse was at his post close by, and there were people awake in several of the surrounding houses. The woman must have been dragged in or carried.'

Burial: A hearse, accompanied by two coaches containing Edward Walker and members of the Nichols family, carried the body of Mary Ann Nichols to the City of London Cemetery, Ilford, where she was buried on 6 September, 1888.

Her grave, in Section No. 318, lies under a grassy area in the memorial garden. There is now a commemorative plaque. This is not over the actual grave, but by the side of the road running through section 318.

Annie Chapman

Ruth Chapman gave birth to her first child, Annie Eliza, about eight months before she married the father, George Smith. Therefore, although she called herself Annie Smith, her actual name could just as easily have been Annie Chapman. She was born in 1841, probably at 29 Montpelier Place, Knightsbridge.

Her future husband, John Chapman, was born in Newmarket, Suffolk. His place of birth probably explains his later employment as a head groom, Newmarket being a major centre for the training of thoroughbred horses.

Annie Eliza Smith - married John Chapman 1 May 1869, All Saints Church, Knightsbridge.

John Chapman was a coachman at the time of the marriage, and the couple were living with Annie's mother at 29 Montpelier Place, Annie's father being dead for some years by this time. In London, Annie and John Chapman had two children:

Emily Ruth - born 1870, Westminster

Annie - born 1874, Westminster

Emily developed epilepsy, and suffered from the fits associated with this disease. In the latter part of the 1870s the family moved to St Leonard's Hill, Clewer, Windsor, where John Chapman was employed as the head groom at a stud farm. The Chapman family lived in a flat above the stables. In Windsor, Annie Chapman had a son:

John - born 1882, Windsor

Sometime after the birth of her son, Annie Chapman separated from her husband, probably moving back in with her mother. John Chapman died on Christmas Day 1886, age 44, Annie's 10/- per week allowance then ceasing. In 1887 she abandoned her children and mother for the East End.

Annie Chapman was living at 35 Dorset Street, Spitalfields, Whitechapel, at the time of her murder.

Killed: 8 September 1888. Body found in the back yard of 29 Hanbury Street, Spitalfields, at 5.55 am. A door from the street gave access to a passageway which led past the stairway up to the rooms of No 29 and into a back yard, where the body was found. Last seen alive at 2.00 am.

Injuries: Lying on her back. Left arm resting on left breast. Legs drawn up. Small intestines and flap of the abdomen lying on the right side above the right shoulder. These were still attached to the rest of the intestines inside the body by a cord. Two flaps of skin from the lower part of the abdomen lying in a large quantity of blood above the left shoulder. Throat cut deeply from left, and back in a jagged manner right around the throat. Handkerchief tied around the neck. The uterus and two thirds of the bladder removed. Not with the body, so they must have been taken by the killers. [More on the taking away of human organs in relation to the murder of Catharine Eddowes.] No unusual noise heard by anyone living nearby.

Blood: A pool of blood above the left shoulder in which lay the skin cut from the abdomen. On the back wall of the house (at the head of the body) at about 18 inches (around 46 centimetres) from the ground - about 6 patches of blood varying in size from a sixpenny piece to a point. And on the wooden paling to the left of the body, near the head, patches and smears of blood about 14 inches (about 36 centimetres) from the ground. The blood spots were 19 mm to 1 mm in diameter. (old sixpence = 19 mm)

The *biggest* patch of blood was *less than* ¾" in diameter. Hardly what would be expected from such violent injuries - the throat being brutally slashed across and the stomach being ripped wide open. The vicinity should have been saturated with blood. And, except for the blood seeping directly from the small intestines, and the blood from the abdominal skin, the few small blood stains were 14" to 18" above ground level.

This lack of blood - as in the case of Mary Ann Nichols - strongly suggests that this could not have been the murder scene. The height of the drops of blood would seem to indicate a body being dropped to the ground, or tipped out of a container.

Two people carrying a body through a passageway to a back yard might seem very risky, but not if the body was wrapped in material of some kind.

71

A reporter on the scene stated that blood could be seen leading along the passageway *from* Hanbury Street. No mention of blood *along* Hanbury Street.

A carriage stopping at the entrance to the passageway, the covered body being lifted out and carried along the passage, could certainly account for this.

Detailed knowledge of local police patrol times would have ensured - as with Mary Ann Nichols - that they did not encounter a constable unexpectedly.

The Pall Mall Gazette, 8 September 1888, mentioned this strange lack of blood:

*'A Mr & Mrs Davis occupy the upper storey (the house consisting of two storeys). The body was found by Mr Davis as he was going to work about six o'clock. The throat was cut open in a fearful manner - so deep in fact that the murderer, evidently thinking that he had severed the head from the body, tied a handkerchief round it so as to keep it on. The body had been ripped open and disembowelled, the heart and abdominal viscera lying by the side. The fiendish work was completed by the murderer tying part of the entrails round the victim's neck. **There was no blood on the clothes.**'* (emphasis added)

A tradition has grown up around Annie Chapman that two brass rings, some pennies (no specific number given), and two new farthings, were laid at her feet. It is a belief which has persisted. In their books on Jack the Ripper, authors such as Daniel Farson and Stephen Knight have stated that this act was carried out. Yet, although many newspapers reported the removal of the rings, there appears to be no newspaper account of the

Annie Chapman murder which offers verification of the ritualistic laying-out of the above-mentioned items.

The Pall Mall Gazette, 8 September 1888:

'The third finger of the left hand bore signs of rings having been wrenched off it.'

The Times, 10 September 1888:

'One or more rings seem to have been torn from the middle finger of the left hand.'

The rings and coins would seem to be an oral tradition. But this tradition must be based on *something*.

The indisputable fact is that rings *were wrenched* from her finger and were missing. This act must have had a purpose. Something strange was afoot. The rings were forced off her finger for a reason by someone involved in the murder - in their case it could not have been theft. Therefore, there must have been another motive - the obvious one being that they were a clue - and this gives credence to the tradition.

If the rings and coins had been arrayed at her feet and had been immediately removed by the police on arrival at the scene, this would account for their disappearance, but individuals were there as well as the police, and would therefore have observed the rings and coins. This probably accounts for the origin of the tradition, because those who saw them would have later mentioned the fact in personal conversations. Various statements were given at the inquest on the Chapman murder. The body of Annie Chapman was discovered by John Davis who lived at 29 Hanbury Street where the corpse was found. Horrified, he ran into the street. 'He at once called two men who worked for Bailey, a packing-case maker of Hanbury-street, whose place was three doors off. *These men entered the passageway and looked at the woman.'* [The Times, 11 Sept 1888]

The two men whom Davis called from Bailey's were James Green and James Kent. *They stood on the steps at the back door.* John Davis also met P.C. John Pinnock. Having viewed the corpse from the passageway, P.C. Pinnock sent the men to Commercial Street Police Station, at least four hundred yards away, for assistance. Inspector Joseph Chandler was on duty, and he hurried back with the men to the back yard of 29 Hanbury Street where he took charge of the situation.

About 6 o'clock, the grandson of Amelia Richardson of 29 Hanbury Street, Thomas Richardson, age 14, said, "Oh, Grandmother, there is a woman murdered!"

*'Witness went down immediately and saw the body of deceased lying in the yard. The police **and several others were in the passageway**, but there was no one in the yard at the time. The police then took possession of the place.'* [The Times, 13 Sept 1888]

Henry John Holland, 4 Aden-yard, Mile End Road:
'Witness went through the passage and saw the deceased lying in the yard. Witness went into the yard and looked at the deceased but did not touch her or her clothes.' [The Times, 13 Sept 1888]

James Green:
'No one was in the yard when the inspector arrived.'
[The Times, 13 Sept 1888]

Inspector Chandler must be the chief suspect for the removal of the rings and coins, but, as has been demonstrated, quite a few people had had a good look at Annie Chapman's corpse during the several minutes

74

which must have elapsed between the discovery of the body and the point at which Chandler arrived and assumed control. The story of the rings, pennies, and farthings lying at Chapman's feet would have circulated, bringing into existence the oral tradition which is still with us. Remember, nobody was in the yard when Chandler arrived, so he would not have known at that point that several people had had a close up view of the body and the items laid out.

The physical evidence was removed, but, in his hurry to pick up the articles, Inspector Chandler was not quite totally successful. Perhaps the smallest items were not so easy to grip.

The Star, 10 Sept 1888:

'Two pills were found near the body.'
'There were also found two farthings, polished brightly.' (emphasis added)

The rings and coins could represent the divesting of all metal prior to a candidate being initiated into Masonic Degrees (Stephen Knight: The Final Solution), the person placing these items therefore disclosing that the killer was a Freemason.

Annie Chapman was divested of all metal, the metal objects then being laid together at her feet. Were the coins actually Chapman's? Surely, if she had been in possession of several coins, this suggests that she already had enough for a night's lodging and a drink, so it would be unnecessary for her to be still touting for business at 2.00 am.

The Times, 10 September 1888:

'She left the lodging-house, 35 Dorset Street, because she had not the 4d to pay for her bed.'

The coins are likely to have belonged to the person who placed them, someone who was assisting the killer. He obviously had a reason, and this seems much more direct than Masonic initiation:

brass rings - the brass: those in charge.

pennies, and farthings - coppers: the police.

The rings and coins were much too dangerous to be allowed to remain at the scene for newspaper reporters to view, because the items pointed the finger directly at the man in charge of the Metropolitan Police, Sir Charles Warren.

A comb and a piece of rough muslin also lay on the ground near her feet. These also seemed to have been set down deliberately.

George Bagster Phillips, divisional-surgeon of police: *'He searched the yard, and in doing so found a small piece of coarse muslin and a pocket comb in a paper case lying at the feet of the woman near the paling; and they apparently had been placed there in order or arranged there.'*

[The Times, 14 Sept 1888]

Again, like the rings and coins, the items must have been put there for a reason. The comb and muslin were clues, with symbolic meaning. The comb hints that someone in Freemasonry is responsible. A comb is made by bees to store honey in their beehive, and both 'bee' and 'beehive' represent 'industry' in Freemasonry. Bees are able to accomplish their task because they work as a group (like the killers), and - only the bees know what goes on within the beehive. Muslin is an old slang word, a derogatory term for women. Coarse muslin: the victim - a common woman with low morals.

The Times wrote on 10 Sept 1888 regarding Annie Chapman that, 'Some years ago she separated from her husband who made her a weekly allowance of 10/- . There were two children, a boy and a girl. The boy is in the Cripples' Home, while the girl is in an institution in France.'

[Emily, the Chapman's eldest daughter, had died, age 12, at Windsor in 1882 from meningitis.]

Even at this early stage the murders held a morbid fascination for many people. The spot where Annie Chapman's mutilated body was discovered became an instant attraction for sightseers:

'For several hours past, the occupants of the adjoining house have been charging an admission of one penny to people anxious to view the spot where the body was found. Several hundreds of people have availed themselves of this opportunity.'
[The Star, Saturday, 8 Sept 1888]

Burial: An unaccompanied hearse took the body of Annie Chapman to Manor Park Cemetery on 14 September. The funeral was private, only her relatives being at the cemetery. Her grave is unmarked. Another burial is said to have taken place over the top of that of Annie Chapman.

Elizabeth Stride

Said to have been born in 1843, Stockholm, Sweden. Her father was Augustus Gustafson. Elizabeth Gustafson came to London in 1866.

Elizabeth Gustifson [sic] married John Thomas Stride 7 March 1869, St Giles' Church, St Giles-in-the-Fields.

At the time of the marriage Elizabeth Gustafson lived at 67 Gower Street, Bloomsbury, and John Stride at 21 Munster Street, Regent's Park. John Stride came from Sheerness in Kent, and was a carpenter. The couple lived at 178 Poplar High Street, later moving to 69 Usher Road, Bow, where they are listed on the 1881 census. No children are listed.

John Stride died, age 63, in 1884. Soon after, Elizabeth was living in Whitechapel. In 1888 she was living at 35 Dorset Street with a man named Michael Kidney, and for a few days before her murder at 32 Flower and Dean Street, Spitalfields, Whitechapel.

Killed: 30 September 1888. Body found at 1.00 am inside the gates of Dutfield's stable yard, 40 Berner Street, by Louis Diemschutz. He returned with P.C. Henry Lamb who then sent for Dr Frederick Blackwell and Dr George Bagster Phillips. Elizabeth Stride last seen alive at 12.45 am. [by Israel Schwartz, age 13]

Injuries: She was lying on her left side, the left arm extended from the elbow. The right arm resting on the stomach. Legs drawn up, with the knees together, and the feet close to the wall. Throat cut deeply across. Blood oozing onto the cobbles. A silk handkerchief was around the throat. The body was warm. No unusual noise heard by anyone living nearby.

A report appeared in the Pall Mall Gazette of 30th Oct 1888 - the details contained therein originating from information given by Stride to Michael Kidney with whom she was living:

'She had lost her husband in the Princess Alice disaster, as well as two children, one of whom was drowned in the father's arms. She herself escaped by climbing up a rope as the vessel was sinking. Her surviving children (she said she had nine) are being brought up in the country at a school connected with the Swedish church.'

This is a very dramatic and exciting story, but it is pure fantasy. *Elizabeth Stride's account of the tragic death of her husband and two of her nine children cannot possibly be true.* The sinking of the paddle-steamer Princess Alice occurred in 1878, when over 600 lives were lost, and, as already stated, John Stride did not die until 1884. No children are recorded for the Strides.

Whether or not Elizabeth Stride had grapes in her hand when her body was found has been disputed. This matter can be cleared up once and for all. It was stated categorically that she did.

The Times, Monday 1st October 1888:

'In her right hand were tightly clasped some grapes, and in her left she held a number of sweetmeats.'

Pall Mall Gazette, 1st October 1888: Statement by Louis Diemschutz, who found the body:

'She had a flower in the bosom of her dress. In one hand she had some grapes and in the other some sweets. She was grasping them tightly.'

Further verification is provided by a resident of the street who was at the scene *immediately,* before the doctor arrived. The doctor's account and that of the eyewitness appear in The Illustrated Police News, 6 October 1888:

'The doctor (Blackwell) who had been called about ten past one by a policeman to 40 Berner Street, said, "Life could not have been extinct for more than twenty minutes. The deceased had on a black velvet jacket and a black dress; in her hand she held a box of cachous, whilst in her dress was a flower." '

The resident: Mrs Mortimer living at 36 Berner Street (My Italics):

"I heard a commotion outside. I went to see what was the matter. I saw the body of a woman lying huddled up with her throat cut from ear to ear. The woman appeared to be respectable judging by her clothes, and in her hand was found a bunch of grapes and some sweets. A man touched her face and said it was quite warm. It was just after one o'clock when I went out, and the only man whom I had seen pass through the street from the Commercial Road was a young man carrying a black, shiny bag, who walked fast down the street from the Commercial Road."

Mrs Mortimer also stated, "I was standing at the door of my house nearly the whole time between half-past twelve and one o'clock, and did not notice anything unusual. There was certainly *no noise* made, and I did not observe anyone enter the gates (of Dutfield's Yard, just inside which Stride's body lay). If

80

a man had come out of the yard before one o'clock I must have seen him. It was *almost incredible* to me that the thing could have been done without the steward's wife (steward of the Socialist Club, close by) hearing a noise, for she was sitting in the kitchen, from which a window opens *four yards* from the spot where the woman was found."

Charles Letchford of 30 Berner Street:
"I passed through the street at half-past twelve, and everything seemed to me to be going on as usual, and my sister was standing at the door at ten minutes to one, but did not see anyone pass by."

We don't know who the young man with the bag was, but we know he was not the killer, because neither Mrs Mortimer, nor the steward's wife, nor Charles Latchford's sister, who were all close by, saw him go into, or come out of, Dutfield's Yard. This young man simply walked down the street.

The inquest into Stride's death only mentioned the cachous, so either the grapes were removed in the 10 minutes or so between the arrival of Mrs Mortimer and the appearance of Dr Blackwell, or they were deliberately left out of the official report.

Grapes refer directly to the physician William Gull. Amongst the medical profession, he was known for his advocacy of the health benefits of grapes. Gull writing in 1877:

'I eat no cane sugar but the sugar of the grape.' 'I never travel, or I may say go anywhere, without raisins.' 'When fatigued, I prefer grapes and raisins.' Grapes, and a box of cachous were in Stride's hands. Sickert, of course, said that drugged grapes were given to the victims by Gull, rendering them unconscious, thereby removing the highly dangerous possibility of screams being heard by someone nearby. Whoever placed the grapes and cachous in her hands did not just *happen to* have them with him, then placing them as an afterthought. The person must have planned his actions.

The grapes obviously alluded to Gull's drugging procedure. Cachous were used to sweeten the breath. They were pills - and 'pills' was street jargon for *a doctor.*

Two pills had been placed beside Annie Chapman's body, but these had been largely ignored. This time the pills were placed in the hand of the victim. Someone involved - almost certainly Walter Sickert, since he left clues in some of his paintings - was leaving pointers.

Berner Street was only around 200 yards long. Elizabeth Stride *was last seen alive* at 12.45 am. Her *dead body* was *found* at 1.00 am.

Mrs Mortimer stood at the door of 36 Berner Street from 12.30 am-1.00 am.

During the same period, the steward's wife sat in her kitchen with the window open *12 feet* from where the body was found at 40 Berner Street.

Charles Letchford's sister, at the door of 30 Berner Street at 12.50 am, saw no one pass.

Three people, not only very close to the spot where Stride's body was found, but *were there when her murder should have been taking place,* yet they heard no sound of anything out of the ordinary, and had seen nothing unusual. *They were amazed that a woman could be murdered right in front of them, yet witness nothing.*

But, if the murder took place in a coach, then the body pushed out as the coach was passing the entrance to Dutfield's Yard, Berner Street, they would have heard nothing, and seen no one enter or leave the yard. A description of injuries sustained by Stride's face, and the position in which she was found, strongly supports this modus operandi.

This report appeared in the Illustrated Police News, 6 October 1888: 'Severe bruises on her left temple and left cheek. When discovered, the body was lying as if the woman had fallen forward, her feet being about a couple of yards from the street, and her head in a gutter which runs down, close to the wall. The woman lay on her left side, face downwards.'

The bruises to her face and her resting position are consistent with her being shoved head-first out of a coach.

The onlookers would have seen no one as the coach was driven slowly through the gloomy darkness past the gates of Dutfield's Yard. *The people in Berner Street were baffled as to how they did not see the killer and the murder. Jack the Ripper had murdered his third victim 'right in front of them' - and they had seen nothing at all.* Coaches passing by in the streets were so common nobody paid any attention to them.

Burial: Elizabeth Stride was buried in a pauper's grave in East London Cemetery, Plaistow, on 6 October 1888. The cost of the funeral was paid by her parish.

The four 'witnesses' who should have seen the murder actually taking place - but saw (and heard) nothing at all:

Mrs Fanny Mortimer, age 48, 36 Berner Street.
Charles Letchford, age 22, 30 Berner Street.
Catherine Letchford, age 20, 30 Berner Street.

Mrs. Diemschutz, 40 Berner Street.

The Steward of the Socialist International Working Mens' Educational Club was Louis Diemschutz. The address of the club, like Dutfield's stable yard, was 40 Berner Street.

All those above should have watched the 'murder' taking place before them. Mrs. Diemschutz at the open window had a ringside seat.

Catharine Eddowes

Catharine Eddowes was born 14 April 1842 at Graisley Green, Wolverhampton. Her parents were George Eddowes, a tinplate worker, and Catharine Evans. They had a family of three sons and four daughters. Catharine was the fourth child of the seven. The Eddowes family moved to Bermondsey in London sometime in 1843. They lived at 35 West Street. In 1855, Catharine's mother died.

Around 1862 Catharine Eddowes met an Irishman from County Mayo, Thomas Conway. Conway has previously been described as an army pensioner. Perhaps he was, but he was only 27. Eddowes called herself Kate. She said her religion was Roman Catholic, and always claimed she had married Thomas Conway who was probably of the same religion. They may well have married in St Mary's R.C. Church, Great Yarmouth, c.1863. However, the marriage registers for St Mary's prior to 1886 are missing.

They had three children:

        Catherine - born 1864, Gt. Yarmouth
        Thomas - born 1868, Westminster
        George - born 1874, London

Thomas Conway worked as a hawker, selling goods around the streets from a horse and cart. In the early 1880s the couple lived at 71 Lower George Street, Chelsea. She worked as a charwoman, probably in Chelsea. Sometime in the mid-1880s Thomas Conway and Catharine Eddowes parted. She moved into the East End. Her final residence was 55 Flower and Dean Street, Spitalfields, Whitechapel.

Killed: 30 September, 1888. Body found in a corner of Mitre Square at 1.45 am. Last seen alive at 1.30 am.

Injuries: Catharine Eddowes was butchered. Body lying on its back. The head turned towards the left shoulder. Arms by the side of the body. Both palms upwards. Left leg extended straight. Right leg bent at the knee. Both thighs naked. A 2ft piece of intestine was placed between the body and the left arm. The throat cut deeply across. Face severely mutilated. Lobe of right ear sliced through. Part of the nose cut off. A cut through the lower left eyebrow. Right eyebrow cut through. Deep cut from the bridge of the nose down to the angle of the jaw on the right cheek. The cut went right into the bone. The upper lip cut through. A 1½" cut on the right side of the mouth. A triangular 1½" flap cut on both cheeks, which peeled up the skin. Cut open from the breast to the pelvis. The liver stabbed, and slit through with a vertical cut. Stomach cut open. Disembowelled. Left kidney removed. Intestines drawn out and placed over the right shoulder. The womb cut through horizontally, leaving only a ¾" stump. Rest of the womb missing. A cut down the right side of the vagina and rectum. Cuts down the inner side of both thighs, forming two flaps of skin up to the groin. The body was warm. The left kidney and the womb were not found with the body.

Blood: Blood on the pavement around the neck and shoulder area. No blood on the pavement except for this. No spurts of blood on the pavement. No spurts of blood on the bricks of the wall where the body was found. No blood on the front of the clothes. No unusual noise heard by anyone living nearby.

A portion of the apron of Catharine Eddowes had been cut off and was missing. At 2.55 am it was discovered in the doorway entrance to the stairway of 108-119 Wentworth Model Buildings, Goulston Street, about 500 yards from Mitre Square.

Thomas Wentworth was executed as a traitor to the State. Likewise, this woman. [Thought to be Kelly]

Above the piece of apron, in chalk, a cryptic message was written on the wall.

There are two versions of this, taken down by policemen at the scene:

The Juwes are the men That
Will not be Blamed for nothing

(Written in the notebook of P.C. Harry Long of the Metropolitan Police)

The Juwes are not the men
That Will be Blamed for nothing

(Written in the notebook of D.C. Daniel Halse of the City of London Police)

(Stephen Knight: The Final Solution): The apron is masonic. And in Masonic legend, the three killers of Hiram Abiff, master builder of Solomon's Temple, were Jubelo, Jubela, Jubelum, known collectively as the Juwes. They tried to obtain the secrets of master masonry from Hiram, which he refused to divulge, so they killed him.

When Sir Charles Warren heard about the chalked message he went to the scene and wiped the message off the wall - the Chief Commissioner of the Metropolitan Police had just removed vital evidence with his own hand!

The popular theory regarding Catharine Eddowes is that the Ripper mistook her for Mary Jane Kelly. [This speculation will in fact be verified later from an excellent source - straight from the horse's mouth, so to speak.] Catharine Eddowes had been picked up at 8.00 pm by the police for being drunk, and had been taken to Bishopsgate Police Station. There, when asked her name, she said that it was Kelly, because she lived with her common-law husband, a man named John Kelly. When a constable checked her pockets he found a pawn ticket with the name M.J. Kelly on it, probably signifying Mrs John Kelly. The killers were looking for Mary Jane Kelly, so if information was being passed to them, this incredible coincidence sealed the fate of Catharine Eddowes. She was released from Bishopsgate Police Station at 1.00 am. If the killers knew she was going to be discharged at that time, they certainly did not want to miss the main target - 'Mary Jane Kelly.' Time was of the essence, so Elizabeth Stride was taken care of as quickly as possible. There was no time to inflict the usual mutilations - the butcher's bloody talents were needed urgently elsewhere.

[Walter Sickert still had enough time to leave another of his clues with Stride though!]

Police constable Edward Watkins walked through Mitre Square at 1.30 am. There was no body in the square. When he returned at 1.45 am the *dissected* corpse of Catharine Eddowes was lying there.

Police Constable William Harvey looked into the square at 1.41 am-1.42 am and saw no body. It means the body appeared 1.42 am-1.44 am.

A lone killer stalking his victim, killing, then mutilating, successfully removing internal organs, and carefully cutting his incisions, those on the cheeks and thighs being almost delicate. All of this done in gloomy darkness while kneeling on a hard stone pavement, and surely accompanied by a constant, nerve-jangling fear of someone entering the square from any direction and being caught in the act. There is *no way* that this was the modus operandi of the killer.

Catharine Eddowes was butchered. The pavement and nearby walls should have been covered with blood, yet this was not the case. She was obviously killed somewhere else, the body then being placed in Mitre Square. Either the killers were extremely lucky beyond belief, or they knew the exact times of the police patrols, and hence the whereabouts of the constables on their beats at all times. But, even if they knew the predictable, as in the case of the police patrols, there was always the unexpected. A passer-by could just chance upon the scene, so surely a lookout would be essential. Catharine Eddowes had been seen in Duke Street near Mitre Square with a man wearing a red handkerchief around his neck.

The mitre and square are masons' tools, and are involved in Masonic ceremonies. And of course Masons are said to be 'on the square', i.e. the chequered square in lodges. A mitre is also a joint formed when two surfaces meet at a corner giving an angle of 90° as in a wall, and Catharine Eddowes was found in the south-west corner of Mitre Square.

The Times, 1 October 1888, stated:

'The fact that he gives proof of the possession of anatomical skill does much to narrow the enquiry. Not one man in a thousand could have played the part of Annie Chapman's murderer. In one of these new cases, if not in both, we have evidence of a similar kind.'

East London Advertiser, 6 October 1888:

'One of the most extraordinary incidents in connection with the crime is that not the slightest scream or noise was heard.'

When P.C. Watkins discovered the body of Catharine Eddowes he ran across the road for help, and returned accompanied by a watchman named Morris, whom he sent for assistance.

East London Advertiser 6 October 1888, re. Morris the watchman:

'The strangest part of the whole thing was that he did not hear the slightest sound. As a rule he could hear the footsteps of the policeman as he passed on his beat every quarter of an hour, so that it appeared impossible that the woman could have uttered any sound without his detecting it. It was only on the night that he remarked to some policemen that he wished the "butcher" would come round Mitre Square and he would give him a doing; yet the "butcher" had come and he was perfectly ignorant of it.'

In the same newspaper article we are told:

'A little while after the finding of the body all traces of blood had been washed away by direction of the authorities.' (emphasis added)

After the murder of the two women on the same night, two letters were made public, one of which had been held back. This was dated 25 September 1888, and was written in red ink. It had been received at the Central News Agency on 27th of September.

'Dear Boss

I keep on hearing the police have caught me but they won't fix me just yet. I have laughed when they look so clever and talk about being on the right track. That joke about Leather Apron gave me real fits. I am down on whores and I shan't quit ripping them till I do get buckled. Grand work the last job was. I gave the lady no time to squeal. How can they catch me now. I love my work and want to start again. You will soon hear of me with my funny little games. I saved some of the proper red stuff in a ginger beer bottle over the last job to write with but it went thick like glue and I can't use it. Red ink is fit enough I hope ha ha. The next job I do I shall clip the lady's ears off and send to the police officers just for jolly wouldn't you. Keep this letter back till I do a bit more work, then give it out straight. My knife is nice and sharp I want to get to work right away if I get a chance. Good luck

Yours truly

Jack the Ripper'

The second message was sent on a postcard postmarked 1 October, i.e. probably sent *after* the double murder of the 30th September.

'I was not codding dear old Boss when I gave you the tip, youll hear about saucy Jacky s work tomorrow double event this time number one squealed a bit couldnt finish straight off. had not time to get ears for police thanks for keeping last letter back till I got to work again,

Jack the Ripper'

Both of these communications were the work of the same person, with the use of the term 'Boss' and the mention of the cutting off the ears. The writer of the first letter is patently educated, as the spelling, use of the apostrophe, and the grammar, are very good. The writer inserted a couple of words - Boss and buckled - possibly trying to make it look as if it was written by a street-person, but he talks of 'being down on whores' and then uses the term 'lady' twice regarding them. He also uses the phrase 'police officers', a rather polite description. One of the hoi polloi would surely have used a term such as copper, peeler, or even rozzer.

He altered his style in the second message, probably realising the first letter was too neat and grammatical. His second communication is more like what would be expected from someone such as the 'Ripper'.

It would not be *too* surprising if a journalist had actually penned the letters and come up with the name.

The name Jack was used for a person or thing without a specific name, as in Jack Straw (a straw

91

effigy), Jack's land (sections of common land), spring-heeled Jack (unidentified individual who terrorised women in earlier Victorian London), Jack-in office (petty official), Jack tar, or even Jack the lad.

Two weeks after her murder, half a human kidney was sent to George Lusk, who was head of the Whitechapel Vigilance Committee in Whitechapel. A letter was enclosed in the parcel with the half kidney:

'From hell
Mr Lusk
Sir
I send you half the Kidne I took it from one women prasarved it for you tother piece I fried and ate it was very nise. I may send you the bloody knif that took it out
if you only wate a whil longer
Catch me when you can
Mishter Lusk'

This letter caused terror when reported in the newspapers. Again, it is a letter written to make it seem as if the writer was semi-literate, with the spelling errors and lack of proper punctuation. But the writer spelt 'half', 'fried', and 'bloody' correctly, words which might have been expected to give problems to an uneducated person. And, although spelt wrongly, the writer knows that 'knif' begins with the letter k.

It has been suggested the half kidney could have been that of Catharine Eddowes because it was gin-soaked. I'm sure that Eddowes did not have the only gin-soaked kidney in Victorian London.

Many ordinary people drank heavily as a temporary release from their daily drudgery, problems, and worries. Heavy drinking was commonplace.

In the extremely unlikely event that the kidney actually belonged to Eddowes, why on earth would the sender have held on to it for *two weeks* before sending?

No, almost certainly the kidney was sent by an outsider - someone such as a medical student as a prank, or a journalist to bestow an even more sensational and gruesome quality to the murder of Catharine Eddowes.

The letters and the half kidney are extremely unlikely to have come from 'Jack the Ripper'.

In the 1970s, West Yorkshire Police received three letters followed by 'I'm Jack' tapes from a man with a Sunderland accent who taunted the police, claiming to be the Yorkshire Ripper. This man was nicknamed 'Wearside Jack'. The police expended a lot of time and effort on the Castletown district of Sunderland, where the tapes were said to have originated from, trying to track him down. In the end, it turned out that he had nothing to do with the murders committed by Peter Sutcliffe from Bradford. (In March 2006, fifty year old John Humble, alias 'Wearside Jack', was sentenced to eight years in prison.)

But there must have been a purpose behind the taking away of Catharine Eddowes' womb and kidney - Mary Jane Kelly's womb and kidney as far as the Ripper was concerned. Their main objective had been achieved, Kelly had been eliminated at last.

Could the reason be connected with the punishment of the Juwes. According to the legend, Jubelo says, "Oh, that my breast had been torn open, my heart and vitals taken from thence and thrown over my left shoulder, carried into the Valley of Jehoshaphat, there to become prey to the wild beasts of the field and the vultures of the air." (Stephen Knight: The final Solution)

Were two of the vital organs of Catharine Eddowes, her womb and kidney, taken away and given to the feral dogs of the streets?

Burial: A funeral procession accompanied the hearse carrying the body of Catharine Eddowes to the City of London Cemetery, Ilford, on 8 September, 1888. The gates of the cemetery were closed against the huge crowd when the cortege passed through.

Catharine Eddowes is buried less than 10 yards from Mary Ann Nichols in Section No. 318. No headstone was erected. Her actual grave lies under a lawn in the memorial garden. There is now a plaque, not over the actual grave, but by the edge of the road running through Section 318.

Mary Jane Kelly

All the background information about Mary Jane Kelly originates from the woman herself. Friends and neighbours simply repeated to others the personal details she had related to them. Probably depending on whom she was talking to at the time, her background story varied slightly. Her basic account of her own life prior to arrival in Cleveland Street was:

'Born in Limerick, Ireland. When she was a young girl, her father, John Kelly, took his family of six (or seven) sons and two daughters and went to Carmarthenshire / Carnarvonshire / North Wales, where he became a foreman in an ironworks. When she was around 16, she married a collier named John Davies or Davis. She became a widow at 18 when her husband was killed in a mine explosion. She then spent some months in a hospital in Cardiff recovering from an unnamed illness / working as a cleaner. In 1884 she came to London. She found board and lodging doing domestic work in a convent in the East End / worked as a prostitute in a high-class brothel in the West End. She had a brother named Henry who was in Scots Guards.'

Little of the above is supported by evidence. No trace of a brother named Henry. No record of her marriage to Davies / Davis. Some of the family information she gave to people is not true. It's as if she invented a new past for herself. Of course, when you are away from home in a strange city you can tell people anything you want about yourself and your family. With her marrying so young, her husband's violent death, her long illness, and her working in a high-class brothel, she may have created - like Elizabeth Stride - a more dramatic, more interesting earlier life for herself to tell people about. In London, Kelly used the first names Mary Jane, Marie, and Marie Jeanette.

Joseph Sickert's account states that Mary Jane Kelly got a job in James Currier's confectionery shop through a solicitor named Edmund Bellord. Sickert asked him if he could recommend someone for the shop to help Annie Crook when she became pregnant.

Bellord, son of a sea captain, was a committee member of the Homeless Poor Refuge in Crispin Street, Spitalfields. (Spitalfields is a district of Whitechapel.)

The refuge was run by the Sisters of Mercy of the Providence Row Charity. It was not solely a women's refuge. In 1881 the refuge contained nearly 200 inmates, 60 of whom were men. Twelve Sisters of Mercy ran the establishment, which employed 10 domestic servants from amongst the women, who worked as such for their board and lodging. Mary Jane Kelly might have been employed there in this way.

When she went to Cleveland Street, Mary Jane Kelly became friends with Annie Crook, and, like Annie, modelled for Walter Sickert. She was employed as nanny to Alice Margaret, to whom Annie Crook had given birth on 18th of April 1885. Mary Jane Kelly was out with the child when the raid which removed Annie Crook from 6 Cleveland Street took place. When she heard what had happened she fled into the East End, leaving the child with Sickert who later returned Alice Margaret to the Crook family.

In the East End, Mary Jane had become friends with three women, Mary Ann Nichols, Annie Chapman, and Elizabeth Stride, eventually sharing her secret with them.

The women's lives were a constant battle against poverty, earning what little they could, when they could, selling their bodies when desperate.

Whoever came up with the blackmail idea, it must have seemed like a heaven-sent opportunity to obtain money to at least get themselves out of the squalid houses in which they had to live, so a letter was sent - most likely to Walter Sickert, probably insisting that it be passed to the appropriate authority - demanding payment in exchange for silence.

Nowadays, it is common practice for people to contact a newspaper to sell their story. If only these women had done likewise. But they didn't. They thought the Establishment would gladly give them a few pounds to keep the royal secret. How wrong they were.

Tracing Mary Jane Kelly now became vital to those in power, not only because she was said to have been a witness at the wedding of Annie Elizabeth Crook and Prince Albert Victor, but because she had taken Annie's copy of the marriage certificate with her when she vanished into London's East End after Annie's kidnapping.

At the time of her murder, Mary Jane Kelly was living at 13 Miller's Court, 26 Dorset Street, Spitalfields, Whitechapel.

Killed: 9 November 1888. Body found at 10.45 am by Thomas Bowyer, the rent collector. *Estimated* time of death about 2.00 am.

If Catharine Eddowes was butchered, what happened to the occupant of 13 Miller's Court was straight from hell. She was virtually gutted and dissected.

Main Injuries: The body, wearing what was left of a chemise, was lying in the middle of the bed. Neck cut right through to the top of the spine. The face was hacked and slashed beyond recognition of the features. Most of the nose, cheeks, ears, and eyebrows removed. Several incisions from the lips down to the chin. The left arm cut off, attached to the body only by skin. Both breasts cut off. All of the flesh on the surface of the abdomen removed. Lower part of the right lung torn off. Intestines, uterus, spleen, kidneys, liver, and heart, removed. Legs wide open, the external reproductive organs removed. The flesh from both thighs removed. The intestines were lying by the right side of the body. The spleen was lying by the left side of the body. The uterus, kidneys, and one breast, were under the head. The liver was placed between the feet. The other breast was lying by the right foot. All of the flesh from the abdomen and thighs had been placed on top of the table next to the bed.

Blood: The right hand corner of the bed clothes was saturated with blood, with a pool of blood about two feet square below this. The wall in line with the neck was splashed with blood.

Recent meal: 'In the abdominal cavity was some partially digested food of fish & potatoes & similar food was found in the remains of the stomach.'

[These details were in the post mortem report of Dr Thomas Bond who examined the corpse. He committed suicide in 1901, age 51, by jumping from a 3rd floor bedroom window of his home in Westminster, falling over forty feet.]

Dr Bond mentioned specific blood patterns in relation to the cutting of her throat, but Mary Jane Kelly's room must have been like an abattoir, with blood splattered over the bed, floor, walls, and table.

Her death certificate lists her name as 'Marie Jeanette Kelly otherwise Davies'.

Her age is stated as being 'about 25 years'. Her personal details have obviously come from Joseph Barnett. Her address is wrongly stated as being '1 Miller's Court' instead of 13 Miller's Court.

It was mentioned at the inquest that Kelly had two children, but that their names and whereabouts were unknown. (Were their surnames Davies or Kelly?) These children are unsubstantiated. Kelly herself obviously never mentioned them, because none of her friends and associates in London knew of any children. Even Joseph Barnett, with whom Kelly had lived for about a year and a half, knew nothing of them. So, *even if* she did have two children, how could the coroner,

Roderick MacDonald, have known this when Joseph Barnett did not?

The information almost certainly came from Inspector Abberline. He kept a diary in which he recorded his detailed background checks on the five Ripper victims - *surely very odd behaviour indeed for a West-End detective in charge of a case where the victims were East End prostitutes. They should have been of little interest, and their deaths of no consequence.* Abberline mentions the 'children' of Mary Jane Kelly in his diary. Presumably he gave this 'information' to the coroner. However, how could Abberline know that Mary Jane Kelly had two children when none of her own friends, or common-law husband of one and a half years, knew?

If she had children when she arrived in London how could Abberline have known of them, because he knew nothing of Kelly's life prior to her arrival in London, and it is extremely doubtful that *even if* she had children that she would have brought them with her. Life would be difficult enough without having to look after children. She worked in Cleveland Street, and no children were mentioned by Sickert.

She fled to the East End where she lived with Joe Barnett until the end of October 1888. Joe Barnett did not know of any children. Perhaps there could be a connection between Kelly being associated with children and the following statement which appeared right after the murder.

The Times 10 Nov 1888:

'Another account gives the following details: Kelly had a little boy, aged about 6 or 7 years, living with her, and latterly she had been in narrow straits, so much so that she is reported to have stated that she

99

would make away with herself, as she could not bear to see her boy starving.' This report goes on: 'The man then accompanied the woman to her lodgings which are on the second floor, and the little boy was removed from the room and taken to a neighbour's house.'

The woman could not have been Mary Jane Kelly, because her room was on the ground floor.

But, even in the final act of death itself, controversy surrounds Mary Jane Kelly. It is conceivable that she survived, and that another woman was cut to pieces in 13 Miller's Court.

According to Joseph Barnett who had lived with her until Tuesday 30th October, the reason why he left Marie Jeanette Kelly (the name *he* knew her by) was because, not only had she returned to earning money by prostitution - she owed 29/- back rent, her weekly rent for her room being 4/6d - but also because she was kind-hearted, allowing prostitutes to stay in the room when she and Barnett were living there. One named Julia was staying with her when Barnett left only ten days ago.

Joe Barnett objected when Mary Jane permitted Julia to sleep in the room, and when another woman, Maria Harvey, also moved in, he moved out. Maria Harvey moved into her own room on 7th November, but there is no mention of the woman named Julia having left.

According to Inspector Abberline (in his diary), another woman had recently moved into the room. This other woman, he stated, was a 20 year old parlour maid named Winifred May Collis, from *Cleveland Street.* He said Collis had moved in because of a pregnancy. He makes it sound so matter-of-fact, but how could Abberline know such details? Was Kelly's

100

address being watched? And, how did this parlour maid from Cleveland Street in the West End know Mary Jane Kelly's address in the East End? Kelly had had other addresses prior to Miller's Court, and the Establishment had been desperately trying to discover where she was living, yet, out of the blue, a Winifred Collis casually turns up at Mary Jane Kelly's door, then moves in with her. This whole scenario seems very odd, to say the least. (More on this later.)

Mary Jane Kelly had several personal encounters with people on the night of 8th November and the morning of 9th November, the people involved giving statements to the police.

At 11 pm on the 8th November Mary Jane Kelly was in the Britannia Public House, and had been drinking heavily. She left with a man around 11.45 pm.

Account given by Mary Ann Cox on 9th November:

At a quarter to midnight, she met Kelly with a man who was carrying a quart of beer. She spoke to Kelly and said that she was drunk. She said that Kelly was wearing a linsey frock (a frock made of linen and wool) with a red cross-over (wrap/shawl) around her shoulders, and no hat or bonnet. Kelly and the man went into 13 Miller's Court. Kelly began to sing a song called, 'A Violet I plucked From My Mother's Grave.' Mary Ann Cox went out shortly after midnight and returned about 1.00 am. Mary Jane Kelly was still singing in her room. Cox went out again just after 1.00 am and returned about 3.00 am. There was no light in Kelly's room, and all was quiet. Mary Ann Cox heard no noise after she returned to her room around 3 o'clock. She said that she did not sleep that night, and would have heard any noise if there had been any, but there wasn't. About 6.15 am she heard a man go out of Miller's Court, but could not be sure which house he came from.

[According to Mary Ann Cox, Kelly was definitely in her room from 11.45 pm until 1.00 am. At around 3.00 am the room was in darkness, and all was quiet. So, Mary Jane could have gone out sometime after 1.00 am.]

Statement of 12th November by George Hutchinson - He said that he was in Commercial Street about 2.00 am on the 9th when he met Mary Jane Kelly who asked him for sixpence, which he did not have. Near Thrawl Street, a man walking in the opposite direction to Kelly tapped her on the shoulder and spoke to her, at which point they both burst out laughing. They walked towards Dorset Street, and as they passed him, George Hutchinson said that the man 'hung down his head with his hat over his eyes. I stooped down and looked him in the face. He looked at me stern.' He stated that the man carried 'kind of a small parcel in his left hand with a kind of strap round it.' Kelly and the man then walked into Dorset Street and stood talking at the corner of Miller's Court for about 3 minutes. He said that Kelly mentioned she had lost her handkerchief. The man 'then pulled his handkerchief, a red one, out, and gave it to her.' Both of them then went up Miller's Court together.

George Hutchinson said he 'went to the court to see if I could see them, but could not. I stood there for about three quarters of an hour to see if they came out. They did not, so I went away.'

Hutchinson gave a detailed description of the man: aged about 34 or 35, height about 5 ft. 6 in., dark hair,

102

dark eyes and eyelashes, moustache curled up at each end. Wore a long, dark coat, with astrakhan cuffs, dark jacket with light waistcoat, dark trousers, dark felt hat turned down in the middle, button boots and gaiters with white buttons. Wore a very thick gold chain, linen collar, black tie with horse-shoe pin. Respectable appearance, walked very sharp, Jewish appearance.

[George Hutchinson's account of the events of early 9th November is suspicious. If all of it was true, Hutchinson must have been the last person, except for the killer, to see Mary Jane Kelly - whom he knew personally - yet he waited three days before going to the police station. He makes no mention of Kelly being intoxicated. In fact, she speaks to him normally, despite being drunk only about an hour previously. If the man she met near Thrawl Street was walking in the opposite direction to Kelly, would he not have been walking towards her? Why, therefore, would he need to tap her on the shoulder?

Hutchinson said he waited around for about ¾ of an hour to see if they came out, then went away. If he was so concerned about Mary Jane Kelly, why didn't he just walk up to No 13 rather than hang about for 45 minutes in the cold of an early November morning. After all, her room was on the ground floor and had a missing window pane. It would have been simple to just stroll past the window to discover if he could see or hear anything.

Hutchinson's statement contains almost a composite of the descriptions concerning the Ripper which had been in newspapers: the man is carrying a package with a strap around it, the man possesses a red handkerchief, he is wearing a long dark coat with astrakhan cuffs, he looks Jewish, he even has a moustache which is curled up at both ends - the only thing missing from this man is a placard hanging around his neck stating, 'I am Jack the Ripper.'

George Hutchinson's powers of observation and memory must have been extraordinary, because the incredible details he gave of the man's attire is truly phenomenal. And all of this gleaned in the gloomy darkness of Victorian gaslight as he passed by. And his encounter is with a sober Mary Jane Kelly, when only an hour before she was singing drunkenly. Maybe he got his days mixed up. Perhaps he was hoping for a share of the rewards.

George Hutchinson's life had gone downhill in recent times: *'George Hutchinson, a groom who is now working as a labourer.'*
Pall Mall Gazette, 14 Nov 1888.]

Account of 9th November given by Elizabeth Prater - She occupied No 20 Miller's Court - her room being directly above that of Mary Jane Kelly. She said that if Mary Jane moved about in her room much, she could hear her. Elizabeth Prater stated that from 1.00 am to 1.30 am no one passed up the court, and she was sure that there was no singing in Mary Jane Kelly's room after 1.30 am or she would have heard it.

Between 3.30 am and 4.00 am she distinctly heard cries of 'murder' two or three times. The sound seemed to come from Miller's Court. She did not take much notice of it, because, 'I frequently hear such cries from the back of the lodging-house where the windows look into Miller's Court'. Elizabeth Prater did not hear the sound of anyone falling. She went back to sleep, rising again at 5.00 am and was in Miller's Court at 5.30 am when she saw no one except two or three carmen harnessing their horses.

[Elizabeth Prater's account states that the singing in Kelly's room had stopped by half past one. So, she *could have* gone out again before 1.30 am. Two or three carmen were in Dorset Street at 5.30 am harnessing their horses. This might seem suspicious, but, in the 1880s many carmen lived in Dorset Street. Besides, 5.30 am was a time when there would have been too many people about for the liking of Jack the Ripper.]

Account of 9th November by Sarah Lewis - She was going to Mrs [Alice] Keyler's place at No 2 Miller's Court. When she came up the court around 2.30 am there was a man standing outside the lodging-house in Dorset Street, on the opposite side from Miller's Court. She could not recall if Kelly's room was in darkness, and silent, or not. Sarah Lewis stated that when she was in Mrs Keyler's, 'Shortly before 4 o'clock I heard a scream like that of a young woman, and seemed not to be far away. She screamed out "murder". I only heard it once. I did not look out the window'.

[It is strange that one woman heard a cry of "murder" two or three times, while the other heard only one cry. These sound like two different incidents, and *neither* can be assumed to be directly connected with events in 13 Miller's Court. Elizabeth Prater stated that cries of 'murder' were often heard in the vicinity.

In these two incidents, neither of the women investigated the screams, but we don't know if anyone else *did*. What we *do* know is that no previous Ripper victim managed to scream, so it is extremely unlikely that the last, and most important one, would be allowed to do so. Would the killers really take the chance on their victim screaming and nobody coming to investigate? How could they be sure that no-one would come to check? They could not. So, it would have been one hell of a chance to take, and so far nothing had been left to chance. They would have taken no unnecessary risks with Mary Jane Kelly, the one they wanted most of all. Besides, Elizabeth Prater heard no sound of a scream in Kelly's room - and she was directly above.

If Mary Jane Kelly's room had been lit, and she was singing, Sarah Lewis would perhaps have remembered. The fact that she did not remember means there was nothing to remember, i.e. nothing stood out for her. Almost certainly, Kelly's room was dark and quiet.

The man standing in Dorset Street at 2.30 am may have been a man just going about his lawful business, but he wasn't doing anything, he was just standing against the lodging-house opposite Miller's Court, which seems a bit odd. After all, he didn't have to go outside for a smoke. He could have been keeping a watch on Mary Jane's place.]

Amid the controversial issues associated with the Miller's Court murder, there is one odd point - *the killers seem to have had a key to 13 Miller's Court.* According to Joseph Barnett, the door key was missing, himself and Kelly letting themselves in by reaching through the broken window and drawing the bolt on the inside of the door.

Yet, when the police arrived after the discovery of the body, they found that the door was locked.

The murder in Miller's Court was different from those of Nichols, Chapman, Stride, and Eddowes. The killers' tried and trusted method of the coach and drugged grapes had so far served them well, so, instead of killing her in the coach, they could have taken the drugged woman back to her room. But, how could they be sure they would not meet someone going in or out when they were taking her from the coach to the room. In any case, trying to carry someone into the court would have been difficult.

The narrow arched passageway to Miller's Court

Miller's Court (26 Dorset Street) was a cul-de-sac. Entrance to it was via an arched passageway shown above, between, presumably, 25 and 27 Dorset Street. This passageway was narrow enough to make it difficult for more than one person to walk through it at a time. It culminated in a tiny square formed by the sides of the half-whitewashed houses. In the court, on the right-hand side were two doors. The first door led to the upper floors of the house in which Kelly lived. The second door opened directly into Mary Jane's room on the ground floor. To take the chance of encountering someone while trying to carry their victim along the passageway, then past the first door of the court, seems very risky, and so far the Ripper had taken no risks.

Perhaps they waited in the room for the occupant to return, but this strategy was dangerous too, because she could have returned with a man.

Or, maybe one of them, say John Netley, picked her up in a public house and went back to her room as a client. But, again there was a problem. Besides the risk of identification for Netley, none of them except Walter Sickert could positively identify Kelly - the Ripper gang could hardly have been given Mary Jane's passport or driving licence to inspect her photograph.

The most likely method used by them would surely have been for a watch to be kept on Kelly's address - *which they obviously now knew.* It is probable that this is what the man in Dorset Street was up to. Mary Jane Kelly could have left her room anytime between 1.30 am and 3.00 am, and there is evidence that Mary Jane Kelly did in fact leave her room.

'Notwithstanding that no evidence was produced at the coroner's inquiry to show that she left her apartment after one o'clock, at which hour she was heard singing, there is every reason to believe that she came out after that hour. This circumstance will account for the fact that no light was observed in the

room after one o'clock, as stated by one of the witnesses at the inquest. The police have received statements from several persons, some of whom reside in Miller's-court, who are prepared to swear that the deceased was out of her house and in Dorset-street between the hours of two and three o'clock on the morning in question.' [London Morning Advertiser, 14 Nov, 1888]

The man in Dorset Street was standing on the opposite side from Miller's Court around 2.30 am.

The carmen were fitting reins to horses, and straps to coaches, about 5.30 am.

Going by the times listed above, the murder could have taken place between 1.30 am and 3.00 am or between 3.00 am and 5.30 am. As can be seen from the accounts of various people, individuals were coming and going during the first period of time. Carmen were busy in the street at 5.30 am, so would have been up and about before this time. Elizabeth Prater was on the go at 5.00 am, and she would not have been the only one. The most likely time period for the butchery would seem to be between 3.00 am and 4.30 am.

Possible modus operandi: The man in Dorset Street (surely Sickert, since, if approached, he could be the working-class loiterer with the correct accent - Netley would be with the coach) is keeping watch on Miller's Court. He sees Mary Ann Cox enter around 3.00 am, and knows that she is not Kelly - Cox would have used the first door to enter the house. When the occupant of 13 Miller's Court returns after 3.00 am, almost certainly drunk, the lookout informs the Ripper and his accomplices who are waiting nearby in a coach, probably in Commercial Street - Dorset Street was a

109

side street leading off Commercial Street. There were almost certainly three men, possibly four, involved in the Miller's Court murder. A small group of men would have been less suspicious, would have drawn less attention, because Jack the Ripper was thought to be a solitary killer who silently stalked the streets. They allow a short time to pass in order for Kelly to have gone to bed and fallen asleep.

They walk the short distance (100 yards) along Dorset Street to the passage. The man retakes his position beside the Commercial lodging house in Dorset Street, directly opposite the passageway entrance, to keep watch, while another takes up position on the first door, locking it to prevent anyone coming out. The Ripper and his accomplice go to No 13. Light from the candle and fire would easily enable the accomplice to check that Kelly is in bed asleep when he gently pulls back the corner of the curtain through the part of the window where the pane is missing. Easing back the bolt, the men enter Kelly's room. First into the room is the Ripper. The room he enters is small, only 12 ft square. In two strides he looms over Kelly. Without hesitation, a razor-sharp surgical knife is drawn powerfully across her throat, slicing through to the top of her spine, instantly severing the carotid artery. Death, swift and silent. No scream. No sound. Having unlocked his door, the man at the first door joins the two men in Kelly's room. The windows are already covered by muslin curtains. They probably hang their coats over them as well. The Ripper cuts the dead woman to pieces. They place their own blood-spattered shirts into the fire which is burning fiercely in the grate. When the Ripper has finished gutting Kelly's corpse, they put their coats back on. Opening the door slightly to listen for footsteps or other sounds of human activity, and receiving a signal from the man in Dorset Street that the coast is clear, the man retakes his position at the first door, locking it. The Ripper and his accomplice then leave 13 Miller's Court, lock the door, and take the key with them. As they pass the man on the first door, again unlocking the door, he joins them. They then leave the passageway, being joined by the lookout stationed in Dorset Street. They walk the 100 yards back to Commercial Street, where the coach awaits them.

Whichever method was used to carry out the killing, was the right woman murdered in Miller's Court? The body was identified by Joseph Barnett as being Marie Jeanette Kelly. He would only have been shown the head area, the rest of the body almost certainly being covered, when brought by the police to carry out the identification. If the hair colour was correct [Kelly had dark hair] what else could he say?

[It has been suggested that Mary Jane Kelly had red hair because she had the nickname "ginger". *Neither Joe Barnett nor any of her neighbours mention Kelly as having this nickname.* Of course, this descriptive name *may have* been used for her. However, as well as referring to someone with red hair, this familiarity was also used for someone who was 'lively' - had plenty of ginger (spirit).]

Reynolds's Newspaper, Sunday, 18 Nov 1888: Joseph Barnett:

> *'I have seen the body, and I identify it by the ears and eyes, which are all that I can recognise.'*

[*There were no ears.* They had been removed. Joe Barnett could not have looked too closely - if he could

111

bear to look at all. Also, *the eyelids of a dead body are always closed when being identified.*]

The face of the corpse was beyond recognition. With the nose, ears, eyebrows, and most of the flesh from the cheeks having been sliced off, would any member of the public have been able to gaze upon it? Like most people, Joe Barnett would have been anxious to get his identification ordeal over as quickly as was humanly possible. The corpse may, or may not, have been that of Mary Jane Kelly. It could just as easily have been the woman named Julia - or the mysterious Winifred May Collis.

There is no mention of the prostitute named Julia having left before 9th November, but according to Abberline, the recently-moved-in Winifred Collis was 'never heard of again'.

As well as the controversy surrounding who exactly died in No 13 Miller's Court, there is another mystery. What happened to the heart of the victim?

The Times, 13 November 1888 (emphasis added):

'Some surprise was created among those present at the inquest in Shoreditch Town-hall by the abrupt termination of the inquiry, as it was well-known that further evidence would be forthcoming.

*No question was put to Dr Phillips as to the mutilated remains of the body, and **the Coroner did not think fit to ask the doctor whether any portions of the body were missing.** The doctor stated to the jury during the inquiry that his examination was not yet completed.*

[Kelly had died on the 9th. This was the official inquest on the 13th.]

His idea was that by at once making public every fact brought to light in connection with this terrible

112

murder, the ends of justice might be retarded. The examination of the body by Dr Phillips on Saturday lasted upwards of six-and-a-half hours.
*Notwithstanding reports to the contrary, **it is still confidently asserted that some portions of the body of the deceased woman are missing.'***

A statement contained in the post-mortem by Dr Bond reads: 'The Pericardium was open below & the Heart absent.' (pericardium - a smooth membrane which surrounds the heart).

Dr Thomas Bond listed the positions in the room of each of the organs which had been cut out of the body, but the heart is not listed. Even the flesh is accounted for, but not the victim's heart. It has to be concluded that it was not in the room when Dr Bond made his post-mortem examination. Obviously, only the killers could have taken it from Miller's Court.

When the room was entered, it was found that a fire had been burning in the grate - hardly surprising, since it was November - and it is said that as proof that the fire must have been fierce 'there was found a large quantity of ashes, and the rim, the handle, and the spout of the kettle had been burnt away'.
[The Times, 12 November 1888]

Perhaps the killers burnt the heart to ashes in the room, but achieving this is probably much more difficult than it sounds. If placed in the kettle a blood-filled organ may well bubble over violently, like milk, and put out the fire - but it is surely unlikely that the killers sat around for some considerable time amid the carnage in order to accomplish this. Even so-called

113

'insane' killers do not hang around beside the body of their victim with the murder weapon in their hand. No matter how 'insane' courts consider them to be, they do a runner. It is much more likely that it was taken away to be dealt with later. The motive for its removal is almost certainly the same as in the case of Catharine Eddowes, whose womb and kidney were taken away.

Now that they had butchered Mary Jane Kelly in 13 Miller's Court, was her heart taken from thence and fed to the wild dogs which roamed the streets?

'At 10 minutes to 4 o'clock a one-horse carrier's cart with the ordinary tarpaulin cover was driven into Dorset-street, and halted opposite Millers-court. From the cart was taken a long shell or coffin, dirty and scratched with constant use. This was taken into the death chamber, and there the remains were temporary coffined. The news that the body was about to be removed caused a great rush of people from the courts running out of Dorset-street, and there was a determined effort to break the police cordon at the Commercial-street end. The crowd which pressed round the van was of the humblest class, but the demeanour of the poor people was all that could be described. Ragged caps were doffed and slatternly-looking women shed tears as the shell, covered with a ragged-looking cloth, was placed in the van. The remains were taken to the Shoreditch Mortuary, where they will remain until they have been viewed by the coroner's jury.'
[The Times, 10 Nov 1888]

Burial: Because Mary Jane Kelly was a Catholic, Joe Barnett, and her landlord, John McCarthy, arranged

114

to have her remains interred with the ritual of the Roman Catholic Church.

East London Advertiser, 24 November 1888: *'On the afternoon of the murder the body was conveyed to the mortuary attached to St Leonard's Church, Shoreditch. As no relatives have appeared, Mr H.Wilton, the sexton attached to Shoreditch Church, incurred the cost of the funeral himself. Mr Wilton has been sexton for over 50 years, and he provided the funeral as a mark of sincere sympathy with the poor people of the neighbourhood. [Henry Wilton was also an undertaker.] The body was enclosed in a polished elm and oak coffin, with metal mounts. On the coffin plate were engraved the words "Marie Jeanette Kelly, died 9th Nov. 1888, aged 25 years."*

The coffin was carried in an open car drawn by two horses, and two coaches followed. An enormous crowd of people assembled, and a large number of police were engaged in keeping order. Wreaths upon the coffin bore cards from friends using certain public-houses in common with the murdered woman. As the coffin appeared at the principal gate of the church, men and women struggled desperately to get to touch the coffin. Women with faces streaming with tears cried out "God forgive her!" Two mourning coaches followed, one containing three and the other five persons. Joe Barnett was amongst them, with someone from McCarthy's, the landlord; and the others were women who had given evidence at the inquest.'

The Daily Telegraph, November 19, 1888 (emphasis added):

'The remains of Mary Janet Kelly, who was murdered on November 9 in Miller's Court, Dorset

*Street, Spitalfields, were brought to the cemetery at Leytonstone, where they were then interred. **No family member could be found to attend the funeral.**'*

Mary Jane Kelly was buried in Plot 10, Grave No 66, Row 66, in St Patrick's Roman Catholic Cemetery, Langthorne Road, Leyton. Her actual grave was only marked in the 1990s, when the superintendent had a memorial erected.

Ironically, Mary Jane Kelly was not a Roman Catholic. Joe Barnett and John McCarthy obviously assumed (or Mary Jane told them) that she was a Catholic, made the funeral arrangements, and had her buried accordingly. It is odd, therefore, that her funeral procession made its way from the Church of St Leonard, Shoreditch. The Parish Church of St Leonard was Anglican. Is it not strange that the burial of a 'Roman Catholic' did not take place from a Roman Catholic church. After all, there was the Church of SS Mary and Michael in Commercial Road about 1 mile away.

But, surely even more convenient for a Catholic funeral would have been the Roman Catholic Apostolic Church situated two streets away from Dorset Street in Lenter Street - *a mere 120 yards from Miller's Court.*

Ripper Rewards

'The most experienced of police officials entertain no serious objections to the offering of rewards on the part of our constituted authorities.

Moreover, eminent police officials of the Metropolitan force frankly avow their unrestricted faith in the utility of public rewards.'
Daily Telegraph, 3 October 1888

'Sir Charles Warren will not commit himself further than to say that, " the matter of rewards in these cases rests entirely with the Home Office," but his experienced subordinates, with very few exceptions, are cordially in favour of Government rewards in such a terrible and mysterious conjuncture of abominable crimes as the present.'
Daily Telegraph, 3 October 1888

'The Home Secretary, Henry Matthews, came to the conclusion that 'the practice of offering large and sensational rewards in cases of serious crime is not only ineffectual but mischievous; that rewards produce, generally speaking, no result beyond satisfying the public demand for conspicuous action, but operate prejudicially by relaxing the exertions of the police. He decided therefore, in all cases, to abandon the practice of offering rewards, as they had been found by experience to be a hindrance rather than aid in the detection of crime.'
Daily News, 13 November 1888

Rewards offered in connection with the 'Jack the Ripper' murders are illustrated by the following examples:

'Colonel Sir Alfred Kirby, J.P., the officer commanding the Tower Hamlets Battalion, Royal Engineers, has offered, on behalf of his officers, a

117

reward of £100, to be paid to anyone who will give information that would lead to the discovery and conviction of the perpetrator or perpetrators of the murders.' [£100 in 1888 = £6,000 - £9,000 now]

'The Lord Mayor, acting upon the advice of Colonel Sir James Fraser, K.C.B., the Commissioner of City Police, will, in the name of the Corporation of London, offer a reward of £500 for the detection of the Whitechapel murderer.'

The prompt action of the Lord Mayor in offering a reward for the apprehension of the Mitre-square murderer has been received with general satisfaction. The sum offered by his lordship, together with £400 which two newspapers offer to supply, the £100 offered by Mr. Montague, M.P., and the £200 collected by the (Whitechapel) Vigilance-Committee, make an aggregate sum of £1,200. It is probable that the reward will be increased to £2,000 as the Lord Mayor has been urged to open a subscription list, and some members of the Stock Exchange seem disposed to take the matter up.'

Illustrated Police News, 6 October 1888

Incredible as it may seem, not only did the Home Office decline to offer a reward for information leading to the capture of Jack the Ripper, but they actually sent back rewards offered by individuals and groups:

'Mr. Marks has sent a cheque for £300 to the Home Secretary on behalf of several subscribers, and requested him to offer that sum, in the name of the Government, as a reward for the discovery of the perpetrators of the murders.'

In returning the cheque, Mr. E.L. Pemberton writes from the Home Office:

"If Mr Matthews (the Home Secretary) had been of opinion that the offer of a reward in these cases would have been attended by any useful result he would himself have at once made such an offer, but he is not of that opinion. Under these circumstances, I am directed to return you the cheque (which I enclose) and to thank you and the gentlemen, whose names you have forwarded, for the liberality of their offer, which Mr. Matthews much regrets he is unable to accept."

The fact that the Metropolitan Police Commissioner and his boss at the Home Office refused to offer a reward in relation to the Jack the Ripper murders, the Home Secretary publicly *opposing* the offering of such rewards, led to the belief that they knew full-well who was responsible for the killings - *and had no desire that he be arrested.*

Chapter 5

Walter Richard Sickert

Walter Sickert was born 31 May 1860 in Munich. He was born into a family of artists. His grandfather, Johann Jurgen Sickert (born 1803 in Flensburg, a Baltic seaport near the Danish-German border) was an artist and lithographer. He was also head of a company of decorators employed by King Christian VIII in the Danish royal palaces. At the Danish Court, Johann would have known Alexandra (born 1844) who later became the mother of Prince Albert Victor.

Walter's parents were Oswald Adalbert Sickert (born 1828 in Altona, near Hamburg) and Eleanor Louisa Moravia Henry. She was the illegitimate daughter of Eleanor Henry, a dancer, and Richard Sheepshanks, an astronomer.

Oswald Sickert was also an artist. He received the patronage of King Christian VIII.

'The astonishing portrait of himself at the age of sixteen certainly justified the gracious interest that was taken in him by HM Christian VIII of Denmark, who conferred on him a travelling purse to Copenhagen.' - Walter Sickert

He too would have known the young Alexandra. Oswald went to Munich in 1852 to complete his studies. In 1868, the Sickert family moved to London where Oswald opened a studio. He became a British citizen, acquiring his wife's nationality by naturalisation. The children born in Germany, including Walter, probably became British citizens when their father became a naturalised subject. Humorously, Walter once remarked to a group of his guests:

'No one could be more English than I am - born in Munich in 1860, of pure Danish descent!'

Walter was the eldest child of six sons and a daughter. He attended King's College School in London, completing his studies in 1878. He decided to become an actor.

As a boy, Walter Sickert loved Shakespeare, and he liked to dress up. Orchestrated by Walter, the Sickert children often acted out scenes from Shakespeare's plays, Macbeth being one of their favourites. Walter's love of acting stayed with him.

At King's College School one year he played a scene from Richard III in the manner of the great actor Sir Henry Irving, then followed that performance by playing the same dramatic scene using his own interpretation of the same part. When he left King's College he decided to become a professional actor. Walter Sickert acted with Isabel Bateman's Company at Sadler's Wells, and toured the country with George Rignould's Company. He was even accepted into Sir Henry Irving's Company, and acted alongside Sir Henry Irving himself who played Hamlet at the Lyceum Theatre in London.

In 1881, Sickert decided to leave the theatre and become an artist. In the words of Osbert Sitwell, "With all its lure, and despite of an undoubted gift for it, Sickert abandoned the stage for painting."

That year he became a student at the Slade School of Art in Gower Street, leaving in 1882 to become an assistant in the studio in Tite Street of the artist James McNeill Whistler.

In 1883, he studied the technique of Edgar Degas in Paris. Sometime in 1883, Walter Sickert opened a studio at 15 Cleveland Street, which was in the centre of the Bohemian quarter of Victorian London known as Fitzrovia.

It was in Cleveland Street that the reason for the eventual emergence of Jack the Ripper was said to have been spawned: Probably through Oswald Sickert, Walter had been asked to take the son of Princess Alexandra, Prince Albert Victor, under his wing, to let him experience the atmosphere of life outside the Court. Annie Crook lived at 6 Cleveland Street, worked in the confectionery shop at No 22, and modelled at times for Sickert in his studio at No 15. She is said to have met the prince, who was pretending to be Albert Sickert, Walter's younger brother.

Annie became pregnant in 1884, but she did not have the Victorian shame of being an unmarried mother. The father of her child was someone she loved, and they would soon be married. Life, no doubt, seemed good to Annie, the future hopeful, yet her own life would soon be devastated as events unfolded, culminating in Jack the Ripper making his appearance on the stage of history.

It has been argued by some that Walter Sickert could not have been involved in the murders because he was in Dieppe from 1885. This argument is simply not true. Sickert only *visited* Dieppe for periods during the summer: (my italics)

'The early Dieppe 'period' extended from 1885 to 1905. Up to the end of the century, however, Sickert's home was in London. *Dieppe remained a summer side-show.*

From '85 to '98 he was much more in London than anywhere else. He and his wife had a house at Broadhurst Gardens, South Hampstead. In addition to a studio on the top floor there, *he rented various rooms in different parts of the city for working.'*

The Life and Opinions of Walter Sickert, by Robert Emmons, 1941.

Being a member of the Ripper coterie, and playing the part of someone who blended into the immediate surroundings would have been easy for Walter Sickert. Being a working-class passer-by or a loitering ruffian on the streets of Whitechapel would have presented no problem at all.

He excelled in the use of make-up, and once said that *when disguised for a part and wearing make-up, his own mother would not be able to pick him out from those around him.*

'When he was already famous, he called one day at Bourlet's, the well-known firm of artists' agents, looking like a tramp, and was nearly thrown out because no one recognised him.'
(Sickert, by Lillian Browse, 1960)

How can an Establishment murder conspiracy be uncovered when documentary evidence of the individuals involved is simply removed *by* the Establishment!

As Joseph Sickert said, the tangled web cannot even begin to be unravelled from an external source. Only from one involved in the plot itself can light be shed on secret events. Walter Sickert left clues, not only at, or near, the sites of at least three murders - Chapman, Stride, and Eddowes - but also in a few of his paintings.

Official documents can be destroyed by the authorities of the time, making it almost impossible for future generations to get at the truth - in the case of Jack the Ripper, without Sickert, totally impossible - *the advantage always lies with the people on the inside.*

But, could there perhaps be a contemporary source which in some way corroborates the Sickert story, one in which the places and people involved in the events which were played out so dramatically in the autumn of 1888 are mentioned? Incredibly, there is such a source.

St John Terrapin

Support for the Joseph Sickert story might seem unlikely because Annie Elizabeth Crook and Mary Jane Kelly, whose activities were centrally connected with the Jack the Ripper murders, were working-class. Like the vast majority of ordinary people, outside of their own family, friends and acquaintances, and a few local shopkeepers and publicans, the existence of individuals such as Annie and Mary would be unknown in a city like London, even within their own level of society, and a woman of the lower classes would certainly not be known by a member of the upper classes.

But, as we shall see, both Annie and Mary *were* known to certain members of the elite.

William Baynes was born 25 May 1863 in Newington, London, son of Oswald and Mary Baynes. Oswald was a greengrocer. When William was twenty he suffered from an attack of scarlet fever, the commonest cause of death in the latter half of the 19th century of children over the age of 1. The attack was almost fatal, but, having survived, he discovered that the scarlet fever had destroyed his hearing. He was now deaf.

William Baynes inherited a small legacy on his father's death, and this gave him the financial independence to live a modest existence. He now decided to change his name to St John Terrapin. In his silent world he became an expert lip-reader - 'I do not think I am being immodest in claiming that few have been able to lip-read with my facility' - living his life vicariously by 'listening' to other people's conversations. He even increased his modest legacy by purchasing shares after 'overhearing' private conversations between financiers and lawyers.

'Of course, one cannot detect what people are saying unless one is able to see their lips moving. But there is a compensation for this - one can see what people are saying when they are so far away that those dependent on their ears cannot hear more than a mumble of sound, especially in a crowded room. Background noise does not affect the lip-reader. Lip-reading is something I would make essential in the training of every spy.'

St John Terrapin became a regular in the Domino Room, a bar-room in the Café Royal, Piccadilly Circus, when he discovered that simply buying a beer enabled you to mix with its distinguished clientele. This establishment was frequented by many of the famous people of the day, including Oscar Wilde, T. E. Lawrence, Lillie Langtry, George Bernard Shaw, Rodin, Marie Lloyd, Toulouse-Lautrec, Virginia Woolf, Arthur Conan Doyle, and Aleister Crowley.

He kept a record of his observations and the conversations of the society regulars in a diary. Each evening he converted his writings in shorthand in the diary onto paper in longhand, with notes. The diaries and papers were given by the only surviving relative of St John Terrapin to the journalist Chapman Pincher. He began to work on them after his retirement from Fleet Street in 1979.

The following are extracts from 'The Private World of St John Terrapin' by Chapman Pincher, published in 1982.

Whistler and Wilde: 'James McNeill Whistler, a jaunty little man with a swarthy complexion, hooked nose, and longish black curly hair with a single white lock which he greatly cherished, was the uncrowned king of the Domino Room when I first began to frequent it in 1886. Whistler and Oscar Wilde, a huge, shambling man with a large head, heavy eyelids, thick lips and a fleshy jaw, met for lunch. Both Whistler and Wilde were excellent raconteurs, though the painter was more long-winded than the writer. Luckily for me they sat, as most people did, side by side on banquette seats, so provided they were facing my table, as they were, I could oversee everything. Whistler, talking about nature, "I take it you agree with me, Oscar, that Nature usually has it wrong? To say to the painter that Nature is to be taken as she is, is to say to the player that he may just sit on the piano."

Wilde replied, "I agree with Bernard Shaw that Wagner's music is the most satisfactory. It is so loud that one can talk the whole time without other people hearing what one says. Still, I concur in principle. Nature is almost always wrong. That is why it is so important for artists like us to put it right."

Whistler, irritated by Wilde describing himself as an artist then said, "I remain surprised, Oscar, that you know so little about art - real art, I mean. You seem to have no more sense of a picture than of the fit of a coat."

Wilde, niggled, since he considered himself a bit of a dandy, retorted, "The true author has every right to call himself an artist. A painter can place any daubs he likes on a canvas and announce that is how he sees things and how others should see them. The writer's words must at least make sense." I almost had to restrain myself from applauding, wrote St John Terrapin.

Wilde, continued, "Is it true, as rumour has it, that you are now charging three hundred guineas for two days' labour?" Whistler replied, "More than that. I ask it not for two days' work but for the knowledge of a lifetime."

At that point Wilde produced a poem which he had written on very thin paper, and handed it to the artist. "That took *me* two days to write," said Wilde, "What would you think *that's* worth?" Inserting his monocle with a theatrical gesture, Whistler read it slowly, then, balancing the paper as though weighing it on his palm, he remarked, "I'd say it's worth its weight in gold," laughing, with his head thrown back. Wilde forced a smile. But he never forgave Whistler.'

Lillie Langtry: 'I saw Bertie [Prince of Wales] leave the Café Royal on many occasions with the Blue Monkey [Portuguese diplomat called the Marquis de Soveral, later to become Prime Minister of Portugal. His heavy five o'clock shadow made his face look blue.] I mention the Blue Monkey because it was through him that I eventually received my first close-up of Lillie Langtry after he had brought her to lunch in the Restaurant in 1892. I have to say that I was rather disappointed, even though she was thirty-nine by that time, and concluded that her beauty had been somewhat exaggerated, as it was with so many beauties of the stage, and later of the screen, who appeared in the Café Royal. She had a flawless complexion, with gold hair shading to auburn, and nice violet-grey eyes, and she walked well, but her nose was not quite straight at the tip, and her chin, with its hint of a dimple, was rather firm. Lillie had love affairs with many men, usually rich or famous. At the time she was even having an affair with the Blue Monkey, for Bertie did not mind if his friends sampled his women as long as he could return the compliment. As became apparent, much later, her illegitimate daughter had been sired not by the Prince but by Louis Battenberg, a distant cousin of Bertie's who later changed his name to Mountbatten, and she was apparently conceived in the cabin of a warship off Cowes!'

Enrico Caruso: 'I have mentioned a number of men with enormous appetites, but in the spring of 1905 I set eyes for the first time on a world-famous Italian who could out-eat them all. His name was Enrico Caruso. I discovered that he had been in the Restaurant during previous visits to the Covent Garden Opera House, but 1905, I think, was his first appearance in the Domino Room. Caruso, who was already fat and stockily built with a very short neck, not only ate a five-course dinner but in between the normal courses demolished three different kinds of spaghetti! I was also surprised to see that Caruso was almost a chain smoker. He was also quite a clever caricaturist and would make lightning sketches on menu cards, which he would often sign and give to the waiters. My waiter friends in the Restaurant upstairs were sometimes even given a free recital, for Caruso would sing quietly into the ear of the wife of his friend Otto Gutekunst, an art dealer, when he was there with both of them.

He was a most pleasant-looking fellow with his smart suits and the carefully upturned moustache he sported during his early visits to London. Unfortunately he tended more and more to use the Restaurant on his later visits, by which time he was richer, fatter and clean-shaven. But on the odd occasions when he did grace us with his unmistakable presence, the Room would rise almost to a man and raise their glasses to him, such was the respect in which he was held.'

T.E. Lawrence: 'He came there first with John [Augustus John] in 1919. I was disappointed by his appearance which in mufti, as we used to call civilian dress in those days, was not that of a man who had been made Prince of Mecca and recommended for the Victoria Cross for his exploits against the Turks. I heard him tell John that he could not understand why he should want to draw the female body when the male was so much better proportioned. Lawrence was only about my size, five feet five or so, but stocky, with an over-size head, unsmiling looks and a hard jaw that could be described as brutal, though he could turn on the charm. Despite his heroic achievements, Lawrence was turned down for the Victoria Cross because the rules require that some British officer has to witness the deed. They wouldn't take the word of any of the Arabs. On Lawrence's word Prince Feisal had been assured that he would be King of Syria, but behind his back the Foreign Office had assured the French that they could have Syria as their share of a carve-up of the Middle

East. It seemed incredible that this little man with the perpetual smile and high-pitched giggle, who so recently had captured the port of Akaba (sic) from the Turks and inflicted many other defeats in brilliant guerrilla actions, should be only in his early thirties.

Incidentally, I noticed another similarity between Lawrence and myself in addition to lack of height - he was withdrawn, through some peculiarity, as I was by my deafness. Whoever he was with in the Café - and he came often enough to become known as the Café Royal Arab - he always seemed to be itching to get away.'

'Of all the habitués who were or became famous, one of the most riveting for me was an artist who had been a pupil of Whistler - Walter Sickert. He was a fascinating man of about twenty-eight when I first saw him: handsome, tall, and a brilliant talker who could hold his audience spellbound, partly, perhaps, because he had undergone professional training as an actor with no less a tutor than Henry Irvine, another occasional visitor to the Domino Room.

There was a particular reason why I enjoyed hanging on his every word over the many years I knew him - he was obsessed with unsolved murders, and especially with the most intriguing murder of all time, that of the man known throughout Britain, and indeed the world, as Jack the Ripper. Such was Sickert's knowledge of the case and his need to talk about it that I have always suspected that he knew the killer's true identity, and I believed that one day I might hear him reveal it in some confidence or other. But first I must set the scene......

Towards the close of my vintage summer of 1888, on 31 August occurred the first of a series of macabre events which were to plunge all London into fear. The newspapers of the following day revealed that the freshly killed body of a woman in a most horrific state of mutilation had been discovered in Buck's Row, a sordid little thoroughfare off Whitechapel. The Star reported that the victim, a middle-aged vagrant called Mary Nichols, had first been killed with a razor or sharp knife, which had almost severed her head, and the body had then been ripped upwards from the groin to expose all the internal organs.

Neither I nor anybody else in the Domino Room paid much attention to the event, for brutal murders were common enough in the East End, which was the haunt of all manner of criminals…. But eight days later the same murderer killed again, leaving his terrible signature on Annie Chapman, another woman so destitute that she could exist only by selling herself to men for a few coppers. Her savaged remains were found in a backyard off Commercial Street, only a few hundred yards from the previous murder. Examination of both bodies revealed that the man must be a fiend of ferocity unprecedented in modern times because, in addition to the mutilations, he grovelled about in the steaming entrails in search of the womb and other parts.

Ever quick to seize on such a sensation, the newspapers soon had an unforgettable name for the unknown killer, 'Jack the Ripper'…. the Domino Room was occasionally patronised by senior detectives. The managers of such establishments were always keen to remain on good terms with the police, since brawls and other minor breaches of the peace might otherwise attract their attention, and over the years I saw many off-duty senior officers of the Criminal Investigation Department and other policemen enjoying themselves in the Domino Room, no doubt at the management's expense. Soon after the second Ripper murder the Commissioner of the Metropolitan Police himself, Colonel Charles Warren, (1) who was to be knighted (2) came in for a quick lunch with a colleague who, I realised…. was Inspector Abberline. The pictures of both men were often in the newspapers, and over the years I was to see Warren arriving and leaving for various functions in the Freemasons' Temples housed in the Café Royal. He was very unpopular among the radicals in the Domino Room because they held him responsible for 'Bloody Sunday' the previous year: about a hundred thousand unemployed had converged on Trafalgar Square for a protest meeting to find themselves confronted not only by the police but by soldiers called in by Warren.

It transpired from the conversation that the two police officers had come straight from a meeting, and would be returning there for further discussion. The murders were causing even greater public concern than they merited because at least three previous killings were being attributed to the Ripper, though the bodies of those victims had not been ripped open, and could have been the work of other violent men…. I recall, for instance, that after some newspaper suggested that the way parts of the body were removed implied some surgical knowledge on the part of the ripper, anybody seen carrying a black bag was subject to harassment. Anyone known to the police to have sexual habits involving violence was also suspect, and this net enmeshed an occasional visitor to the Café Royal, the poet Algernon Swinburne, who was addicted to flagellation by women. Fortunately for him he was by that time safely in the custody of the writer Theodore Watts-Dunton, who for his own good kept him almost incarcerated in a house in Putney.

It soon became clear that from the tenor of the conversation between Warren and Abberline that the Home Secretary, described by the Daily Telegraph that very day as helpless, heedless, and useless, was venting his anger on them.

"This business is getting hopelessly out of hand," Warren said between mouthfuls of omelette, always his favourite lunch. "It's these blasted mutilations that have incensed the public. They are so unnecessary."

"I agree, sir. What is the point of them?"

"That, Inspector, I am not permitted to explain. We'll just have to go on living with these horrors, though not for long, I hope."

Abberline shrugged resignedly. "It's just that, having seen the state of these bodies, it makes me wonder what they'll do next." They! Did Abberline know that the Ripper was not a lone killer, but a gang? If so, what kind of gang? Self-righteous people fanatically opposed to prostitution? Though the phrase was hardly applicable to me, suddenly I was 'all ears'.

"Whatever *they* do, I know what *we're* going to do," Warren said emphatically. (3) "We shall have to go through the motions of using bloodhounds."

Abberline looked doubtful as Warren, a dapper figure with his smart suit and monocle, smoothed his military-style moustache. "I'm afraid it will be obvious that bloodhounds could do no good in Whitechapel, sir. It's full of alleys already stinking to high heaven with stable yards, slaughterhouses and earth closets."

"I have been to the scene of the murders," Warren reminded him loftily. "At least the public will see that we are trying everything. Another thing we can be seen to be doing is eliminating all the doctors in the area from our inquiries. Particularly left-handed doctors…

We need to keep that theory going in the newspapers." (4)

Abberline nodded, and I wondered why the police would want the public to believe that the Ripper was left-handed simply because his victims' throats had been slashed from left to right. Surely that would be the way a *right-handed* man would do it if he grabbed a woman from behind?

"We've covered all the doctors in the immediate vicinity," Abberline said. "Apart from that Russian lunatic Michael Ostrog, who doesn't seem to be in the area, I see no suspect."

"Well, track down Ostrog if you can, but don't arrest him. Just keep tabs on him until these killings are finished. (5) Then he could be a godsend. And don't relax your watch on Cleveland Street. That woman could still turn up there." (6)

It sounded as though both Warren and Abberline *knew* that the Ripper would strike again. And why were they looking for a woman in Cleveland Street? The only Cleveland Street I knew had nothing to do with Whitechapel: it was in 'Fitzrovia', the artists' quarter round Fitzroy Square, off Tottenham Court Road. The mystery was compounded when, while waiting for his bill, Warren remarked with a heavy sigh, "All hell is going to be let loose when the next body is found." (7)

When the next body is found? Not *if.*

All hell *was* let loose on the night of Saturday 1 October when the Ripper killed *two* prostitutes. The Sunday newspapers told us that he had not mutilated his first victim, apparently because he had been disturbed, but had then directed his thwarted ferocity on the second woman, whose body was found not far away in an appalling state of dismemberment. Never in my

134

recollection had the newsboys such bloodcurdling contents to exploit as they shouted, "More 'orrible murders in Whitechapel.... two disembowelled women found.... mutilation murders special..." Once again, in spite of the bloodbath, the Ripper had vanished on a clear, early autumn night.

At lunchtime that day Walter Sickert was in the Domino Room wearing one of the rigouts which he said he favoured so that he could not possibly be confused with the Decadents, led by Oscar Wilde. It was a Norfolk jacket and breeches topped by a long tweed coat and a deerstalker cap. As he took his seat he was the perfect description of a young man, alleged by the newspapers to have been seen leaving the scene of one of the murders! I also knew from his conversations that he regularly haunted the Whitechapel area, making sketches for his paintings. The Domino Room was convenient for Sickert because his studio happened to be in Cleveland Street. (8)

So here was a further connection with the Ripper inquiries. Coincidence, of course - surely his background ruled out any connection with the crime. I had heard how his father and grandfather had been court artists in Denmark and how, as a result, he had met Princess Alexandra since she had come to live in England. (9)

That day Sickert was joined by George Moore, then a little-known Irish writer..... Immediately he tried to interest Moore in the Ripper, but with no success, even when he hinted that if all the facts were known they could be made into the novel of the century. "You might find royalty involved," Sickert said, darkly. (10)

"Royalty has been overdone," Moore replied. "I prefer to write about the predicament of ordinary people." This he did to great effect a few years later in his novel *Esther Waters* about a servant girl.

I could have hit Moore on the head for his lack of interest. With a little more encouragement Sickert might have said far more. What had he meant by royalty? There was already a crazy rumour that the Ripper was Prince Eddy…. who was known to the public, affectionately I believe, as 'Collar and Cuffs' because of his habit of wearing very deep, starched collars to hide his over-long neck, matched with shirt cuffs protruding several inches from his jacket sleeves. Eddy was a wild young man, but the suggestion that the future heir to the throne of England could be a homicidal maniac was preposterous. The rumour seemed to be based on nothing more than a much reproduced photograph showing the Prince wearing a deerstalker!

Following the double murder the public outcry became so deafening that there were demands for the resignation of the Home Secretary and the appointment of someone who would get the job done. These views were reiterated through the Domino Room by intellectuals who would normally have held themselves aloof from such muck-raking. There were also those customers with their own theories about the murders, the most interesting being that of the young Scottish author, Arthur Conan Doyle, later to become immortal as the inventor of the greatest detective of all time, Mr Sherlock Holmes. Conan Doyle, who was soon to use the Café Royal in a Holmes novel, The Illustrious Client, was already a frequent visitor to the Domino Room and had made a considerable name for himself with novels such as A Study in Scarlet. His theory, which was taken seriously, was that the Ripper

136

disguised himself as a woman, so that he could not only approach his victims but escape without suspicion.

Another Domino Room theory suggested that the Ripper must be a Freemason who was killing his victims according to Masonic ritual. (11) This was supposed to be why each victim's throat was cut from left to right and the entrails were flung over the shoulder. Apparently, according to Masonic legend, three apprentices who killed a Master Mason building Solomon's Temple were executed in this manner. I did not pay much attention to this theory because I knew that the man propounding it was an Irish Catholic who hated Freemasonry.

George Bernard Shaw, another occasional customer, made use of the murders in a characteristic way - to draw attention to the dreadful social conditions in the East End, where it was alleged eighty thousand women were driven to live by prostitution. (This figure, announced by some bishop or other, caused a tremendous outcry, but did not surprise me because the whole of London was infested with such women, even children being available in the side-streets off Haymarket.)

Meanwhile Commissioner Warren's experiments with bloodhounds had degenerated to farce. After specially selected dogs had been quickly trained, with the fullest publicity they were let loose for a trial run on Tooting Common. Instead of following the trail which had been laid, the bloodhounds ran off and police everywhere were looking for them instead of the Ripper!

Shortly after the double murder Inspector Abberline came in with a stranger who turned out to be another policeman transferred to assist him with the Ripper case. By that time every murder of any woman in London was being attributed to the Ripper, and the strain was showing on Abberline's face.

"What an extraordinary room," the stranger remarked as Abberline motioned him to the table he had booked for a quick working lunch.

"Yes, but it has advantages," Abberline replied. "We don't get a bill. I thought I would bring you here privately to mark your card. The fewer who know in the office the better. Nobody can overhear us at this table, but watch it while the waiter's about." I could scarcely resist a smile at this remark as I briefly transferred my gaze to another part of the room.

"I can't tell you too much, but you already know that there's politics behind all this?" Abberline remarked.

"Vaguely. But why bring me in at this stage? I thought that four was the finish."

"It should have been, but the bloody fools got the wrong woman. The one that matters most, Mistress Kelly, is still alive. They thought the last one was Kelly but she just happened to be living with a man named Kelly. But what would you expect with amateurs?" (12)

"So the case shouldn't last much longer?"

"I hope not, but with all this outcry we have to go through the motions - carry on hauling in the doctors and all that stuff. As a matter of fact I called you in because the Queen has suddenly intervened. "

"The Queen!?"

"Yes. She's cottoned on to the theory that Jack the Ripper is a slaughterman and a foreigner, so she wants us to check on all the cattle boats."

"So though it's a waste of time, we'll have to be seen doing it?"

"For a while," Abberline replied.

"Surely the Queen can't know the full truth," his companion observed.

"Does she know about the P.A.V. connection?"

Abberline looked startled. "How did you hear about P.A.V.?"

"On the Yard bush telegraph."

Abberline shook his head despairingly. "Well, for God's sake don't mention it to anybody else. His name must be kept right out of it. And any mention of Cleveland Street or Annie Crook. (13) Warren and the Home Secretary are in enough trouble."

"What's Warren like to work with? At close quarters, I mean."

"He's alright, but it's of no consequence now. He's going to resign."

"Resign! The Commissioner! But why?"

"He just can't take any more of this revolting caper, and I don't blame him. The Assistant Commissioner is taking over - anything for promotion."

It was all most intriguing information. There was Cleveland Street again! Who was this woman Kelly? How did they know that someone had been murdered in mistake for her? Who was Annie Crook? What was the extent of Queen Victoria's involvement? And who or what was P. A. V.?

For the rest of the day and in bed that night I racked my brains for an answer to the last riddle, with no success. Then next morning, without conscious thought, the meaning came to me. Prince Albert Victor! That was the official title of Prince Eddy. So Collar and Cuffs was mixed up in it! What had I got my nose into! Or rather my eyes?

Sure enough Warren resigned, and on that very day, 8 November, Jack the Ripper perpetrated his most wanton orgy. When I saw the billboard headlines and the newsmen calling I could not part with my halfpenny quickly enough to see the victim's name. There it was - Mary Kelly! Her body had been so ripped and cut to pieces that it had to be taken to the mortuary in parcels. So the murders *had* been arranged. The police *had* somehow known about them in advance. And, somewhere, Prince Eddy *had* been involved. But who had committed the dreadful mutilations, and why? The obvious explanation that they were to prevent identification of the body could hardly be correct, for Mary Kelly was not killed on the street but in her hovel of a home!

Such was the public revulsion at the Ripper's deeds and the failure of the police to catch him that thousands of people flocked to the funeral of poor Mary Kelly, for whom nobody had cared much in life. A few days later a drawing of 13 Miller's Court, the dreadful slum dwelling where the murder was committed, appeared in the Penny Illustrated paper, which I read in the Café. It showed a poorly dressed young woman letting in a top-hatted man, obviously well to-do and carrying a black bag. Because of my secret knowledge I could not resist going down to the East End to see the murder room. I was not alone when I entered that dreadful alley off Dorset Street: There were a dozen equally curious people trying to peer through the broken window into the squalid little room where Mary had taken the Ripper and had met her end. Looking round at their questing faces I felt that some of them might be wondering whether I was the wanted man, who had been unable to resist the compulsion to return to the scene of his ghastly crime.

I wandered around the area to some of the other places where the Ripper had struck. It became obvious that he, or they, must have had a house or rooms nearby into which to sneak to wash and dispose of clothes, unless the departure from the scene had been facilitated by the police and accomplished, perhaps in a cab.

The memory of that dreadful area, the like of which I had never seen before, remains vivid to this day, as does any place which one explores with a purpose rather than merely for sight-seeing. As I walked westwards from the Whitechapel Road I felt confident, from my inside knowledge, that the Ripper would not strike again. And if he did not it would be proof that some appalling mission with official backing had been completed.

My hunch was justified. After some months without a recurrence the police let it be known, through the newspapers and rumour sources, that their chief suspect had committed suicide. They refused to name him because of the effect it would have on his innocent relatives. One rumour had it that he was an insane Russian doctor, whom I assumed to be the man Ostrog mentioned by Inspector Abberline, but Walter Sickert circulated a different story in which he gave the Ripper a name like Drewitt, which I did not hear him spell. This Drewitt was supposed to have drowned himself in the Thames less than a month after the murder of Mary Kelly. I also overheard policemen putting this Drewitt tale about, but if it were true why did Sickert go on talking about the murder of Mary Kelly?

To me it seemed a cover story for the truth which I knew to be much more complicated, and a false explanation of why the police had abruptly ended their inquiries into the killings. (14)

141

My suspicions were intensified when the police raided a male brothel where a relay of GPO telegraph boys offered their services. Though the authorities tried to hush up the scandal it soon became known that several prominent men had been among the haul of regular patrons. They included Lord Arthur Somerset, Lord Euston, and, most important of all - Prince Eddy. Further, the brothel was situated in Cleveland Street, near Sickert's studio, so once again there was a connection between Prince Eddy, Cleveland Street, Sickert and sex. (15)

Clearly, Prince Eddy enjoyed the pleasures afforded by young boys, but if the rumours about him had any foundation he was interested in women too. I heard more than one artist allege that he had an illegitimate daughter by one of Walter Sickert's models. *Jacob Epstein even called the model Annie Crook - the very name which had been mentioned by Abberline in connection with the Ripper murders.* So, Sickert must have been connected with them, along with Prince Eddy. (16)

I have spent many hours trying to solve this intriguing riddle, believing that I was on the brink of the solution, but got no further than the conviction that the murders had been politically inspired in connection with some event in Prince Eddy's private life which had to be concealed. As for the horrific mutilations, they could have been a cold-blooded part of the cover-up - to throw the blame on some unknown madman. In that case, of course, the letter alleged to have been sent by a man calling himself Jack the Ripper may have been fabricated by the police.

If Collar and Cuffs was privy to the truth he died with the secret. I continued to hang on Sickert's words

142

for any mention of Annie Crook, but without success. Like the rest of the Ripper saga, the truth was locked away in the minds of a few who are already dead or soon will be.'

---

(1) Charles Warren's rank is often stated as being that of General at the time of the murders. He was Lieutenant-Colonel.

(2) Although he was already *Sir* Charles Warren [having received the K.C.M.G. in 1883], another knighthood [the K.C.B.] was conferred on him in 1888.

(3) Warren and Abberline know that the murders are not the work of one man. And who will not *permit* the Commissioner of the Metropolitan Police to explain the mutilations - even to a colleague 'in the know'? The Prime Minister?

(4) The pointless use of bloodhounds is to be authorised in order to deceive the public into believing the police will use every means to track down 'Jack the Ripper'. And, in order to further conceal the truth, the police are going to impress on journalists that they know the murders are the work of a left-handed doctor.

(5) Two lowly prostitutes, Mary Ann Nichols and Annie Chapman, have been killed in isolated incidents. The victims are supposed to be unconnected. Yet Warren and Abberline know that their murders are part of a series, with more to come. They know the murders are prearranged. They know everything. The police are to keep under surveillance an individual

named Michael Ostrog, a man they obviously regard as being insane. [Michael Ostrog, age 54, was Polish - and a surgeon. In the late 1870s-early 1880s Ostrog had been incarcerated in 'Her Majesty's Convict Prison' in Portland, Dorset.] If the murders needed to be blamed on someone, Michael Ostrog would be ideal as a patsy. The perfect fall guy.

(6) Warren confirms the Joseph Sickert story that the East End 'Jack the Ripper' murders are in fact directly connected with Cleveland Street in the West End. The expression 'that woman' shows that Warren knows the identity of the main target.

(7) The Chief Commissioner of the Metropolitan Police knows another murder will soon take place.

(8) St John Terrapin, a contemporary, states that Walter Sickert's studio *was* situated in Cleveland Street - a fact disputed by some.

(9) Confirmation that Princess Alexandra and Walter Sickert knew each other.

(10) Walter Sickert makes the royal connection.

(11) A Masonic ritual connection with the murders is actually suggested in 1888.

(12) Kelly is actually mentioned by name by Abberline. Mary Jane Kelly has been propelled from total obscurity in the East End to the attention of the highest in the land.

The government is revealed as being behind the murders. Abberline confirms that Eddowes was mistaken for Kelly.

The Chief Commissioner of the Metropolitan Police criticises the work of the killers as being unprofessional for failing to murder Mary Kelly, and displays annoyance that she is still alive.

Four women, identities already known, hunted down and murdered by sanction of the government with the collaboration of the police. They never stood a chance.

No regret is expressed for the 'wrong woman' who is simply regarded as what would now be called 'collateral damage'.

This conversation between the top policeman and a police inspector sums up the so-called 'mystery' of Jack the Ripper. They know exactly what is behind the killings, the identities of the women earmarked for murder, and who is doing the killing.

It is all so casual, matter-of-fact. To those 'in the know' there was no mystery at all attached to Jack the Ripper. He just never existed.

(13) The Prince Albert Victor, Cleveland Street, Annie Crook connection is verified. The name of the low-born Annie Crook is also known in upper-class circles.

(14) This is Montague John Druitt. His body was discovered in the Thames (suicide or murder?) on 31 December 1888, and the police spread the cover-story that he was Jack the Ripper. Montague John Druitt was an even better scapegoat than Michael Ostrog - because he was dead.

145

(15) The Cleveland Street Scandal began less than a year after the Whitechapel murders, in July 1889.

(16) Prince Albert Victor - Annie Crook - a daughter. *The truth seemed almost common knowledge* within Walter Sickert's artistic circle.

The Red Handkerchief

Annie Chapman: A handkerchief round her neck covered the jagged cut which had all but decapitated her.

Elizabeth Stride: Her throat cut across. A silk handkerchief around the throat.

Catharine Eddowes: The throat cut across. Below the throat was a neckerchief.

George Hutchinson: George Hutchinson's statement said that the man with Mary Jane Kelly had a red handkerchief. This shows that a red handkerchief was an item connected with the Whitechapel murders.

The Times, 2 October 1888:
'The following is a description of a man seen with a woman who is supposed to be the victim of the murderer in the city. The man was observed in a court in Duke-street, leading to Mitre-square, about 1:40 a.m. on Sunday. He is described as of shabby appearance, about 30 years of age and 5ft 9in in height, of fair complexion, having a small fair

*moustache, and wearing a red neckerchief and a cap
with a peak.'*

Walter Sickert connected a red handkerchief with
Jack the Ripper. Marjorie Lilly was a contemporary
and close friend of Sickert. She wrote: 'He had two
fervent crazes at the moment, crime and the princes of
the church; crime personified by Jack the Ripper, the
Church by Anthony Trollope.'

[Anthony Trollope was Anglican, with a liking for
the High Church with its emphasis on rituals. He was
drawn to the Oxford Movement, although not a full
supporter of its views. His sister Cecilia, though,
became a Puseyite.]

'Thus, we had the robber's lair, illumined solely by
the bull's-eye lantern; when he was reading Trollope
we had the Dean's bedroom, complete with iron
bedstead, quilt and bookcase. The ecclesiastical flavour
so congenial to him was somewhat marred by the red
Bill Sykes handkerchief dangling from the bedpost; but
the presence of this incongruous article in the Dean's
bedroom was not a passing whim; it was an important
factor in the process of creating his picture, a lifeline to
guide the train of his thought, as necessary as the
napkin which Mozart used to fold into points which
met each other when he too was composing.

Sickert was working now on one of his Camden
Town murders, and while he was reliving the scene he
would assume the part of a ruffian, knotting the
handkerchief loosely round his neck, pulling a cap over
his eyes and lighting his lantern.

Immobile, sunk in his chair, lost in the long shadows
of that vast room, he would meditate for hours on his
problem. When the handkerchief had served its purpose

it was tied to any doorknob or peg that came handy to stimulate his imagination further, to keep the pot boiling. It played a necessary part in the performance of the drawings, spurring him on at crucial moments, becoming so interwoven with the actual working out of his idea that he kept it constantly before his eyes. How it affected his preoccupation with church dignitaries I cannot presume to say, but there seemed to be some mysterious connection here too. Even Mrs Parminter (Sickert's landlady) respected the red handkerchief, and left it where she found it whenever she invaded the Frith.' (The Frith was what Sickert called a later studio at 15 Fitzroy Street. The name meant sanctuary.)

Walter Sickert attached great importance to the red handkerchief. It obviously had strong personal significance for him. To possess the inside knowledge that Walter Sickert had, he must have been bound up closely with those who carried out the killings. We know he could identify Mary Jane Kelly, and he probably helped to track down the other women, but he must also have had a more personal involvement with the murders. He was very likely a lookout, but he may have been the one who approached the victim to inform her that a 'client' was waiting in the coach. After all, Gull was hardly likely to get out, and Netley was up-top in charge of the coach - and we *do know* that Catharine Eddowes was seen with a man on his own shortly before her murder, a man wearing a red handkerchief.

Perhaps Netley and Sickert placed the corpses of the victims in the spots where they were found - this would surely be a two-man job, and again, Gull was unlikely to have left the coach.

According to Marjorie Lilly, Sickert not only equated the red handkerchief with Jack the Ripper, but also with church princes.

The church (Roman Catholic Church) princes are the cardinals. They wear red robes, and are potential successors to the papal throne. The red handkerchief represented Jack the Ripper and the potential Catholic succession to the British throne.

The Dean's Bedroom

In the Roman Catholic Church, a dean is in charge of the process which brings about a papal successor from the cardinals. The Dean, President of the College of Cardinals, summons them to a conclave where an heir (to the papal throne) is produced. The Dean, too, wears red. The Dean never succeeds.

The 'Dean' of Walter Sickert's 'The Dean's Bedroom' is Prince Albert Victor. The bedroom - his sexual activities. Through Prince Albert Victor a Catholic heir (to the throne) was produced. Prince Albert Victor did not succeed.

The red handkerchief was necessary for Sickert to focus his mental energies, to set the imagination flowing. If he was the man who had worn the red handkerchief, its presence would have transported him mentally and emotionally back to the dark streets of Whitechapel, immersing him once again in the highly-charged atmosphere leading up to a Jack the Ripper murder.

Sickert Paintings

Little Dot Hetherington at the Old Bedford
c1889

Little Dot Hetherington is on the stage of the Old Bedford Music Hall singing, 'The Boy I Love is up in the Gallery'.

Prominent in the foreground, in the audience, are three people. Only their headgear can be seen. The man on the left wears a bowler hat, the man in the centre is wearing a top hat, and the woman wears a fine, black feathered hat.

Music hall was too vulgar, too working-class, for people of high social rank.

Right down the centre of the painting, directly in front of the two toffs, is a large pillar. The 'pillar of society' mixing with commoners. [Prince Albert Victor]

Little Dot Hetherington, bathed in the spotlight which shines onto the stage, points upwards to the gallery to the right of the spotlight. Just above, to the left of where the spotlight emerges sits a mysterious male figure. This man is in the highest position, remote from the activities taking place, but he oversees everything. [The Prime Minister]

A woman wearing a black dress and hat has opened the stage curtains on the right. Only one side of her face can be seen, and her eye is closed. Dot Hetherington can see the boy she loves (up in the gallery), but the woman is unable to see (the boy *she* loves).   [Annie Crook]

Gallery of The Old Bedford
c1897

Symbols of compass and square extend along the front of two balconies. A triangle projects at the corner of the balcony on the right in which a group of men are standing. One of these men stands out as being taller than the others (Walter Sickert was 5 ft 11 in). On the wall behind him is a motif in the shape of a shadow of a woman wearing a crown.

The motive (motif) is the monarchy. But the queen is unaware of what's taking place - looking away, in the opposite direction.

Although the motive behind the murders was the preservation of the monarchy, Queen Victoria had no knowledge of those in the fore-front - the murder group.

Ennui
c1918

This is the second of Sickert's paintings called Ennui, and contains symbolism which is missing from his original Ennui of 1914.

A married couple are in their living room. The painting has an atmosphere of total silence. The man sits at a table, smoking, looking to the right. The woman stands at the back of him, leaning on a chest of drawers, looking to the left.

The painting portrays a married couple who no longer communicate. [Prince Albert Victor and Annie Crook]

The tablecloth on the table in front of the man bears a design containing a single eye. [The All-Seeing Eye of Freemasonry]

A painting of Queen Victoria hangs on the wall. On her left shoulder stands a gull. [William Gull]

On the chest of drawers on which the woman leans sits a glass display case containing several small, stuffed birds, resembling finches. [Songbirds silenced – the dead women]

Amphitryon or Xs Affiliation Order
1925

A woman who looks like a servant stands in what appears to be the room of a mansion house or stately home, since the room contains a pillar, a sculpted bust, and a painting above a large fireplace. She stands next to the pillar, the palm of her right hand against her right cheek, as if worried. A set of buffalo horns is on her right.

Amphitryon: The Greek legend of Amphitryon tells how Zeus, ruler of humanity, came down to earth disguised as a normal human being. He seduced a woman, who then bore him a child. [Prince Albert Victor – Annie Crook]

X's Affiliation Order: X, the unknown person - the missing name on Alice Margaret's birth certificate where the name of her father should have been.

An Affiliation order is a court order requiring the man judged to be the father of an illegitimate child to pay towards its support.

Buffalo horns: The Royal and Ancient Order of Buffaloes, from whom needy families could receive relief payments.

[Not only was the child born in a workhouse, and stigmatised as illegitimate, but Annie Crook received no financial support.]

Lazarus Breaks His Fast
c1927

[Sickert used a photograph of himself to portray Lazarus.]

Lazarus - the man who 'rose from the dead' - is seated at a table, eating black grapes from a spoon which he holds in his right hand. His left hand is not visible. Instead of a napkin tucked into his collar, an apron tied at the back of his neck hangs down in front of him, covering his upper body.

Grapes are strongly associated with William Gull: 'I never travel, or, I may say, go anywhere, without raisins.' 'When fatigued, I prefer grapes and raisins and water.'

Lazarus is Gull. William Gull's death was announced, and his burial took place, in 1890. Sickert is stating [spoon-feeding the information] that Gull did not die in 1890.

153

On the one hand [right hand] alive, but on the other hand, sinisterly [left hand] concealed [under the table] out of public view - Sickert said that William Gull's burial was a sham, and that he was actually confined in an asylum.

With the apron covering the front of Lazarus, Sickert is stating that it was all a Masonic cover-up.

The Servant of Abraham
1929

[Sickert used a photograph of himself to portray the subject.]

The painting simply features the head.

Abraham said: 'and lo, my servant, born
in my house, shall be my heir.'
The word of the Lord came to him saying:
'He shall not be thy heir.'
Genesis XV: 3-4

Alice Margaret was the daughter of the eldest son of the heir to the British Crown. When her grandfather, King Edward VII, died in 1910, Prince Albert Victor was the rightful successor. If he was dead, his only child was next in line. Those 'on high' would not allow her to succeed to the throne.

Walter Sickert had an affair with Alice Margaret. This resulted in the birth of Joseph Sickert in 1925. The son of the woman who was denied her birthright in 1910, like his mother, he too would not inherit.

Jack and Jill
c1936

This painting is a Walter Sickert creation based on the gangster film 'Bullets or Ballots', starring Humphrey Bogart, Edward G. Robinson, and Joan Blondell. The film was released in 1936.

The painting depicts head and shoulder views of Robinson and Blondell. Edward G. has a cigar in his mouth. Although both are looking forwards, Blondell stares fixedly ahead. Robinson looks confident, Blondell has her left hand pressing on his left shoulder as if trying to move behind him afraid of what she sees in front of her. He has an air of calm control, she of trepidation.

This painting depicts Jack *(Jack the Ripper)*, narrow-eyed, with a self-satisfied smile. Jill looks vulnerable, she needs a shoulder to lean on. Jill is afraid of what is approaching - Jill is *Mary Jane Kelly*.

They did not meet each other by chance. They were two of the three main characters cast together. Each had their part to play. Jack looks relaxed, pleased at what lies ahead - looking forward to it. Jill, aware of what is heading her way, wears a look of wide-eyed apprehension.

Chapter 6

The Real Mary Jane

Mary Jane Kelly's birth and christening details are intriguing, in that they are not to be found. From census records, she was born 1851-1852, but even with these records there is conflict of information. On the earliest census she is listed as being born in the place where you would have expected her to have been born, in the city where her first six siblings were born, but the next two censuses give her birth-place as Ireland.

1861 census - age 9 - born Liverpool, Lancashire
1871 census - age 19 - born Dublin, Ireland
1881 census - age 29 - born Dublin, Ireland

According to the first census on which her name could appear, she was born in Liverpool like her elder sister and five younger brothers and sisters. This would seem probable, to say the least, yet the next two records disagree with the first.

Mary Jane had six brothers and three sisters. It seems odd, that of all the Kelly children, she was the only one listed as being born in Ireland, hence making her the only child whose birth details are difficult to ascertain. Sometimes a wife went to her parents, or her husband's parents, to give birth to her first baby, but neither of Kelly's parents came from southern Ireland, never mind Dublin, and Mary Jane was not the first-born child. Also, *if* Mrs Kelly was in Dublin (for whatever reason), and *if* the birth of her second child was unexpectedly premature, Mary Jane would nevertheless have been christened in St Peter's, Liverpool, like her brothers and sisters. She wasn't - at least there is no record of her christening.

Also, Mary Jane Kelly's Irish place of birth, Dublin, is ambiguous, because this means that her birth could have taken place in the City of Dublin, or in the County of Dublin.

With regard to checking her background, this could be Sod's law in action - the most inconvenient thing is the most likely to happen.

There is no birth registration 1851-1852 for Mary Jane Kelly in Liverpool. Also, there is no christening record for her (1851-1853) in the Parish Church of St Peter, Liverpool. Perhaps this is another example of Sod's Law rearing its ugly head again - *but the registration situation surrounding Mary Jane Kelly does bring firmly to mind the missing birth and christening details of Annie Elizabeth Crook.*

Her parents were John Kelly and Mary Colville. They had the following children:

Sarah born 26 April 1847 Liverpool
          chr. 30 May 1847 St Peter's, Liverpool

Mary Jane born
          chr.

William born 21 Oct 1853 Liverpool
          chr. 20 Nov 1853 St Peter's, Liverpool

Elizabeth born 8 Jan 1856 Liverpool
          chr. 17 Feb 1856 St Peter's, Liverpool

Maria born 26 May 1858 Liverpool
        chr. 13 Jun 1858 St Peter's, Liverpool

John Colville born 30 Jan 1861 Liverpool
        chr. 5 May 1861 St Peter's, Liverpool

Philip Colville born 8 Jan 1863 Liverpool
        chr. 22 Feb 1863 St Peter's, Liverpool

Thomas born 3 Feb 1865 Chester

John born 18 Aug 1867 Chester

James Charles born 15 Jul 1870 Chester

Mary Jane's father, John Kelly, a metal turner, was from Armagh in Northern Ireland, and her mother, Mary Colville, like Annie Crook's mother, was Scottish (Fife). Her parents being from Northern Ireland and Scotland makes Mary Jane's Dublin-listed birth seem somewhat out of place. There seems no obvious reason why Mrs Kelly would be in Dublin for the birth of her second child - her parents, brothers and sisters (Colville family), were all living in Liverpool in 1851. It is all very strange.

The Kelly family lived at several addresses in Liverpool in the 1840s and 1850s. They moved to Chester, where John Kelly became a foreman in an engineering works, about 1864. Around 1876, the Kellys moved to Hawarden, Flintshire, North Wales, where (as Mary Jane said) he became a foreman in an ironworks - almost certainly the Ratcliffe Iron Works, Hawarden.

Inspector Frederick George Abberline checked into the family background of Mary Jane Kelly, together with those of the other victims of Jack the Ripper. Abberline's diary notes on the personal details of Mary Ann Nichols, Annie Chapman, Elizabeth Stride, and Catharine Eddowes are straightforward, and pretty accurate. His notes on Mary Jane Kelly are not so straightforward, and are rather bewildering. For Kelly, he gives the following information:

Inspector Abberline's Diary Excerpts
(The Ripper & The Royals, by Melvyn Fairclough)

1) Marie Jeanette Kelly. August 1865 - Nov 1888. [Actual name Mary Jane Kelly, born 1852]

2) Abberline received a letter from a Miss Nora O'Brien of Roofer Castle, Limerick, Ireland, which stated that Mary Jeanette Kelly was her niece, daughter of her brother who was in the army. This letter stated that her real name was Mary Jane O'Brien.

[We don't see this letter. Inspector Abberline *says* that he received it. It 'contains' information which could send investigators in the wrong direction. If there was a letter, it is *possible* that Abberline thought that it might be genuine, since he could not trace Kelly's past as he had with   the other four women - *so, how could he 'know' that Mary Jane Kelly was born in the month of August?*

Significantly, neither Limerick County Archives nor Limerick City Reference Library could find any trace of such a place as Roofer Castle. The suggestion of it

159

being the name of a pub seems very dubious. Like the Windsor Castle, if Roofer Castle was the name of a pub, it suggests that there was a place named Roofer, which it would seem is simply not so.

However, the address from which this 'letter' is said to have originated is rather interesting. Roofer - A letter of thanks for hospitality received by a guest. Castle - A move in chess to protect the King. Limerick - The place claimed for Mary Jane Kelly's birth.

Interpretation of the letter:

"Thanks to the woman from Limerick for the welcome and entertainment in Miller's Court which safeguarded the monarchy." Scornful humour, mocking the murder victim.

3) I now know she was never an unfortunate. No record of Workhouse or Infirmary or any other help or assistance.

[Abberline is stating that he knows that Kelly was not a prostitute, but *how can he know this*? He had no way of checking her personal life in detail. He also found no evidence of her having been in any workhouse, etc. Again, *how could he know*? Abberline could not possibly know that Kelly had received no help from any workhouse, infirmary, or hand-out from a parish. There must have been hundreds of workhouses, infirmaries, and parishes in London. He claims more knowledge of Kelly than he actually has.]

4) The Bellord Domestic agency helped her to acquire service to a West-end family as a nanny in Cleveland Street.

[From St John Terrapin, we know that Abberline knew about the real goings-on in Cleveland Street, and the politics behind the murders. Yet, this entry in his diary mentions Kelly taking up a domestic position as if it was a run-of-the-mill post of no great importance with a 'West-end family' of little matter. There is more significance in what he *does not write.* Even although it was his personal diary, he makes no mention of Prince Albert Victor, Annie Crook, or a child. For someone purporting to tell the truth, this is highly illuminating. He does make the connection between Kelly and Cleveland Street, and states that she was a nanny there, but he might have mentioned this fact in case the connection was made by someone else, perhaps someone *from* Cleveland Street. The diary may well have been written in order to give misleading information, its purpose being that its contents would be later revealed - as has of course happened.]

5)   Had made friends with a house parlour-maid - Winifred May Collis, 20, of 27 Cleveland Street off Great Portland Street, who went to stay with Mary Jane Kelly in Dorset Street in November   1888, due to an unwanted pregnancy. Never heard of again.

[Abberline knows that Kelly had made friends with a Winifred May Collis in Cleveland Street, yet, *when Mary Jane Kelly was in Cleveland Street, Inspector Abberline was ensconced in the police station at 160 Commercial Street, Whitechapel. Abberline did not become involved in the machinations until Mary Jane had gone back to Whitechapel,* yet knows that Kelly had made friends with a parlour-maid in Cleveland Street some months before. A watch would have been kept on the activities in Cleveland Street before his involvement. Perhaps he read the notes. Abberline says that Winifred May Collis was 20, but we are not entirely sure if she was that age when Kelly became friends with her in Cleveland Street, or she was 20 when she moved in with Kelly in Miller's Court.

There is no record of the birth of a Winifred May Collis in England or Wales 1857-1872. Of course, there is no record of Annie Elizabeth Crook's birth either - but there is a good reason for Annie's being missing. Although the missing birth record does not prove that Winifred May Collis did not exist, simply meaning that there is no record of a birth for her, she does not appear on the 1881 census. According to the rate books for 27 Cleveland Street, Thomas Hitt was the ratepayer in the 1880s - normally, only ratepayers would be listed, therefore the rate books would not include people who were living in a property - and Hitt is still listed as such in 1886. In 1887 no person is listed on the rate book. Rate arrears of £8 18s 2d are listed as having been paid, presumably by Thomas Hitt.

So, 27 Cleveland Street was unoccupied in April 1887, therefore Winifred May Collis could not have been working there as a parlour-maid at that time - it seems doubtful if Collis would have been a parlour-maid working at this address, because Thomas Hitt was a carpenter. She could have rented a room there. She could have been living at 27 Cleveland Street in 1886, and just possibly for part of 1887 - the period (as will be shown) of Mary Jane Kelly's time in Cleveland Street.

Abberline says that Winifred May Collis moved into the room with Mary Jane Kelly in Dorset Street in November 1888, but does not give the day this took place. With the 'never heard of again' quote, he

162

strongly hints that Collis was the one who died in Miller's Court, not Kelly. Abberline is saying that he kept his suspicions that Mary Jane Kelly was not killed in Miller's Court to himself - not a snowflake's chance in hell.

As we now know, Inspector Abberline was privy to inside knowledge concerning the motive behind the Whitechapel murders.

If Abberline believed that Mary Jane Kelly had not died in Miller's Court, it is certain that, as happened after the murder of Catharine Eddowes, the hunt for Kelly would have been renewed.]

6) She was not an unfortunate, and she never lacked money.

[Inspector Abberline again emphasizes that Kelly was not a prostitute. He then states that, although she made no money from prostitution, she was never short of money. He is hinting that all is not above-board regarding Mary Jane Kelly, that there is more to her than meets the eye. He is strongly insinuating that he knows more than he is saying. Why doesn't he just say what he means. It is *his* diary, after all.]

7) She mysteriously appeared from nowhere, then disappeared.

[Abberline makes Kelly out to be a bit of an enigma, strongly implying that the authorities had no idea of her origins. Maybe they didn't. Then again, maybe they did. He gives Mary Jane an air of mystery as having appeared 'from nowhere'. Inspector Abberline seems to have forgotten the Kelly story about Limerick and Wales - yet it was in the newspapers and it was told at the inquest. His use of the word 'disappeared' rather than the phrase 'was murdered' once more gives a not-so-subtle hint that she was not killed in Miller's Court.

8) I believe she was a P.A.

[We finally arrive at what Inspector Abberline was hinting at with his previous insinuations about Mary Jane Kelly. He believes she was a Police Agent. *Surely he was in a position to know if she was or she wasn't!*]

9) I was advised not to pursue any more to this investigation.

[Pursue. Investigation. One can almost picture the intrepid Inspector Abberline doggedly following up every clue in a determined solo effort to track down the evil perpetrators à la Sherlock Holmes, then being warned off because his tenacious investigations have come dangerously close to uncovering the truth. This from the man who said, 'the bloody fools got the wrong woman. The one that matters most, Mistress Kelly, is still alive. But what would you expect with amateurs.' (St John Terrapin)]

10) Abberline said that Kelly had 2 children.

[Joe Barnett, Kelly's common-law husband, knew of no children, and one of her landladies before she moved into Miller's Court said she did not have a child.]

In the case of Mary Jane Kelly, the details contained in the diary appear designed to deliberately confuse.

Even although those responsible had been completely successful in achieving their objectives through the Ripper murders, perhaps it was decided to leave misinformation behind - almost certainly to mislead, to muddy the waters for future investigators. Nothing, it seems, was to be left to chance.

If it had not been for the one unknown factor, their cuckoo in the nest - the lip-reading St John Terrapin - the information in the diary regarding Mary Jane Kelly would have totally succeeded in its purpose - to deceive.

We know that Mary Jane Kelly came to London from North Wales, the names of her parents, brothers and sisters, and that she was probably born in Liverpool (or Dublin). Little is known, however, of her life between her arrival in London and the period of her residence in Miller's Court.

Using personal accounts published in newspapers, many of Mary Jane Kelly's movements in the city can be traced. The following statements help to build up the picture of her life in London:

'He had lived with her at 13 room in Miller's Court about eight months, and ceased to live with her on October 30.'
(The Times, 13 Nov 1888)

'He had lived in Miller's-court, Dorset-street, for eight or nine months with the murdered woman.'
(The Times, 10 Nov 1888)

Kelly and Barnett had moved into Miller's Court in February-March 1888.

'Joseph Barnett, who for about 20 months lived with the murdered woman.'

165

(The Times, 12 Nov 1888)

'Barnett says he has lived with Kelly for a year and a half.'
(The Star, 10 Nov 1888)

So, they had been together from around the period March-May 1887.

Statement by Joseph Barnett to Coroner's Jury:
'Did she ever tell you where she was born and brought up?

Yes, she said she was born in Limerick, and was taken to Wales when very young. She came to London about four years ago. Her father was a foreman in some ironworks in Wales. She said she had one sister who was respectable, and who followed her aunt's occupation of travelling from market place to market place with materials. She said she had six or seven brothers, six at home, I think, and one in the army. I never saw one of them to speak to.

Was she ever married? Yes, when very young, about 16, in Wales, to a colliery owner or collier, but I have never been in those parts and don't know which. She said her husband's name was Davis, and that he was killed in an explosion. After her husband's death she went to Cardiff, and was in an infirmary there between eight and nine months. She followed a bad life at her cousin's in Cardiff, and I have often told her that was the cause of her downfall. After leaving Cardiff she came to London, and was in a gay house in the West-end. There, a gentleman came to her and asked her if she would like to go to France. She went to France, but did not stop there long, as she did not like the part.

166

After her return to England she went to the Ratcliffe-highway and lived opposite the gasworks with a man named Morganstone. Then she went to Pennington-street, I believe, and lived in a bad house there. In connection with that house she mentioned the name of Joseph Flemming, a mason's plasterer, of whom she was very fond. He used to often visit her. I picked up with her in Commercial-street one night when we had a drink together, and I made arrangements to see her on the following day. We then agreed to live together, and I took lodgings in a place in George-street. I then lived with her up to when I left her, just recently.'
[The Star, 12 Nov 1888]

[Barnett says Kelly claimed to have had only one sister who was respectable. Seems rather harsh!

An aunt travelling to market places with materials has been added to the original Kelly 'story'. This aunt, and Kelly's cousin in Cardiff - all very vague, nothing specific. Yet, the fact that Kelly *'has'* a cousin in Wales seems odd, since her father was from Northern Ireland, her mother from Scotland, and the Kelly family only moved to Wales around the mid 1870s.

For someone who did not know Mary Jane Kelly at that period, Joseph Barnett displays great knowledge of Kelly's movements. When they lived together, it would seem that Kelly made sure they discussed her personal life prior to when they met.

Kelly, whilst seeing the man she is sweet on, Joseph Fleming*, immediately agrees to shack-up with complete stranger, Joseph Barnett!*

Barnett and Kelly take lodgings together in George-street, later moving to Miller's Court in Dorset Street.

167

Joseph Barnett has provided the inquest with details of Mary Jane Kelly's personal life, and her various places of abode, but - *no mention of Cleveland Street! Either Barnett did not know of her time in Cleveland Street, or he has deliberately left out that period of her life from his account.*]

Joseph Barnett's time-scale for Kelly

West-end gay house - c1884-1885

Ratcliffe-highway - 1885 - (Morganstone)

Pennington-street - 1887 - (Joseph Fleming)

George-street, Commercial-street - March/May 1887 - Feb/March 1888

Miller's-court - Feb/March 1888 - 9 Nov 1888

Another Joseph Barnett statement shows that a person can only pass on to others what he has been told:

'Her father came from Wales and tried to find her there (i.e. in her lodgings in Pennington-street), but hearing from her companions that he was looking for her, Marie kept out of the way. A brother in the Second Battalion Scots Guards came to see her once, but beyond that she saw none of her relations, nor did she correspond with them.'
(The Star, 12 Nov 1888)

[This is obviously what Kelly has told Joe Barnett, because he did not know her when she lived in

168

Pennington-street. If Kelly 'did not correspond' with her relatives, *how on earth could her father and brother have known that she was living in Pennington-street. Another Mary Jane story.]*

Statement by *Mrs Elizabeth Phoenix, residing at 157 Bow Common-lane, Burdett-road, Bow, who called at the Leman-street Police-station (main police station of the Whitechapel Division, under Superintendent Thomas Arnold) last evening and made a statement to the officers which it is thought will satisfactorily establish the identity of the murdered woman:*
'She stated that about three years ago a woman, apparently the deceased, resided at her brother-in-law's house at Breezer's-hill, Pennington Street, near the London Docks. She describes the lodger as a woman about 5 ft 7 in in height, and of rather stout build, with blue eyes and a very fine head of hair which reached nearly to her waist. At that time she gave her name as Mary Jane Kelly, and stated that she was about 22 years of age, so that her age at the present time would be about 25. There was, it seems, some difficulty in establishing her nationality.
She stated that she was Welsh, and that her parents, who had discarded her, still resided at Cardiff, whence she came to London.
On other occasions, however, she declared that she was Irish. About 2 years ago she left Breezer's-hill and removed to Commercial-road.
It has been stated more than once that Kelly was a native of Limerick, **but a telegram received from that place last night says that inquiries made in that city have failed to identify the latest Whitechapel victim as a native of that town.**

169

*There is little doubt that Kelly came to London from
Cardiff some five or six years ago. It would appear
that on her arrival in London she made the
acquaintance of a French lady residing in the
neighbourhood of Knightsbridge, who, she informed
her friends, led her into the degraded life which has
brought about her untimely end. She made no secret of
the fact that while she was with this lady she drove
about in a carriage, and made several journeys to the
French capital, and in fact led the life of a lady. By
some means, however, at present not exactly clear, she
suddenly drifted into the East-end. Her first experiences
of the East-end appear to have commenced with Mrs
Buki, who resided in one of the thoroughfares off
Ratcliffe-highway, now known as St George's-street.
Both women went to the French lady's residence, and
demanded Kelly's box, which contained numerous
costly dresses.*

*From Mrs Buki's place, Kelly went to lodge with
Mrs Carthy at Breezer's-hill, Pennington-street.
This place she left about 18 months or two years ago
and took up her quarters in Dorset-street. (journalistic
error - Mrs Phoenix stated that Kelly left Mrs Carthy's
for Commercial-road, not Dorset-street.)*

*As to her ever having a child, the testimony is
conflicting.* **Mrs Carthy declares positively that she
never had one.**

*Mrs Carthy states that the deceased, when she left
her place, went to live with a man who was apparently
in the building trade, and who she (Mrs Carthy)
believed would have married her.*

*It appears from inquiries made at Carmarthen and
Swansea, that after leaving the former place for the
latter, Kelly, who was then only 17 years of age,*

170

entered the service of a Mrs Rees, who stands committed to the next assizes on a charge of procuring abortion, and who is the daughter of a medical man formerly resident at Carmarthen.'
(The Star, 12 Nov 1888, emphasis added)

Mrs Elizabeth Phoenix's time-scale for Kelly

West-end gay house - c1883-1884

Road off Ratcliffe-highway (Mrs Buki) - 1884-1885

Breezer's-hill, Pennington-street (Mrs Carthy) - 1885-1886

Commercial-road - 1886-1887 (with man in building trade: Joseph Fleming)

[Mary Jane Kelly was quite tall. Mrs Phoenix does not mention red hair. Just as has been inferred earlier, the name 'Ginger' - *if* it was used in relation to Mary Jane - must have been used in reference to her enthusiasm, her natural disposition.

The normal 'Kelly story' - with the usual Kelly variations - is given by Elizabeth Phoenix. Limerick is just part of the 'story'. She corroborates the Barnett account that Kelly went to Ratcliffe-highway (Mrs Buki's) but she makes no mention of Morganstone whom Barnett said was living with her.

Kelly then goes to Pennington-street (Mrs Carthy's) - Joseph Barnett's so-called 'bad house'. There is no

171

evidence that Mrs Carthy ran a house of ill-repute. It is unlikely that the place was as bad as Barnett made it out to be, because Joseph Fleming, who liked her a lot, and wanted to marry her, didn't mind visiting Mrs Carthy's regularly. If it had been such a 'bad house' he would surely have insisted that she leave there. But he didn't. *Mrs Phoenix makes no mention of Kelly working as a prostitute at Mrs Carthy's or Mrs Buki's.* She leaves Pennington-street to live with a man whom Mrs Carthy believed would have married her. This man, presumably, is Joseph Fleming (in the building trade) but, *Joseph Barnett has already stated that Kelly left Pennington-street to live with him.*

Mary Jane Kelly must have *told* Mrs Carthy that she was leaving the Pennington-street lodgings to go and live with *Fleming. At no time does Mrs Phoenix mention Joseph Barnett.* It may reasonably be supposed that she has never met him. She almost certainly *didn't* meet Joseph Barnett.]

There are discrepancies between the dates given by Barnett and Phoenix for the time when Kelly left Pennington-street. And why would a woman who is sweet on the man she is seeing regularly move in with another man almost as soon as she meets him?

We know when Kelly and Barnett moved into Dorset-street. We can be pretty sure of the time-period when Kelly moved into Pennington-street, because Pennington-street was the home of Mrs Phoenix's sister, Mrs Carthy, and her brother-in-law.

So, we have a conflict of dates, Barnett saying Kelly left Mrs Carthy's in 1887, and Mrs Phoenix saying that she left in 1886, but - *Joseph Barnett has left no time period in his account when Kelly could have been in Cleveland Street.*

Mrs Phoenix said that Mary Jane Kelly left Mrs Carthy's for Commercial-road, to live with a man in the building trade but *she can only be relating what Kelly said to her sister, Mrs Carthy, when she was leaving her lodgings.*

She couldn't have gone to Commercial-road (actually Commercial-street). *This was when she went to Cleveland Street.*

Joseph Barnett is only relating *what Mary Jane Kelly told him.* When they met in the spring of 1887 and had a drink together, Kelly must have told Barnett she was in Mrs Carthy's 'bad house' in Pennington-street. When they met the following day, Barnett suggested she move out of this 'bad house' and into lodgings with him.

Kelly's immediate acceptance of this offer is now not so strange. The man seeing her regularly is not being inexplicably left for a complete stranger - because Joseph Fleming's visits to meet Kelly in Mrs Carthy's house took place more than a *year before!*

When Mary Jane Kelly fled from Cleveland Street, she returned to the area she had come from. When she met Joseph Barnett she was almost certainly living in the Homeless Poor Refuge in Crispin Street, run by the Sisters of Mercy of the Providence Row Charity. Rather than arriving in Cleveland Street *from* this establishment, she sought sanctuary there when she *left* Cleveland Street - and she is said to have left the Annie Crook marriage certificate with the Sisters of Mercy for safe-keeping.

Joseph Barnett and Mary Jane Kelly moved into lodgings in George-street in the spring of 1887. George-street was just off Commercial-street. It ran from Flower & Dean-street, through Thrawl-street, to

Wentworth-street - it was only about 200 yards from Dorset-street and the Britannia Public House, where Mary Ann Nichols, Annie Chapman, and Elizabeth Stride, drank. The blackmail note must have been sent when Mary Jane Kelly was living in George-street.

Unknowingly, Mrs Elizabeth Phoenix and Joseph Barnett have revealed the time spent by Mary Jane Kelly in Cleveland Street: *1886 to around March 1887.*

Barnett met Kelly, not when Mary Jane left Pennington-street - when she left *Cleveland Street,* although Joseph Barnett could not have known that.

Mrs Phoenix says that Mary Jane Kelly was in service to Mrs Rees in Carmarthen when she was 17 - *when she was supposed to be married to Davies the collier*!

The Cleveland Street raid, when Annie Crook was abducted, most likely took place around March 1887. The blackmail note was almost certainly sent in July 1887 - *because Inspector Abberline was suddenly transferred from Whitechapel to Scotland Yard on the 25th of July 1887.*

The time-scale for Mary Jane Kelly

West-end gay house (if true) - c1883-1884

301 Cable-street (Mrs Buki i.e. Mrs Heinbokel) - 1884-1885

138 Pennington-street, Breezer's-hill (Mrs Mary McCarty) - 1885-1886

Cleveland-street - 1886 - circa March 1887

174

Homeless Poor Refuge, Crispin Street - circa March 1887 - April/May 1887

George-street, Commercial-street - April/May 1887 - Feb/March 1888 (Joseph Barnett)

Miller's-court, Dorset-street - Feb/March 1888 - 9 Nov 1888 (Joseph Barnett)

Joseph Barnett, a man aged 29 in 1888, is variously described as a general labourer, porter, or fish porter. But Mary Jane Kelly, aged around 36, besides accusations of occasional prostitution, no occupation, besides her time working as a nanny in Cleveland Street, is attributed to her. Mrs Phoenix does not say that Kelly was an 'unfortunate' when living at Mrs Buki's or Mrs McCarty's, nor does she mention any job which Kelly was employed in.

[It is not beyond the bounds of possibility that she worked as a nurse in The London (Royal London Hospital) on Whitechapel Road, which was less than ¾ of a mile from Pennington-street.

As for her landlady not mentioning where she worked - on a personal basis, when I lived in London I stayed in six different flats at various times, and not one of the private landlords knew (or asked) where I worked. What interests landlords is that you pay the rent on time.]

Mrs Phoenix has stated that Mary Jane Kelly was quite tall, being around 5 ft 7 in, but there is a description of her general appearance from a neighbour in Miller's Court, Elizabeth Prater - (My Italics) "She lived in No 13 room, and mine is No 20, which is almost over hers. She was about 23 years old. I have

175

known her since July - since I came to lodge here. *She was tall and pretty, and as fair as a lily."* (The Star, 10 Nov, 1888)

The term 'fair as a lily' is rather ambiguous, and surely refers to Mary Jane having a clear, pale complexion. If she had had *fair hair*, surely Mrs Phoenix would have mentioned this when she said Mary Jane 'had a very fine head of hair which reached nearly to her waist.' The fact that she did not think it worth mentioning almost certainly means that Kelly's hair was normal, i.e. dark.

A momentary glimpse into the background of Mary Jane Kelly can be had from two quotes.

'The young woman Harvey, who had slept with the deceased on several occasions, has made a statement to the effect that she had been on good terms with the deceased, whose education was much superior to that of most persons in her position in life.'
(The Times, 10 Nov, 1888)

'She is stated to have been an excellent scholar and artist.'
(The Star, 12 Nov 1888)

Mary Jane Kelly was tall and attractive, with a smooth, pale complexion, and had a youthful appearance, enabling her to claim to be younger than she actually was. She had been educated to some degree, and had an aptitude for art.

John Kelly was an engineer, and must have ensured that all his children received an education, as he himself had had through his father. Mary Jane's grandfather, Philip Kelly, had been manager of a cotton mill.

So, Mary Jane Kelly certainly attended school, as did her brothers and sisters. They probably left around the age of fourteen - her sister Sarah is listed as 'scholar' when fourteen, while sister Elizabeth is working at the same age. Mary Jane's brothers became engineers.

In her teens, Mary Jane worked in Liverpool as a 'fitter of shoe tops', as did her sister Elizabeth.

When the Kelly family moved from Chester to Wales around the mid-1870s, it is unlikely that Mary Jane went to Wales with them, because she had joined, or was soon to join, the nursing profession. In 1881, she is listed, age 29 - *unmarried*, not a widow - as a nurse in Chester General Infirmary, St Martin in the Fields, Chester. In those days, at the time of their engagement, nurses had to be no younger than twenty-four and no older than thirty, so, when twenty-four in 1876, Mary Jane Kelly probably enrolled as a nurse at Chester General Infirmary. Of course, this was the period when her parents and younger siblings moved to North Wales. She had to remain in Chester. As a new nurse, Mary Jane would have been provided with the following uniforms: five pink dresses, six aprons, and five caps.

Although Mary Jane Kelly did not move to Wales with her parents, but later used the country as part of her background story to people, there is evidence to show that she *visited* Wales on at least one occasion - for her sister's wedding.

Maria Kelly married William Evans 24 May 1881, The Mother Church, Parish of Hawarden, County of Flint [St Deiniol's] (Anglican). Witnesses: Philip Colville Kelly, Mary Jane Kelly.

Let's go back. The story was that Walter Sickert asked the solicitor Edmund Bellord if he knew of a woman who would be suitable to help Annie Crook.

So, Sickert asked Bellord if he could recommend someone. Edmund Bellord would not know any of the inmates of the refuge for the poor. He was a committee member, he did not actually work in the building. Would an unknown inmate of a refuge in the East End really be given a position as a nanny? In any case, this story is no longer reliable, because Mary Jane Kelly did not go to Cleveland Street from the Homeless Poor Refuge in Crispin Street - *she came from Pennington-street.*

Rather than through Edmund Bellord himself, more likely Mary Jane Kelly obtained the post of a nanny in Cleveland Street through the Bellord Domestic Agency. Abberline said she did. If Kelly had been aged 22 in 1885-1886, there is little chance that a reputable domestic agency would have given her a position as nanny to a West End family. She no doubt told them she was a nurse, but, unlike her later acquaintances, Mary Jane must have given the agency her real age, 33. Even so, it still seems unlikely that an agency would take on a person such as Kelly, living in common lodgings in run-down Whitechapel, and then send her to be a child's nanny in a house in London's West End, but it becomes perfectly feasible, if, in order to obtain the position as nanny from the Bellord Domestic Agency, Mary Jane did what she was good at - she altered her background story to suit her purpose.

[Although Kelly almost certainly obtained her position as nanny in Cleveland Street from the Bellord Domestic Agency, Inspector Abberline has hinted at a more sinister purpose for this – that she was sent to Cleveland Street as an agent for the police.]

Mary Jane Kelly arrived in Cleveland Street near the beginning of 1886. Cleveland Street was already under surveillance because of Annie Crook and her paramour, Prince Albert Victor. Kelly acted as nanny to Annie's child, Alice Margaret, who was born 18 April 1885 in St Marylebone Workhouse, so she would have been about 9 months old. If Mary Jane Kelly was a witness at the marriage of Prince Albert Victor and Annie Crook, then the marriage must have taken place in early 1886, because Mary Jane did not reside in Cleveland Street until then.

Rather than the marriage taking place 1884-1885, the year 1886 is surely much likelier for the event, because Kelly fled Cleveland Street in the spring of 1887. Also, if the wedding of Prince Albert Victor and Annie Crook had taken place in 1884 or 1885, would the authorities actually have waited two or three years to take action ?

The marriage was the critical event which triggered those in authority into action. Before the marriage, Prince Albert Victor had fathered a child by a commoner, albeit a Roman Catholic one. It was of little consequence.

The marriage had upped the stakes considerably, as the heir to the throne was now *married to a Roman Catholic and had a legal heir,* forcing the hand of the Establishment. Separating the couple was now of paramount importance to them, and it is pretty certain that their scheme set up to accomplish this was put into action around March 1887, because that was the time when Mary Jane Kelly, seeing an opportunity when Annie Crook's abduction from Cleveland Street took place, fled with Annie's marriage certificate back to the streets of Whitechapel.

Abberline suggests Kelly was a plant, presumably to pass on information about Annie and the Prince, and he knew that she had befriended a Winifred Collis.

It is possible that Kelly *could have* passed on information which enabled the raid to take place successfully, but, *if she was a police agent, surely she would have handed over the marriage certificate*. There would no longer have been any problem for the Establishment - apart from Annie Crook, of course - and no need for Jack the Ripper to have ever existed.

Inspector Abberline seems to be accusing Mary Jane Kelly of being a police agent who then *ran off with the evidence*!

Timing of Events:

Mary Jane Kelly arrives in Cleveland Street around the beginning of 1886.

If Kelly was a witness at the wedding, the marriage of Annie Elizabeth Crook and Prince Albert Victor must have taken place sometime in early 1886.

When the couple went through their marriage ceremony, action by the Establishment became inevitable. The one thing which would have been absolutely necessary when this action was initiated, would have been someone they could totally rely on to be in place as head of the police.

The marriage, with Mary Jane Kelly as a witness, takes place sometime in February 1886.

Sir Edmund Henderson resigns as Commissioner of the Metropolitan Police on 26 February 1886. In

March, Sir Charles Warren is appointed in his place.

March 1887: Annie Crook is abducted. She and Prince Albert Victor never see each other again. Mary Jane Kelly flees back to Whitechapel.

On 28 June 1887, Prince Albert Victor is awarded the K.P. [made a Knight of (the Order of) St Patrick]. The motto of the Order is Quis Separabit? - Who Will Separate Us?

On 25 July 1887, Inspector Abberline, who has been in Commercial Street Police Station, Whitechapel, since 1878, is suddenly transferred to Scotland Yard.

The first blackmail demand from Mary Jane Kelly must have been sent from Whitechapel in July 1887.

The murders are about to begin. Assistant Commissioner James Monro is replaced by Warren's friend Robert Anderson on 31st August 1888 - the day of the first murder.

When she returned to Whitechapel, Mary Jane Kelly could not go back to nursing. She had to keep a low profile because she was 'on the run'. She almost certainly stayed in the Homeless Poor Refuge in Crispin Street, in which place she is said to have deposited the marriage certificate with the Sisters of Mercy for safe-keeping.

Around April/May 1887 she met Joseph Barnett, and agreed to move in with him. She did not have to wait for several years before sending her first demand for money in exchange for silence. Why would she? Kelly knew that Annie Crook had been taken away because the authorities were worried. Soon after she had settled into George Street with Joe Barnett she sent her first demand for hush-money - within three months of Annie's abduction. Over those three months Mary Jane must have become acquainted with Mary Ann Nichols, Annie Chapman, and Elizabeth Stride, probably through using the nearby Britannia Public House at the corner of Dorset Street and Commercial Street, the blackmail note being sent to Walter Sickert from George Street, Whitechapel, in July 1887, resulting in the sudden transfer of Inspector Abberline from Whitechapel on the 25th of that month.

How to collect the money? She could hardly go in person. Only Mary Jane Kelly's signature would have been on the blackmail demand, *so how did the authorities know who the other women were?* If Kelly shared her secret with three women, heavy drinkers, tongues loosened by alcohol, it is pretty certain her 'secret' would not have been secret for too long, and she would have been speedily tracked down and killed. If the four women were operating as a cabal, tracing one of them must lead to the other three. And, if there are four women in a closely-knit blackmail group, and one of them, then a second, is slaughtered, surely it would be pretty obvious what was happening, and that the writing was on the wall for the other two. Yet the third victim (Stride) didn't run from her imminent fate. She appeared to act normally, as if the Nichols and Chapman murders were unconnected with her. The obvious reason for this is that Elizabeth Stride *saw no pattern in the previous murders - because she was not a member of any group.* The most critical and dangerous part in any blackmail attempt must surely be the point when the money has to be collected. Someone has to physically turn up to pick it up. Mary Jane Kelly would not have been so foolish as to do this personally.

Homeless Poor Refuge in Crispin Street

Run by the Sisters of Mercy of the Providence Row Charity, it was less than 35 yards from Miller's Court.

A much more likely scenario is that she arranged for the blackmail payments to be picked up by others, to whom she then gave a small payment. This would explain why Elizabeth Stride did not run for her life. She obviously saw no link between Mary Ann Nichols, Annie Chapman, and herself, because the women were individually selected at random by Mary Jane to pick up the blackmail payments - this was what Abberline was alluding to in his diary when he stated that Kelly appeared never to lack money. Of course, those picking up the cash would be unaware that it was blackmail money - Mary Jane would have spun them a story.

Only Mary Jane Kelly was privy to the secret, only she understood the murder pattern. There was no 'group' of conspirators as such - remember, the Ripper had problems locating Kelly, even killing the wrong woman. To those paying the blackmail, of course, the individual women picking up the payments were part of the plot, and Nichols, Chapman, and Stride, had to be eliminated - *but because they were not working as a group, none of them led back to Mary Jane.*

Joseph Barnett and Mary Jane Kelly moved the 200 yards from George Street to Dorset Street and Miller's Court during the period Feb-March in the fateful year of 1888. If the marriage certificate was still with the Sisters of Mercy in Crispin Street, it was conveniently handy, because Miller's Court was only about *100 feet* from Crispin Street.

The murder of Catharine Eddowes might have thrown Kelly for a short while, might have given her a straw to grasp at because Eddowes had not been one of her couriers, but when she found out that Eddowes was living with a man named Kelly, she knew beyond any shadow of a doubt that she had been the intended victim. She knew she was next to be cut to pieces. Terror should have stalked her every waking moment. Anyone in such a position would surely flee for their life. Of all the victims, Kelly was in the best position to abscond to a relative. Nobody knew the truth of where she had come from. Even Abberline, who tracked down many of the details of the victims, could not trace her background.

Mary Jane Kelly could have vanished back to her parents in Flintshire - both were still alive in 1888 - or to one of her brothers or sisters. It beggars belief that she continued to live in Whitechapel.

184

Outwardly, Mary Jane seems to have carried on after the murder of the three women as if nothing had happened. A question put to Joseph Barnett at the Kelly inquest:

'Did you ever hear her say she was afraid of anyone? Yes, she used to get me to bring her evening papers and see if there was another murder.'
(The Star, 12 Nov 1888)

[Hoping that, if there had been another murder, the victim was not her latest courier? Clutching at straws, in desperation.]

For someone who is the main target of the Ripper, someone who knows that she is next on the list to be bloodily butchered, Mary Jane's behaviour is extremely unexpected, to say the least. She hangs around when the blatantly obvious course of action is to flee from Whitechapel as quickly as is humanly possible. Mary Jane Kelly carries on as normal despite the murders, almost as if she was unconnected with the whole affair.

(a) Mary Jane Kelly knows she is destined for bloody death at the hands of Jack the Ripper.

(b) Mary Jane Kelly's actions are not those of someone in fear of her life.

These two statements are true, but are completely at odds with each other. Something has changed. The only possibility for Kelly's conduct is *she has given back the Prince Albert Victor-Annie Crook marriage certificate.*

She no longer lives in fear. The threat of imminent slaughter no longer hangs over her like the sword of Damocles. The butchery of Catharine Eddowes (Mrs Kelly) must have been the last straw, the certificate being finally handed over in exchange for her life. She could hardly have strolled into Scotland Yard to give back the marriage certificate. Almost certainly she took the paper which had caused such mayhem to Walter Sickert, asking him to pass it on to the Establishment.

Sickert no longer had his studio at No 15 Cleveland Street (gone during 1887), but he was still in that locality, because, although the exact address of his new workroom is unknown, St John Terrapin has already stated (1888) that 'his studio happened to be in Cleveland Street.'

But, of course, this was dangerous territory for Mary Jane, because, unbeknown to her, Sir Charles Warren had already given instructions that a watch be kept on Cleveland Street as 'that woman' might yet turn up there, which is precisely what she did. She had no choice, since she was trying to save her life, but her return to Cleveland Street was her undoing.

When she left Sickert's place she was almost certainly followed back to 13 Miller's Court - *this was how the Ripper finally discovered where she was living.*

Mary Jane Kelly was deluded. Giving back the marriage certificate would no longer have been sufficient. She simply knew too much.

Besides, *Mary Jane would surely have to pay for the trouble she had caused to the Establishment.*

The Miller's Court Victim

Statement to Police by Caroline Maxwell:
At 8.30 am on the morning of 9th November (when the mutilated corpse was lying undiscovered in No 13) she stated that she met Mary Jane Kelly *in Dorset*

Street at the corner of Miller's Court. Mrs Maxwell asked her why she was up so early, and Kelly replied that she had the horrors of drink upon her. Mrs Maxwell suggested that she go to the Britannia Public House and have a half-pint of beer. Kelly said that she had already done so, and that she had vomited it up, pointing to some vomit in the road. Caroline Maxwell then went to Bishopsgate, returning around 9.00 am. She again saw Mary Jane Kelly, this time outside the Britannia talking to a man who was dressed like a market porter. Mrs Maxwell said that Kelly was wearing a 'dark dress, black velvet body, and a coloured wrapper round her neck.'

[See Mary Ann Cox's description of Kelly's attire made in darkness just before midnight on the eve of the murder. (p.101)]

From The Times, 12 November 1888 -

'Mrs Maxwell, the deputy of the Commercial lodging-house, which is situated exactly opposite Miller's-court: saw Mary Jane Kelly standing at the entrance to Miller's-court at half-past 8 on Friday morning. She expressed surprise at seeing Kelly at that early hour, and asked why she was not in bed. Kelly replied, "I can't sleep. I have the horrors from drink." Mrs Maxwell further stated that after that she went into Bishopsgate-street to make some purchases, and on her return saw Kelly talking to a short, dark man at the top of the court.

When asked by the police how she could fix the time of the morning, Mrs Maxwell replied, "Because I went to the milk-shop for some milk, and I had not before

187

been there for a long time, and that she was wearing a woolen cross-over that I had not seen her wear for a considerable time." On inquiries being made at the milk-shop indicated by the woman her statement was found to be correct.

Another young woman, whose name is known, has also informed the police that she is positive she saw Kelly between half-past 8 and a quarter to 9 on Friday morning.'

A man named Maurice Lewis is positive he saw Mary Jane Kelly twice that Friday morning.

The Times, 10 November 1888 -

'A tailor named Lewis says he saw Kelly come out about 8 o'clock yesterday morning and go back.'

Lewis lived in Dorset Street. It is most unlikely that Lewis was talking about Kelly's room. He could not have seen Kelly coming out of No 13, as will be seen. Most likely, he saw her *come out of the passageway* leading from Miller's Court into Dorset Street, then *turn and go back down.* Did Kelly go to the door of her room, glimpse the horror within, turn and walk away, then have go back to the window to confirm that what she saw was real, and not her mind playing tricks on her? This would certainly account for her vomiting in the street just before she met Mrs Maxwell.

Illustrated Police News, 17 November 1888 -

'Maurice Lewis, a tailor living in Dorset Street, stated that he saw Kelly the previous night (Thursday) in the Horn of Plenty in Dorset Street, between 10 pm and 11 pm. She was drinking with some women and a

188

*man named "Dan" (an orange seller). One of the
women he saw was known as Julia.*
*Soon after 10 o'clock in the morning (Friday the
9th, when the corpse was found) he was playing with
others at pitch and toss in McCarthy's-court when he
heard a lad call out "Copper," and he and his
companions rushed away and entered a beer house at
the corner of Dorset Street known as Ringer's (the
Britannia Public House run by Matilda Ringer,
formerly with her husband Walter Ringer who died of
consumption in 1881, age 41). He was positive that on
going in he saw Mary Jane Kelly drinking with some
other people, but is not certain whether there was a
man amongst them.'*

[Mrs Maxwell is positive that she spoke to, then saw
Kelly, around 8.30 am and 9.00 am, times when the
corpse was lying in pieces in No 13. She remembers
her clothing, which attire was not the norm for Kelly -
only a woman could have noticed such a thing. *Her
story was checked at the milk-shop and this was
corroborated.*

Another female witness, whose name the Times
does not divulge - presumably because she did not want
it to be - states that she saw Kelly between 8.30 am and
8.45 am that same morning, backing up Mrs Maxwell's
account.

Maurice Lewis is positive he saw Mary Jane on two
occasions, around 8.00 am at the entrance to Miller's
Court, and just after 10.00 am in the Britannia, on that
Friday morning - the corpse was discovered at 10.45
am.]

Three individuals - and they are the ones we *know* about, the ones who made statements - who gain nothing by coming forward to make their statements.

Of course, these witnesses claiming that they saw Kelly after the murder would have been dismissed as deluded idiots. They are ignored by officialdom, by those 'investigating' the murder.

We also hear nothing of any police attempts to identify the women whom Maurice Lewis states he saw drinking with Kelly in the Britannia, nor do we hear of any inquiries being made to Matilda Ringer.

The woman named Julia who was drinking with Mary Jane Kelly on the eve of the murder in the Horn of Plenty could not have been the neighbour of Kelly's named Julia who sometimes visited her:

The Times, 13 November 1888: (The Inquest) –
'After a short adjournment, Julia van Teurney, a laundress of No 1 room, Miller's-court, was called, and said she knew the deceased and Joseph Barnett. She last saw the deceased alive about 10 o'clock on Thursday morning. Witness slept in the court that night, retiring to bed about 8 o'clock.'

So, the woman in the pub with Kelly only a few hours before the murder is almost certainly the same Julia who was staying with her in No 13, the woman who caused Joseph Barnett to move out because Mary Jane was now earning money by occasional prostitution.

Kelly now *had to* earn money from prostitution, because, after the murder of Catharine Eddowes, and the surrender of the marriage certificate, she no longer had any blackmail money coming in to support herself.

190

Then there is the strange entry in Inspector Abberline's diary (The Ripper & The Royals, by Melvyn Fairclough) which states that a Winifred May Collis had recently moved into No 13. Abberline strongly hints that Winifred May Collis was the victim in Miller's Court, not Mary Jane Kelly.

Inspector Abberline knows that Collis is pregnant, and has come to Kelly's seeking an abortion - he is extremely well-informed.

He states that Winifred May Collis moved in with Mary Jane Kelly in November 1888 - to know this implies that he knew where Kelly lived - but he does not mention the fact that the woman named Julia is living with Kelly - and she has been from at least 30th October when Joe Barnett moved out because of her. We only have Abberline's account about Collis - and *Abberline was 'in the know' about the Ripper.* The existence of Winifred May Collis is highly dubious.

Of course, it could be that 'Julia' *was* Winifred May Collis. A woman seeking an abortion would be unlikely to be using her real name. If 'Julia' was pregnant, and had come for an abortion, this would go some way to explain why Kelly allowed her man, Joseph Barnett, to move out rather than turn her away.

With murder victims, obliteration of the features was usually carried out to prevent identification of the corpse. The previous victims had been badly disfigured, especially Catharine Eddowes, but the face of the corpse in No 13 Miller's Court had been so violently attacked that the features were all but erased.

The body was badly mutilated, so it would be impossible to know if the victim had been pregnant.

The body was discovered at 10.45 am, but the police did not enter the room until 1.30 pm. And a fire had been burning in the grate for several hours during Friday 9th November. Loss of heat starts immediately after death, the body (i.e. a whole body) becoming the same temperature as the surrounding air after 12 hours. But in this case the body was cut wide open, was in pieces, a fire had burned for several hours in a small room - it would have been impossible to determine the time that had elapsed since death occurred.

There are two subjects of controversy which crop up after the discovery of the mutilated remains. Was the door to No 13 locked? And, why did the police take almost three hours to enter the room?

Barnett stated at the inquest that the key had been lost some time ago and that when Kelly or he wished to get into the room they pushed back the bolt on the back of the door through the broken window.

Concerning Kelly's room, Inspector Abberline's diary writings give the following - *The door was not locked. The bolt could not be drawn because the door had a heavy washstand pushed up against it. The murderer left by way of the window after pushing the washstand up against the door.*

The Times, 10 November 1888 (emphasis added):
'*At quarter to 11 yesterday morning, the landlord, Mr McCarthy, sent John Bowyer, a man employed by him as rent collector, to No 13. Bowyer did as he was directed, and knocking on the door was unable to obtain an answer.* **He then turned the handle of the door and found it was locked. On looking through the keyhole he found the key was missing.**'

13 Miller's Court

The rent collector looked through a window. The broken pane through which the bolt could be drawn is top-right (first window).

The Star, 10 November 1888 (emphasis added):
> *'Mr McCarthy said to John Bowyer, "Go to No 13 and try to get some rent." Bowyer did as he was directed, and on knocking at the door was unable to obtain an answer.* ***He then tried the handle of the door and found it was locked.'***

[John Bowyer, the man on the spot, states that the door was indeed locked - contrary to what Abberline wrote several years later.]

The length of time which lapsed before the police entered 13 Miller's Court seems suspicious, but, in this particular instance at least, there may well have been no hidden, sinister reason, for it.

The Times, 10 November 1888:

'McCarthy sent John Bowyer to the police-station and he brought back Inspector Back (sic). He then despatched a telegram to Superintendent Arnold, but before Superintendent Arnold arrived, Inspector Abberline came and gave orders that no one should be allowed to enter or leave the court. The inspector (presumably, Beck) waited a little while and then sent a telegram to Sir Charles Warren [Warren had tendered his resignation the previous day, on the eve of the Miller's Court murder] to bring the bloodhounds, so as to trace the murderer if possible.

So soon as Superintendent Arnold arrived he gave instructions for the door to be burst open.

'I (the landlord, John McCarthy) at once forced the door with a pickaxe, and we entered the room. The sight we saw I cannot drive away from my mind. It looked more like the work of a devil than of a man. I had heard a great deal about the Whitechapel murders, but I declare to God I had never expected to see such a sight as this. It is most extraordinary that nothing should have been heard by the neighbours, as there are people passing backwards and forwards at all hours of the night, but no one heard so much as a scream.'

The Times, 13 November 1888:

'Frederick George Abberline, detective-inspector, Scotland-yard, having charge of this case, said he arrived at Miller's-court about 11:30am on Friday. He did not break open the door as Inspector Beck told him that the bloodhounds had been sent for and were on the way, and Dr Phillips (Divisional Surgeon of Police) said it would be better not to break open the door until the dogs arrived. At 1:30 pm Superintendent Arnold

194

arrived, and said the order for the dogs had been countermanded, and he gave orders to force the door.'

The Times, 13 November 1888:

'Dr George Bagster Phillips: Having ascertained that it was advisable that no entrance should be made into the room at that time, I remained until about 1:30, when the door was broken open, by Mr McCarthy I believe. I know he was waiting with pickaxe to break open the door, and I believe he did it. The direction to break open the door was given by Superintendent Arnold. I prevented its being opened before. *I may mention that when I arrived in the yard the premises were in charge of Inspector Beck. On the door's being forced open it knocked against the table. The table I found close to the left-hand side of the bedstead.'*

[John McCarthy had to smash open the door with a pickaxe. No mention of any object such as a washstand preventing the door from being opened. If a washstand - hardly a grand piano, or even a chest of drawers - had lain against the door, it would have been quite easy for a man to push the door open! There would have been no need to break the door with a pickaxe! When the door was burst open it simply banged into the table next to Kelly's bed in the small room.]

The Star, 12 Nov 1888:

Itemised the contents of Kelly's room as, two old tables, a broken chair, a bedstead, and an old fender (a metal guard in front of the fireplace to stop burning coal from falling out).

The Times, 10 Nov 1888:

195

Listed the furniture contents of No 13 as 'an old bedstead, two old tables and a chair.' *A washstand is conspicuous by its absence.*

Unlike so much involved in the so-called Jack the Ripper murders, the long delay in entering Kelly's room *appears to be* due, not to some hidden factor, but to Dr Phillips simply following correct scientific procedure regarding the bloodhounds, which, as it turned out, did not make their appearance. If the room had been entered at 10.45 am instead of 1.30 pm, would it have made a difference? The crime scene was undisturbed. The butchered remains still lay around the room, slightly colder no doubt, but exactly as they were at 10.45 am - or for several hours before.

Although items in Mary Jane Kelly's room such as tables and a chair had been listed, no mention was made in the Times or Star of a print hanging on the wall above the fireplace. This print was named 'The Fisherman's Widow'. It appears in sketches made of Kelly's room, and is in Reynold's Newspaper, Sunday, November 18, 1888.

This is an *extremely* odd item for Mary Jane to have on her wall, and is highly suspicious. The Fisherman's Widow is a mythical tale of a Prince of the Royal House of Atlantis who marries a woman from another world, the poor widow of a fisherman. Shades of Prince Albert Victor and *his* woman from another world, Annie Elizabeth Crook. This is too close for comfort, just *too much* of a coincidence, that, of all prints, this one hangs on the wall in Mary Jane Kelly's room. *Was the print placed in No 13, blatantly declaring the reason for the murder - but only decipherable to those 'in the know'?*

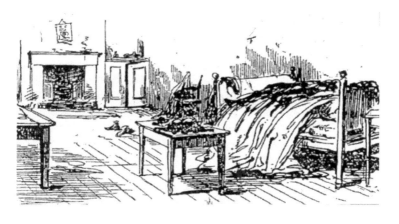

The sketch above the fireplace in Kelly's room

The Times, 10 November 1888:

'A correspondent who last night saw the room in which the murder was committed says it was a tenement by itself, having been the back parlour of No 26 Dorset-street. A partition had been erected, cutting it off from the house, and the entrance door opened into Miller's-court. The two windows also faced the court, and, as the body could be seen from the court yesterday morning, it is evident that, unless the murderer perpetrated his crime with the light turned out, any person passing by could have witnessed the deed. The lock of the door was a spring one, and the murderer apparently took the key away with him, *as it cannot be found. The more the facts are investigated, the more apparent becomes the cool daring of the murderer.'*

[With the door locked, muslin cloth, plus perhaps clothing, covering the windows, and the fire blazing in the grate, there would have been plenty of light - and no passer-by could have seen anything. Those inside would have had complete privacy.]

It has already been illustrated that two women were sharing 13 Miller's Court. One of them lay in pieces on the bed in the room. The question is, *where was the other woman?*

If the corpse was Julia's, Kelly being seen by various people would not be too surprising, and three witnesses swore that they saw Mary Jane Kelly on that Friday morning, one of them talking to her, while the body lay in No 13.

But, the Ripper was sure that Kelly had at last been eliminated. This strongly suggests that he did not know that two women had been living in the room.

If the corpse was Mary Jane Kelly, where was the woman called Julia? *Above all other witnesses, surely the most vital of all was the woman who was staying with Kelly - yet no attempt appears to have been made to trace her.* Again this demonstrates that they did not know about the second woman in the room - Julia's name only seems to crop up at the inquest when it is mentioned by Joseph Barnett.

Julia had been drinking with Mary Jane Kelly on the eve of the murder, yet after the murder she appears to have vanished into thin air - *unless hers was the corpse lying in Miller's Court.*

On the eve of the murder, Mary Jane was having a drink with friends, seemingly free from care. When she saw the carnage within her room, instinctively she would not have gone to the police. To have done so would be like walking into the lion's den. She now knew that she had been double-crossed by the Establishment, knew full well that she was the intended victim regardless of any deal she thought she had struck. But she then did what seems to be incomprehensible - *she hung around.*

She obviously waited for someone else to find the bloody remains, and, surely in shock, she took the normal course of action - she went to the pub to try to calm her nerves, and to be with people. To be seen with people at this time might seem a completely illogical thing to do, but Mary Jane was *expecting her friend Julia to be named as the victim. She was waiting for her friend's murder to be declared.* When she heard the butchered corpse within 13 Miller's Court named as *herself,* Mary Jane Kelly saw her golden opportunity, and fled at last from Whitechapel. She was free, and vanished from recorded history.

After the murder of Catharine Eddowes by mistake, the Ripper would have wanted to make doubly sure that the woman in No 13 was the correct one - not because of any scruples or conscience that another innocent woman might be killed, but because he would not wish to repeat his previous mistake.

Walter Sickert was the only person within the exclusive Ripper circle who could positively identify Mary Jane. Sickert must have been involved with the murder party. He would have been needed to verify that the woman who entered the room of 13 Miller's Court was indeed Mary Jane Kelly. They knew *it had to be her because this was her address,* but in view of the previous blunder, nothing would be left to chance. Sickert - *surely the lookout man standing in Dorset*

Street opposite Miller's Court - must have deliberately confirmed Julia as Mary Jane.

Walter Sickert had to make a decision no-one would wish to make, but, if you can only try to save the life of one person, whom do you make an effort to save - a complete stranger, or someone you knew as a friend?

Reference to the woman Julia, of whom brief mention was made at the inquest by Joseph Barnett, would surely not have perturbed those involved in the Kelly murder too much. From their perspective, this 'Julia' woman *must have* moved out of No 13 before November 8th, because there was only one occupant of the room then, Mary Jane Kelly, and *she had been positively identified* - and she was dead.

Despite Abberline's insinuations - penned a few years after the murders, c1892 - that someone named Winifred May Collis had been killed instead, those behind the murders were sure that Kelly had not survived, that she died in No 13.

Abberline knew that it would later be taken for granted that the writings in the diary were from the perspective of a police inspector deeply immersed in trying to solve the mystery of the Jack the Ripper murders. This assumption, as has been demonstrated, is a total misconception.

The various Mary Jane Kelly background hypotheses; the survival suggestion; the Collis information; all seem to have been inserted in order to complicate and confuse later examiners of the killings.

If the Whitechapel murders had been random killings by a lone psychopath - the theory offered up by the Establishment and the Police - and Kelly was still alive, *she would simply have turned up to ask about the murder of her friend Julia.*

Would not Inspector Abberline himself have interviewed the *surviving* Mary Jane Kelly as the main witness in the aftermath of the 'Julia' / 'Winifred May Collis' murder?

No, those who conceived, directed, and carried out the Whitechapel murders for their own ends, were positive that Kelly died in Miller's Court. Is it not the supreme irony, therefore, that Mary Jane Kelly survived. Again, the unknown factor, that unbeknown to the killer et al, another woman had in fact recently moved in with their quarry. This unknown factor - the woman called Julia - died in place of Kelly.

Sickert verified the occupant of No 13 as Mary Jane Kelly, but how could he be sure that Kelly would not come back to her room while the Ripper and his accomplices were still there. Was it chance that Mary Jane stayed out until morning, or, before he took up his post of lookout (he was already there at 2.30 am) did Walter Sickert seek out Kelly sometime between 1.30 am and 2.30 am in either the Britannia or the Horn of Plenty and make sure she had enough money to keep drinking in the pub for another two or three hours? Sickert the actor, remember, said that *when dressed for his chosen role, his own mother would not know it was him.*

Kelly was an incredibly lucky woman. Her life was saved on two occasions by the death of innocent women. Someone, it would seem, was watching over her. This time, almost certainly, it was Walter Sickert.

After Mary Jane Kelly absconded from Whitechapel, she could have gone to one of her relations, where she would almost certainly have been safe, because no one knew where members of the Kelly family lived - *no relatives could be found to attend her funeral.*

201

More likely, perhaps, Mary Jane chose to start a new life elsewhere. If she decided to go to pastures new, she could use any name she wanted, give any background details she wished, to her new acquaintances.

Chapter 7

The Cleveland Street Brothel

[Three of the participants linked with the 'Jack the Ripper' plot were connected with the Cleveland Street scandal which broke less than a year after the Whitechapel murders.]

The affair began with a trivial incident which took place elsewhere. Some small amounts of cash had been stolen from people working in the General Post Office building in St Martin's-le-Grand in the City of London. On the 4th July 1889, Luke Hanks, a Post Office constable, questioned various employees, amongst whom was Arthur Swinscow, a 15 year old GPO messenger boy. Swinscow had 18/- on him, which was a lot more than he should have had, since it was about a month's wages (His wage would have been 4/- to 5/- per week.)

Rather than be accused of the thefts, Swinscow admitted that he had been recruited to work, along with other boys, Algernon Allies, and Charles Thickbroom, in a male brothel at 19 Cleveland Street which was run by a Charles Hammond. Swinscow said he had been taken to this brothel by Henry Newlove, another Post Office employee, who also worked in the male brothel. In these premises the boys were paid 4/- a time to go to bed with gentlemen of the upper class.

[Henry Newlove recruited boys for the brothel in association with George Veck, a former Post Office employee. Veck lived in 19 Cleveland Street with Charles Hammond - who was married to a French prostitute called Madame Caroline, with whom he had two sons!]

Hanks's report was passed to Inspector Abberline, who was appointed head of the investigation.

When questioned by Abberline about the clients of the male brothel, Swinscow stated that two of the names of the toffs he knew were Lord Arthur Somerset and the Earl of Euston.

[Lord Arthur Somerset, age 38, son of the Duke of Beaufort, Major in the Royal Horse Guards, and Superintendent of the Prince of Wales' Stables.

Henry James Fitzroy, age 41, Earl of Euston, eldest son of the Duke of Grafton.]

Inspector Abberline ordered a watch to be kept on 19 Cleveland Street for several days. When he 'felt he had a good case,' Abberline applied for a search warrant, and the police finally raided the premises. Hammond was not there. He had gone to France. From there he went to Belgium. He did not return to England.

It was later suggested that aristocratic clients had been 'tipped off' about the raid in order for them to be elsewhere when it took place.

Henry Labouchere M.P. accused the Prime Minister, the Marquess of Salisbury, in the House of Commons, of passing on information to Lord Arthur Somerset that a warrant was about to be issued for his arrest, and that Somerset went to France that same night.

Charles Swinscow, Algernon Allies, and Charles Thickbroom, swore information against Lord Arthur

Somerset (who was not in the country), and were under 'police protection' leading up to the trial.

Somerset instructed his solicitor, Arthur Newton, to notify the Director of Public Prosecutions that if he, Somerset, was ever prosecuted, *he would name an individual even higher in social rank as being a client of the brothel at 19 Cleveland Street - Prince Albert Victor.*

The Director of Public Prosecutions informed the Prime Minister, the Marquess of Salisbury.

Henry Du Pré, M.P., stated in the House of Commons, "I cannot help thinking that if the government had been in earnest, they might have obtained the extradition of Hammond, because our Extradition Treaties, both with France and Belgium, cover such charges as those of indecent assault, either by the principal or by accessories."

Lord Arthur Somerset was never extradited - neither was Charles Hammond, keeper of the male brothel. Instead, those who were prepared to give evidence naming upper-class clients of the brothel were charged with prostitution.

George Veck, Henry Newlove, Arthur Swinscow, Algernon Allies, and Charles Thickbroom went on trial at the Old Bailey in September 1889. The names of the Earl of Euston and Lord Arthur Somerset were suppressed.

George Veck received 9 months with hard labour, while Henry Newlove, Arthur Swinscow, Algernon Allies, and Charles Thickbroom each received 4 months with hard labour.

[Regarding the extradition of Charles Hammond, the decision rested with the Foreign Office, and, as well as being Prime Minister, the Marquess of Salisbury was also the Foreign Secretary. *Salisbury decided that Hammond should not be extradited, thereby ensuring that no damaging revelations would be forthcoming in court from the man who knew the names of all the patrons of the male brothel at 19 Cleveland Street.*

In October 1889, Charles Hammond sailed, unhindered, for America - no doubt to the great relief of the British Establishment.]

After the conviction and imprisonment of the minor participants, the newspapers did not let the matter rest. On the 16th November 1889, Ernest Parke, editor of the North London Press, published the names of two of the aristocrats who were involved, and whose identities were shielded at the trial, under the following headline (my italics):

The West End Scandals

Names of Some of The Distinguished Criminals Who Have Escaped

The men to whom we thus referred were the Earl of Euston, eldest son of the Duke of Grafton, and Lord H. Arthur C. Somerset, a younger son of the Duke of Beaufort.

The former, we believe, has departed for Peru; the latter, having resigned his commission and his office of Assistant Equerry to the Prince of Wales, has gone too. These men have been allowed to leave the country and thus defeat the ends of justice because their prosecution would disclose the fact that a far more distinguished and more highly placed personage than themselves was inculpated in their disgusting crimes. The criminals in this case are to be numbered by the score. They include two or three members of Parliament.

The Earl of Euston told his solicitor to sue Ernest Park for libel, and Parke's trial opened in January 1890 at the Old Bailey. Several witnesses for the defence swore on oath that the Earl of Euston had certainly been at 19 Cleveland Street on many occasions. One of these witnesses, who worked in the male brothel, actually gave details of his sexual encounters with Euston there.

The judge, Mr Justice Hawkins (Sir Henry Hawkins), said of this *witness* that he could not imagine 'a more loathsome object.'

The jury found the newspaper editor guilty of libel charges against the Earl of Euston. Ernest Parke was sent to prison for twelve months.

The downfall of Ernest Parke in the libel trial was brought about by the statement he published, declaring in print, that at the time of the trial of Veck, Newlove, Swinscow, etc, the Earl of Euston had 'departed for Peru', making it look as if Euston had fled the country. In fact, he had not left for Peru. He was still in London.

Despite the fact that witnesses swore on oath that the Earl of Euston had often been in the male brothel, the 'departed for Peru' declaration was legally decisive. It actually *made certain that Ernest Parke would be convicted* for libel.

However, not only did it seal the fate of the editor of the North London Press, it ensured that the Press in general would now be very wary of revealing any further 'disclosures' and would effectively back off from the whole story.

The fact that Ernest Parke boldly published the statement that Euston had fled to Peru means that his information came from an authoritative source. Parke's informant must have been in a position to know just such a thing, therefore Parke assumed that the information was totally reliable. So, he published with confidence - *and was doomed.*

Being a journalist, Ernest Parke refused to name his 'source'. This, of course, was exactly what he would be expected to do. *Parke's 'source' was strongly suspected to be Inspector Abberline.*

* * *

Prince Albert Victor - *Again,* he was the central figure. *Again,* his personal actions instigated intrigue and cover-up at the highest level, resulting, in the case of the Cleveland Street scandal, not in madness and murder, but in the jailing of the working-class troublemakers.

Salisbury, the Prime Minister - *Again,* he manipulated behind the scenes to protect royalty. Warned the aristocrats who patronised 19 Cleveland Street when the premises were going to be raided. Made sure, at all costs, that Prince Albert Victor's name was kept out of the exposé of the male brothel.

Inspector Abberline - *Again,* had premises watched - à la 13 Miller's Court - this time in a situation where, as a result of information received, quick action was called for. The deliberate slowness in acting was designed to allow those in high places, already pre-warned, to make their escape.

Again, although investigating the crimes, Abberline is actually working with those behind the cover-up. He is the main suspect for being the informant who passed on the 'inside information' to the newspaper editor that the Earl of Euston had fled the country, resulting in the libel case which Ernest Parke was *guaranteed to lose,* thereby ensuring that newspapers would thereafter view the Cleveland Street brothel story as a bit of a hot potato, and drop their interest in it.

Police 'investigations' and court cases resulted in the lawfully-guilty aristocrats going scot-free, while those who were to give evidence against them were sent to prison.

St John Terrapin wrote of the Cleveland Street male brothel scandal when it took place (my italics): 'By 'coincidence' the policeman in charge of this case was my old friend Inspector Abberline, and *once again the main villains of the piece were allowed to escape prosecution.* Prince Eddy was sent on a naval cruise to get him out of the way, while others moved to the Continent for a few months. *Yet another cover-up to protect top people!* '

As well as the Joseph Sickert story, and the verification by St John Terrapin, this scandal provides *additional* proof, that Prince Albert Victor was a regular visitor to Cleveland Street. The scandal was not uncovered until 1889, *but Charles Hammond had operated the brothel there from 1885.* The male brothel at No 19, visited by Prince Albert Victor, was only two doors away from Sickert's studio at No 15 Cleveland Street, and it was across the street from James Currier's confectionery shop at No 22, where Annie Crook worked.

[As well as being a regular visitor to Cleveland Street, Prince Albert Victor was also an habitué of an exclusive club in the Cleveland Street neighbourhood. This was The Hundred Guineas, a transvestite club in Portland Place, about 300 yards from Cleveland Street.

209

Humorously, he went under the assumed name of 'Victoria' when on club premises. In The Hundred Guineas, its clientèle could dance until 2.00 a.m., the lights then being lowered to allow illicit sexual liaisons to take place. The club closed at 6.00 a.m.]

Lord Somerset spent the remainder of his life on the Continent, settling on the French Riviera. The Earl of Euston, a prominent Freemason (Provincial Grand Master of Huntingtonshire and Northamptonshire at the time of the Cleveland Street affair and the Ernest Parke libel trial), was made an aide-de-camp (confidential assistant) by King Edward VII (Prince Albert Victor's father) in 1901.

William Withey Gull

Born 31 December 1816, Colchester, Essex.
Bap. 9 February, St Leonard's, Colchester.
Parents: John Gull, Elizabeth ------

The Joseph Sickert story of the Jack the Ripper murders named Sir William Gull and John Netley as being the central people involved in the Whitechapel killings, and there is no reason to doubt that this was so. Sickert's information so far has been accurate. Cleveland Street in the West End - a woman named Annie Crook - Prince Albert Victor - Mary Jane Kelly - all directly connected with the murders in the East End and their involvement confirmed by Sir Charles Warren and Inspector Abberline. The gull on Queen Victoria's shoulder in the painting Ennui by Walter Sickert.

Four of the murders carried out in a moving coach the only method which fits the killings - the lack of blood where the bodies were found - nothing ever seen - nothing ever heard. It was as if the killer was invisible, and of course he was, being inside a coach. Feeding the victims drugged grapes guaranteed silence.

William Gull and John Netley were the front line, the operational unit of the plot to prevent the Roman Catholic marriage becoming public knowledge, Gull being the man who did the cutting and mutilating, Netley his coachman and right-hand man.

Although theirs was the active, bloody side of things, they were not exactly popular with their masters, Gull being responsible for inflicting the 'blasted mutilations that have incensed the public' on the victims, which Sir Charles Warren deemed as 'so unnecessary.' And, having killed the wrong woman, both Gull and Netley were the object of Inspector Abberline's disparaging remarks, ''The bloody fools got the wrong woman, but what would you expect with amateurs.''

Besides William Gull being named by Sickert as the man who did the killing and mutilating, two other people point the finger at him.

Involvement by the psychic, Robert James Lees, in the hunt for Jack the Ripper has been mentioned at times in films and books of recent years, most notably 'Jack the Ripper' starring Michael Caine, and 'Jack the Ripper: The Final Solution' by Stephen Knight, but generally it has been played down, almost dismissed as being of any relevance because the story is said to have first made its appearance in the early 1930s, about fifty years after the events. However, this is not so. Details of Robert Lees' connection with the murders appeared in print in 1895 in the Sunday Times-Herald of Chicago.

Robert Lees, born in Hinckley, Leicestershire in 1849, is reputed to have developed great psychic abilities when a young boy. He is said to have conducted private séances for Queen Victoria after the death of her husband, Prince Albert.

The gist of the newspaper article telling the story of the involvement of Robert Lees in the case of Jack the Ripper is as follows:

One day, when travelling with his wife in an omnibus from Shepherd's Bush towards Oxford Street, a man boarded the omnibus at Notting Hill. Lees said to his wife, "That is Jack the Ripper." The man left the omnibus at Marble Arch, and Lees followed him. About half way down Park Lane the man, presumably realising he was being followed, decided to take a cab, and was driven off. Robert Lees told the police that he could track the killer. Accompanied by a police inspector and policemen, he led them to a house in the West End, and told them that this was the home of Jack the Ripper. The inspector, knowing that a distinguished physician lived there, and wary of losing his job if he accused the occupant, told Lees that if he could describe what was in the entrance hall to him - Lees never having been inside - he would enter the house. Robert Lees duly gave a description of items which he said were in the hall. The inspector knocked at the door which was opened by a servant. After quickly verifying what Lees had told him, he asked to see the doctor, whom the servant said was in his bed. He then asked if he could see the doctor's wife, which request was granted. The inspector spoke to her, and during this conversation she admitted that she thought her husband was mentally unstable. She also stated that her husband had not been at home when any of the murders in Whitechapel had taken place.

Arrangements were made for the doctor to be examined by experts on insanity. The doctor admitted that there had been occasions when he had no memory of what he had been doing. When told he was suspected of having committed the murders in Whitechapel during these periods of memory loss, the doctor, horrified, said that his nature would not have allowed him to commit such terrible deeds. It is said that everyone involved in the discovery of the identity of Jack the Ripper, including Robert James Lees, were sworn to secrecy.

The Sunday Times-Herald of Chicago also tells the story of Dr Benjamin Howard. The following quotes are from the article, published on 28 April 1895:

'The story recently told by Dr Howard, a well-known London physician, to William Greer Harrison of the Bohemian Club in San Francisco in regard to the fate of Jack the Ripper, and which is at last given to the world, unseals the lips of a gentleman of this city, ...

has resulted in fixing the identity of the famous Whitechapel murderer beyond the shadow of a doubt. When 'Jack the Ripper' was finally run to earth, it was discovered that he was a physician in good standing, with an extensive practice. He had been, ever since he was a student at Guy's Hospital, a keen vivisectionist.'

1837 - William Gull became a medical student at Guy's Hospital.

1841 - Graduated M.B. (Bachelor of Medicine degree).

- Given the post of medical tutor at Guy's.

213

1843 - Appointed Medical Superintendent of the lunatic ward at Guy's.

1848 - Gained his M.D. (Doctor of Medicine degree).

A vivisectionist. Staunch supporter of experiments on live animals.

'Through some extraordinary contradiction, instead of the sight of pain softening him, as is the case of most devotees of scientific experiments, it had an opposite effect.

This so grew upon him that he experienced the keenest delight in inflicting tortures upon defenceless animals. One of his favourite pastimes was to remove the eyelids from a rabbit and expose it for hours, in a fixed position, to a blinding sun. He would take a seat near it, totally forgetful of meals, of the passage of time, and of everything except the exquisite sensations he experienced in watching the agonised contortions of his victim. He had scarcely been married a month before his wife discovered that he had a mania for inflicting pain.'

1848 - William Gull married Susan Anne Lacy (18 April) in Guernsey.

    They had the following children:
        Susan Charlotte Mary Gull born 1849
        Caroline Cameron Gull born 1851
        William Cameron Gull born 1860

In testifying before the commission (of lunacy) she gave the following extraordinary evidence:

'One night we were sitting in the drawing room. It was quite late. I arose to go to bed. When I arrived upstairs I remembered that I had left my watch upon the drawing room mantelpiece. I descended the stairs. As I approached the drawing room I heard the sounds of a cat mewing piteously. Looking through the door, which happened to be open, I was horrified to see my husband holding a cat over the flame of the moderator lamp (oil-lamp). I was too frightened to do anything but retreat upstairs. When my husband came to bed along towards daylight I felt that I was occupying the same couch as a monster. I discovered later that he had spent almost the whole night in burning the cat to death. The next day he was as kind and loving as possible.

I discovered later that he was subject to an unconquerable mania for inflicting pain. It was quite possible for me, as I studied him closely, to tell when these moods were coming on. On such occasions some apparently trivial act would put me on my guard. He was apt at such times to begin by catching a fly and twirling it impaled upon a pin. He was a strange contradiction. When our little boy, only four years old, imitated him once in this respect, the father was actually shocked and was so indignant that he gave the child a sound whipping. As the boy screamed with the pain of the punishment, the ferocious side of my husband's nature asserted itself. He would in all probability have beaten the child to death if I had not interfered. In his normal moods he was an excellent husband and father, and one of the gentlest and most tractable of men. I have frequently heard him express sincere sympathy with persons in misfortune.'

'The Dr Howard referred to was one of a dozen London physicians who sat at a court of medical enquiry or as a commission in lunacy upon their brother physician, for at last it was definitely proved that the dreaded 'Jack the Ripper' was no less a person than a physician in high standing, and in fact was a man enjoying the patronage of the best society in the west end of London.'

The status of William Gull certainly matched the above description.

1888:   Consultant Physician at Guy's Hospital.
        Physician to Queen Victoria.
        A Governor of Guy's Hospital.
        Served on the Senate of the University of
            London.

A man of strong physique, William Gull had his famous stroke in 1887. A great deal of importance has been placed on this fact in order to claim he would have been unable to carry out his role in the murders. This was patently not so, because that same year Gull was appointed Physician in Ordinary to the royal household - i.e. he was in regular attendance on Queen Victoria until his death was announced in 1890. He also remained Consulting Physician at Guy's Hospital until 1890.   Furthermore, in 1887, he was made a governor of Guy's. He also continued in his position on the Senate of the University of London. William Gull's workload in 1888 was not that of a man with a severely impaired constitution.

'An exhaustive enquiry before a commission in lunacy developed the fact that while in one mood the doctor was a most worthy man, in the other he was a terrible monster.

When it was absolutely proved beyond peradventure that the physician in question was the murderer, and his insanity fully established by a Commission de Lunatico Inquirendo, all parties having knowledge of the facts were sworn to secrecy. Up to this time of Dr Howard's disclosure this oath had been rigidly adhered to.

He was at once removed to a private insane asylum in Islington, and he is now the most intractable and dangerous madman confined in that establishment.

None of the keepers know that the desperate maniac who flings himself from side to side in his padded cell and makes the long watches of the night hideous with his piercing cries is the famous 'Jack the Ripper'. To them and to the visiting inspectors he is simply known as Thomas Mason, alias No. 124. In order to account for the disappearance of the doctor from society a sham death and burial were gone through.'

It was officially announced that he had died at his home at 74 Brook Street, Grosvenor Square, a burial then taking place at Thorpe-le-Soken, Essex – these events made easier by the fact that William Gull's death certificate was signed by Dr Theodore Dyke Acland, Gull's son in law. *This was highly unethical.* (Caroline Cameron Gull married Theodore Dyke Acland 12 April 1888.)

'A London clubman, now in Chicago, who is acquainted with Dr Howard, is of the opinion that, being in a foreign country and perhaps under the influence of wine, Dr Howard has permitted his tongue to wag too freely. I notice that Dr Howard has not revealed the name of the physician who committed the murders. For this he has reason to be thankful, for such an act would have resulted in the total destruction of his London practice. As it is, he will doubtless be privately reprimanded by the Royal College of Physicians and Surgeons, as an oath administered under such

217

circumstances is considered of the most sacred and binding nature.'

[Dr Benjamin Howard later denied disclosing this information. Well, he would, wouldn't he? What else could he do.]

Gull's ferocity in killing the women went way beyond what was expected. As has been seen, his employers were displeased with the public outcry he had created. Perhaps he was punished for his excess. Or, more likely, William Gull became truly insane - hardly surprising considering the bloody butchery he immersed himself in. He would have been a dangerous liability to his masters, therefore he was confined in an asylum - under the derisive name of Thomas Mason.

There are three possible hospitals for Gull's confinement: St Mary's Islington Infirmary; the London Fever Hospital, Liverpool Road, Islington; the Great Northern Central Hospital, Caledonian Road, Islington.

St Mary's was not founded until 1900. The London Fever, although it moved to the Islington site in 1849, dealt with contagious fevers (typhus, scarlet fever, smallpox) as its name suggests.

Almost certainly, Gull was incarcerated in a private room in the Great Northern Central Hospital. The hospital's President - *H.R.H. Prince Albert Victor.*

John Charles Netley

John Netley, the coachman from hell. John Charles Netley was born 19 May 1860, Paddington, London, son of John Netley and Mary Ann Terry. John Netley Snr, born in Pulborough, Sussex, in 1831, was a (horse-drawn) omnibus conductor, then an omnibus proprietor, later becoming a hackney carriage driver. John Netley and Mary Ann Terry married 2 June 1857, St James' Church, Paddington. They had the following children:

George Alfred born 1858, Paddington
John Charles born 1860, Paddington
William Henry born 1860, Paddington
Albert James born 1863, Paddington
Francis Luke born 1865, Paddington
Mary Ann born 1868, Paddington
Margaret Lydia born 1870, Kensington
Alfred Ernest born 1871, Kensington
Agnes Louisa born 1874, Kensington

Four of John and Mary Netley's surviving sons - George, John, Francis, and Alfred - all followed in their father's footsteps, becoming hackney carriage drivers (coachmen), while the other son, Albert, became a railway carman (driver). These railcars were powered carriages controlled by an operator.

In his early twenties, before becoming a coachman, John Netley worked as a railway carman like his brother, and may well have been in charge of one of these carriages on London's underground railway.

Netley worked as a coachman for contractors. Exactly how he became involved as the coachman for William Gull may never be known for sure, but the two men became partners in bloody murder.

John Netley never married. He lived at the following London addresses:

1860 -1863 - 3 Cambridge Place, Paddington.
1863 - 1865 - 41 Pickering Place, Paddington.
1865 - 1868 - 18 Pickering Terrace, Paddington.
1868 - 1870 - 5 Pickering Place, Padddington.

1870 - 1875- 99 Westbourne Park Road, Paddington.
1875 - 1903 - 3 Amberley Road, Paddington.

John Netley died, aged only 43, on 20th September, 1903. He was driving his growler - a four-wheeled horse-drawn cab - in Park Road, Regent's Park, when he had an accident.

The Marylebone Mercury & West London Gazette, 26 September 1903:

'One of the wheels of the van collided with a stone rest, and he was thrown from his seat into the roadway. As the deceased lay on the ground, one of the horses kicked him on the head and the wheel passed over him. '

By the sound of this account, a coach wheel hit a bollard in the road, Netley then being thrown forwards between the horses who kept going, trampling on him, then the wheels of the coach ran over him.

No eye-witnesses are mentioned, so we don't know if Netley was found lying in the road and it was *assumed* that an accident had taken place as above, or if there were witnesses to an *actual* accident, but their names were then left out of the report.

His death certificate simply states: 'Fracture of skull and other injuries. Fall from his van under the wheel of it from colliding with rest in roadway – Accidental.'

Netley is said to have attempted to murder Alice Margaret, daughter of Annie Crook, by running her down with his coach, failing to kill her, but injuring her in the process.

If the Establishment had wanted her killed it would surely not have been at all difficult. John Netley's life does not appear to have improved in any way since his time as coachman and right-hand-man to William Gull during the Whitechapel reign of terror. Netley *must have* felt he had been unjustly treated - after all he had done for them!

He *must have* felt badly let down, *must have* wondered why he had not received the recognition his services deserved. Had he simply slipped their mind? Netley maybe took it upon himself to kill the girl in order to remind his former employers and masters that he was still around - *and to jog their memory of the debt they owed him.*

John Netley's death occurred near an entrance to Regent's Park named Clarence Gate - Albert Victor became *Duke of Clarence in 1890, and henceforth was known by that name.* Could it have been a million to one coincidence that, of all the places in London for Netley's accident to have taken place, it happened at Clarence Gate?

Perhaps Netley tried a bit of blackmail of his own. In a desperate attempt to get what he considered was long overdue, did he stick his head above the parapet and have it shot off? Was the death of John Netley the removal of a problem, or was it 'just one of those things'?

Pickering Place - Now part of Queensway on the Porchester Road side of Westbourne Grove.

Pickering Terrace - Now Pickering Mews, parallel to the above.

Clarence Gate entrance

By the look of the streetlamp, this could be the actual traffic island where Netley died in 1903.

Chapter 8

Clarence Guy Gordon Haddon

When the scandal of the Cleveland Street brothel was at its height (autumn 1889) Prince Albert Victor (accompanied by his younger brother George) was sent overseas on a tour of India - to get him out of the way.

At a ball in India he met Margery Haddon. Daughter of a civil servant, she was married to a civil engineer, Henry Haddon. Prince Albert Victor and Mrs Margery Haddon are said to have become lovers. The following year, 1890, she gave birth to a son who was significantly named Clarence Guy Gordon Haddon. Perhaps Margery Haddon named her son Clarence after his father - Prince Albert Victor had become Duke of Clarence on 24 May 1890, thereafter being known by that title.

His death was announced as having taken place on 14 January 1892, so if Albert Victor had syphilis, the signs must surely have been evident in 1891. Many years after Clarence's birth in 1890, neither Margery Haddon nor her son are mentioned as having any particular health problems, so the Duke of Clarence must have contracted the disease in 1891. It would, therefore, appear to be unconnected with any of his Cleveland Street activities. If he was still a patron, perhaps he caught the infection in the Hundred Guineas transvestite club.

After her divorce, Margery Haddon came to Britain, claiming that she was the mother of the Duke of

Clarence's son. Patrick Quinn, head of Special Branch, led a secret enquiry into the claim, which was taken seriously enough for William Carrington, Keeper of the Privy Purse, to contemplate paying her off. What happened instead, is that letters written to Mrs Haddon by Prince Albert Victor - *named in the Haddon divorce proceedings* - were 'acquired' (procured for cash, no doubt) by the legal firm of Lewis and Lewis who had acted for the Duke of Clarence during the said divorce action.

Matters came to a head in 1914, when Margery Haddon was arrested at the gates of Buckingham Palace where she was publicly proclaiming that she was the mother of the Duke of Clarence's illegitimate son.

It was generally agreed (i.e. by Special Branch and royal courtiers) that it would be better (for them) if Margery Haddon left the country. Clothes were bought for her through an account, a passage back to India arranged - and she was given £5.

On 20 February 1915, Margery Haddon sailed for India, and into obscurity. Her disappearance did not, however, result in the final closure of the matter the Establishment hoped for.

In the 1920s, Clarence Haddon himself came to London. He asserted that his father was the Duke of Clarence, and he was determined that this fact be accepted by the Royal Family. He was dismissed as a crank, his claim rejected because he had no proof to back it up. There was, of course, no possibility of Clarence Haddon having proof of his claim - *because the documentary proof of the association between his mother and the Duke of Clarence was already in the hands of royal lawyers, having been 'obtained' some years before.* Legally, Clarence Haddon's claim was doomed.

However, he did not give up. He wrote a book - My Uncle, King George V- which was published in 1929 - in America.

He also wrote to King George V to bring to his attention the 'unjust' and 'underhand' treatment which had been meted out to him by those in authority. No reply is known.

Hoping to be rid of him once and for all, a passage to America was arranged for him - the cost of the trip again being paid from police funds. The plan did not quite work out, because, after taking his free trip to America, Clarence returned to England and resurrected his campaign for recognition.

In 1934 he was arrested, and he appeared at a hearing at the Old Bailey where he was bound over for three years by Mr Justice Charles on condition that he dropped his claim to be son of the Duke of Clarence.

Haddon breached the conditions, and was jailed for 1 year. Wearied from his efforts, and gradually worn down with the hopelessness of his cause, Clarence Haddon became a sad figure. He was said to have died a broken man.

Also named during the Margery Haddon divorce proceedings was Lieutenant George Rogers, military aide to Prince Albert Victor. It is almost certain that Rogers set up the meeting with Margery Haddon for him. It was implied that Lieutenant Rogers was the father of Clarence, not the prince, but Rogers was a smokescreen, taking the blame for his master.

Incredibly, *although knowing that Lieutenant George Rogers was not the child's father, the Rogers family agreed to pay maintenance for Clarence*

Haddon, in order to protect the name of Prince Albert Victor.

The Rogers family bearing the cost of the upbringing of someone else's child, followed by Clarence Haddon's struggles in vain for truth and justice, bring to mind John Wardle's unsuccessful efforts of more than half a century before.

The lives of Margery Haddon and her son Clarence, like those of Annie Crook and her daughter Alice Margaret, were destroyed by a man whose actions literally sowed the seeds for the creation of 'Jack the Ripper' - the man who never was.

Files Released in 2005

Patrick Quinn, head of Special Branch, met with Sir William Carrington at Buckingham Palace in July 1914:

'He (Carrington) invited my opinion on the question of making a payment ....He was afraid she might have some proof.'

Re. 'embarrassing' letters which Margery Haddon once had: Special Branch Report, July 1914:

'There were grounds for thinking Lewis and Lewis obtained these letters from her upon payment.'

The family of Lieutenant George Rogers had in fact told the police a different story to that which had been claimed. They actually said that Lieutenant Rogers had been a 'scapegoat' for the clandestine royal relationship, and that his family had made maintenance payments for the child Clarence even although Rogers was not his father.

The Death of the Duke of Clarence

During the scandal of the Cleveland Street male brothel (1889), when it was suggested that Prince Albert Victor was one of those who had frequented the establishment, the New York Times declared:

'It is not too early to predict that such a fellow will never be allowed to ascend the British throne.'

As events turned out, the newspaper's prophecy was correct, because in 1892 it was announced that the Duke of Clarence (Albert Victor) having contracted influenza, had died at Sandringham, Norfolk, on the 14th of January that year.

[This must have been the Asian Flu 1889-1890. The outbreak was not of Spanish Flu 1918-1919 proportions, when about 40 million people died. It seems to have been of Asian Flu 1957-1958, and Hong Kong Flu 1968-1969, proportions, when around one million people died (worldwide). The flu of 1889-1890 disappeared in March 1890, but the infection recurred in January 1892. The Royals were at Sandringham before and after the Christmas/New Year period. Queen Victoria, together with her children (she had 9) and grandchildren (she had more than 30), catered for by numerous household servants - *yet only Albert Victor, age 28, is fatally struck down.* How unlucky.]

It was later rumoured that he had not in fact died, that his death had been fabricated, and that he was hidden away until his death, which, according to Walter Sickert, did not take place until 1933.

A falsely concocted death strongly implies that it was thought absolutely necessary that Prince Albert Victor be prevented from succeeding to the throne. There must have been a reason for this course of action - it wasn't as if the prince was Jack the Ripper. He may have, unwittingly, been the cause, but he would not have been involved in any way with the murders. In fact, he would almost certainly have been unaware of the motive behind them. The names Mary Ann Nichols, Annie Chapman, Catharine Eddowes, and Elizabeth Stride, would have meant nothing to him, because he had never heard of them. He may well have met *the* Mary Jane Kelly, but the fact that the fifth Ripper victim was thought to be named Mary Jane Kelly again, would probably have meant nothing to him.

He had married a Roman Catholic and fathered a child by her, but this was *private information,* it was not publicly known. Besides, all those involved had been taken care of (so the Establishment thought) via the Whitechapel murders. Problem resolved.

It had also been implied that the prince had been involved with the male brothel in Cleveland Street, but his entanglement could not be proved. His connection with the whole affair had been hushed up. Again, the problem had been resolved.

Any heir to the throne was expected to marry and provide heirs. Could the reason for removing Prince Albert Victor from the succession be connected with what St John Terrapin wrote of him at the time (My Italics): 'Homosexual or not, he became engaged to the beautiful Princess Mary of Teck who was half-English being the daughter of Lady Mary Cambridge by the German Prince of Teck.

But two weeks before the proposed wedding, in February 1892, Eddy caught pneumonia and died, aged only twenty-eight. *By then it was rumoured that he had other complaints acquired from his habits, which seem to have been bisexual, and though appearances can be misleading he certainly looked dissipated. The Princess, who eventually married Eddy's younger brother George instead and later became Queen Mary, may have had a very lucky escape.'*

If Prince Albert Victor had contracted a venereal disease such as syphilis, this would certainly have been a vital motive for removing him from the direct line of succession to the throne. He could not be allowed to marry and have children, for obvious reasons. Therefore, he could not provide the necessary heirs. Just cancelling his marriage to Princess Mary would have been completely ineffectual, because he would still have remained heir to the throne - the problem would simply have been prolonged. Much more convenient for everyone, indeed the only practical solution, was an official statement that the death of Prince Albert Victor had taken place (déjà vu Sir William Gull) after a short illness.

The prince's fiancée was then betrothed to the next in line to the throne. Prince Albert Victor would, of course, have to be hidden away somewhere.

The information passed on to Walter Sickert (Melvyn Fairclough, The Ripper & The Royals) was that the prince was kept in Glamis Castle. The castle is on the outskirts of the village of Glamis, about four miles from Forfar, in the county of Angus, Scotland, and is most famous for its connection with

Shakespeare's Macbeth and the secret room which housed the so-called 'Monster of Glamis' - said to have been Thomas, the first-born son of George Bowes-Lyon, Lord Glamis. Legend says that the boy was born deformed in 1821 - Thomas was said to have been born covered in black, matted hair, with tiny arms and legs. After a story was circulated that he had died the day he was born - legend says that, incredibly, he lived for around 100 years - he was locked up in a room about 15 ft by 10 ft, lit very dimly with small windows.

There is no doubt that Prince Albert Victor could have been kept secluded in Glamis Castle, but as his place of concealment it had one major drawback - the castle is the family home of the Earls of Strathmore and Kinghorne (Bowes-Lyon family), not the Royal Family. Is it likely that knowledge of the sham death would have been immediately shared with others? Surely the fewer people who knew of this the better. And of those who did know, as few of them as possible knowing his true whereabouts would surely be preferable - perhaps this is why Walter Sickert was told that the prince was kept in Glamis Castle.

Is it not more probable that Prince Albert Victor would have been hidden away in a royal residence, the secret therefore being kept in-house, so to speak - and there is in fact a royal residence associated with him after the announcement of his death.

Local tradition states that Prince Albert Victor, Duke of Clarence, died in Osborne House, Isle of Wight, in 1930.

Osborne House was built 1845-1851 for Queen Victoria and her husband, Prince Albert. Less than five miles from Osborne House was Carisbrooke Workhouse and Asylum. This building, also known as

Forest House because it stood in the forest of Parkhurst, opened around 1803, and was originally a workhouse, but in 1831 part of the building was licensed as an asylum. In 1867, this part of the building housed 16 male and 19 female inmates.

Osborne House seems a much more credible candidate for the hiding-place of the Duke of Clarence. Albert Victor was, after all, Queen Victoria's grandson, and Osborne House, built for privacy, and to provide seclusion from public life, was the private home of Victoria - she also died in Osborne House (1901).

Another of its advantages, of course, was that Osborne was not far from Carisbrooke Asylum, where Albert Victor could be sent during the periods when his condition was severe. Symptoms such as an ulcer at the site of the infection, sores, and swollen glands, are endured before the next indications of the disease, a rash and fever, makes their appearance around two months later.

The final stage of the affliction - and years could elapse before they appear - can consist of masses of tumour-like nodules in the skin or muscles, arterial disease such as thickening of the arteries, mental failure, a stroke, or paralysis. The nodules could even develop in the spinal cord, or in the brain. I dare say that being able to send a patient afflicted with such a disease to an asylum, especially in the latter stages, would be a godsend for those trying to care for him.

A sham death, the individual then vanishing from sight is by no means a one-off event in the Royal Family.

In 1986, a member of the Royal Family, Nerissa Bowes-Lyon, died aged 66. She was the niece of the Queen Mother (Elizabeth Bowes-Lyon), and a cousin

231

of the Queen. Nothing surprising in the death of someone in their mid-60s, it may be thought - *except that Nerissa Bowes-Lyon was supposed to have died in 1940.*

Nerissa and her sister, Katherine Bowes-Lyon, were born mentally handicapped with impaired mental development. When in her late teens, Nerissa was said to have had the mental age of a girl of six.

In 1941, the two Bowes-Lyon sisters, Nerissa (age 22) and Katherine (age 15) were put into the Royal Earlswood, a psychiatric hospital in Redhill, Surrey. Nerissa's death being fabricated - *i.e. that she had died during the previous year.* She spent the next 46 years there, until her *real death on 22 January, 1986.*

She was buried in a pauper's grave. The grave in Redhill Cemetery was marked with a 6" high (15.24 cm) white plastic tag. On the tag were two strips of sticky tape bearing the reference number M 11125 and the name Bowes-Lyon. A headstone was later put up - after the story appeared in the press.

The death of Nerissa's sister, Katherine Bowes-Lyon, occurred in 1961 - *or rather Burke's Peerage, the family tree of British aristocracy, was informed in 1961 that she had died.* She was still alive.

The Royal Earlswood Hospital closed in 1997 and Katherine Bowes-Lyon was moved to Kentwin House Surrey, a care home for the mentally disabled. However, this closed in 2001, and she is now in another (unnamed) care home in Surrey. As far as can be known, she is still alive (Jan 2010).

In 1987, when the shocking truth appeared in The Sun newspaper, a hospital insider revealed that neither of the sisters had ever received a visit from any member of the Royal Family, that the only people who had visited them had been members of the hospital's League of Friends, who came to see them because they had been abandoned.

Appointment with Death

Important people are determined that Mary Jane Kelly be tracked down so that they can have her killed. The police are keeping a watch on Cleveland Street: Sir Charles Warren, "And don't relax your watch on Cleveland Street. That woman could still turn up there." Which is precisely what happened. Kelly did return to Cleveland Street, almost certainly to see Walter Sickert and hand over Annie Crook's marriage certificate for him to pass on to those who were trying to kill her. Kelly's trip back to where it all began must surely have occurred fairly soon after the murder of Catharine Eddowes on 30th September, so her meeting with Sickert almost certainly took place in the early part of October. Of course, this was her undoing, because she would have been followed back to Whitechapel, thus revealing where she was living. Those searching for her had traced her at long last. They were desperate to eliminate her, and they now knew where she lived - yet, for a month, perhaps more, they just waited, and had a watch kept on her house. From information passed on from the plain-clothes policemen who took turns to watch the entrance to Miller's Court (they could not have stood in the cul-de-sac that was Miller's Court, directly outside her house) Abberline would have been informed of the comings and goings of people who went in and out of the passageway, not Mary Jane's actual home, at various times. Also, they could hardly have kept a watch on the passageway twenty-four hours a day - if there was someone standing opposite the entrance all day and night, it would be far too suspicious, not to say blindingly obvious.

Mitre Square, seemingly their designated spot for Mary Jane Kelly, had already been used for Catharine Eddowes (Mrs John Kelly) whom they mistook for their target. They could hardly place another MJK body there! And, presumably, they could not surpass that particular location. So, something else, something special, would have to be arranged for the real Mary Jane.

They had Kelly's address. They had Walter Sickert who could identify her for sure on the night - now wishing another Eddowes fiasco on their hands - so why delay for several weeks until the 9th of November? Although they were anxious to kill her, they hung back from carrying out the deed. There must have been a very good reason for postponing Mary Jane Kelly's murder. They must have been waiting for a specific date, an important date, on which to kill their main target.

Sir Charles Warren founded Quatuor Coronati, a Lodge for Masonic research (Stephen Knight: The Final Solution). It seems an unusual title, but, strangely, it is not unique.

Oddly, the Roman Catholic Church also has Quatuor Coronati (Latin: The Four Crowned Ones). They use the term to signify The Four Crowned Martyrs, said to be Christian stonemasons who refused to build a pagan idol or temple for the Emperor Diocletian in the late 3rd century/early 4th century AD. They were then beheaded. Dedicated to them is the Church of the Quattro Coronati (Italian: The Four Crowned Ones) in Rome.

is claimed that this church is held in great esteem by builders and stone-cutters in Rome, since carved effigies of the four have stone-masons' tools such as chisel, mallet, rule, and square, at their feet.

The Quattro Coronati Church is known as Church of the Four Crowned Brothers. These Four Crowned Brothers were said to have been put to death on the 8th of November - close.

In the second half of the 1860's, Charles Warren led an expedition to the Holy Land to undertake excavations. His party engaged in an archaeological dig on the Temple Mount in Jerusalem, site of the Temple of Solomon, then the Temple of Herod the Great.

The Babylonian army of King Nebuchadnezzar invaded the Kingdom of Judah, conquering Jerusalem and totally destroying the Temple in 586 BC. The destruction of the Temple of Solomon took place on the 9th of Av that year. On the Hebrew calendar, Av is the eleventh month of the civil year. The ninth day of the eleventh month - the 9th of November. Did they wait for the day of the utter destruction of the Temple of Solomon to carry out the utter destruction of Mary Jane Kelly?

Almost certainly.

Appendices

Appendix I

Mrs Carthy's

Elizabeth Phoenix stated that Mary Jane Kelly had lived for a time in the house of a Mrs Carthy in Pennington-street. It was while she was there that she had been 'sweet on a man in the building trade' (Joseph Fleming). This would have been 138 Pennington Street, the house of John and Mary McCarty. Mary Jane probably drank in the local pub, the White Bear in Breezer's Hill, a short street at the west end of Pennington Street.

Montague John Druitt

The body of Montague John Druitt was found in the Thames on 31st December 1888, and it had been in the water for 'upwards of a month'. So, Druitt probably 'suicided' in November 1888.

The police hinted that they had their suspicions of his being Jack the Ripper. As we know of course, he was not, as we also know that the police knew he was not. He was to be the 'get out of jail free card' if he was needed. Which he wasn't.

Montague John Druitt was not a doctor, but a barrister who had given up the legal profession and was working as a schoolteacher. He did have convenient medical connections however, if the matter ever needed to be raised in a court of law. Which it didn't. Both his father, William Druitt, and his uncle, Robert Druitt, had been medical practitioners, F.R.C.S. (Fellow of the Royal College of Surgeons).

Winifred May Collis

Further to details given earlier (p 161-163) regarding the Winifred May Collis who Inspector Abberline stated was a parlour maid at 27 Cleveland Street when she met Mary Jane Kelly, as has been shown, she is most unlikely to have been employed as a parlour maid at this address as it turned out to be a property leased by Thomas Hitt, a carpenter, who let rooms for rent.

In 1886, Thomas Hitt is the ratepayer. In April 1887, no individual is listed on the rate book. So, it would appear that, sometime between April 1886 and April 1887, 27 Cleveland Street became empty, i.e. it was *uninhabited in April 1887.*

On the 1891 census, the numbers 25-35 for Cleveland Street are not even listed as uninhabited - they do not appear on the census at all. So, No. 27 must have been *pulled down between April 1887 and 1891.* So, how could a Winifred May Collis have been living at 27 Cleveland Street in 1888?

Appendix II

Sarah Annie Crook

Regarding Sarah Annie Crook and Annie Elizabeth Crook it has been stated that Sarah was born on 31 August 1838 at 22 Great Marylebone Street, and that Annie was born in London on 10 October 1862.

This information about the birth of Sarah Annie Crook, mother of Annie Elizabeth, appears on the International Genealogical Index of the Church of Jesus Christ of Latter-Day Saints as follows:

Sarah Ann Crook.   Birth: 31 Aug 1838, 22 Great Marylebone Street, London.
Death: 18 Nov 1918 [Sarah Annie Crook's death certificate gives 17 Nov 1918.]
Record submitted after 1991 by a member of the LDS Church.
No additional information is available.

So, someone placed this data about Sarah Ann Crook on the I.G.I.   The problem with the above information is - is it genuine, or is it false?

With Sarah, we know that her birth should have taken place 1838-1839, so, even although Sarah is listed on census records as being born in Scotland Berwick-on-Tweed, this birth information is tempting to believe.

Regarding the statement that Sarah was born on 31 August at 22 Great Marylebone Street - there is no record of this birth in Westminster Register Office.

In any case - Crook was Sarah's *married* name. She was born *Sarah Annie Dryden* - not Sarah Annie Crook.

Annie Elizabeth Crook

Like Sarah, information regarding the birth of Annie appears on the I.G.I. as follows:

Annie Elizabeth Crook. Birth: 10 Oct 1862 St Pancras Parish, London.
Parents: Mother: Sarah Ann Crook.
Death: 23 Feb 1920.
Record submitted after 1991 by a member of the LDS Church.
No additional information is available.

We know that Annie's birth is missing from the registration of births. We know she was born during the period 1862-1864. So, again the birth details are enticing.

The details on the I.G.I. for Annie list no father for her, thus making her appear illegitimate - *hence, no Roman Catholic marriage, and of course, no Roman Catholic baptism.* There is no record of this birth.

William & Sarah Crook's other children

Two of William and Sarah Crook's four daughters died young:

Sarah Mary Crook died 30 June 1867, age 14 months.
Cause of death: measles and pneumonia.

Catherine Crook died 9 October 1871, age 14 months.
Cause of death: diarrhoea.

Appendix III

Alice Margaret Crook

Daughter of Annie Elizabeth Crook and Prince Albert Victor, Alice Margaret Crook was born on April 18th 1885 in the St Marylebone Workhouse, Northumberland Street, off Marylebone Road. Northumberland Street is now Luxborough Street, and the University of Westminster buildings occupy the site of the old workhouse.

She suffered from the hereditary disease otosclerosis, which causes progressive hearing loss over the years.

<u>? indicates afflicted by otosclerosis</u>

King Christian IX of Denmark m Princess Louise
                                                    Wilhelmina (?)
_____|_____
Frederick Alexandra (?) Vilhelm Dagmar Thyra
                                                    Valdemar
                        m
        Edward, Prince of Wales
_____|_____
Albert George   Louis Victoria Maud Alexander John
Victor (?)
    m
 Annie Crook
_____|_____
Alice Margaret Crook (?)

241

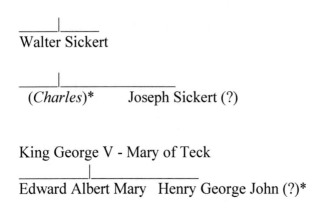

Walter Sickert

(*Charles*)*   Joseph Sickert (?)

King George V - Mary of Teck

Edward Albert Mary   Henry George John (?)*

The Claim

The baby Charles was taken from the Crook family and substituted for Prince John, who had died when a baby.

Alice Margaret Crook married William Gorman 14 July 1918 in St Aloysius Roman Catholic Chapel, St Pancras. He was a fish curer. His father was Patrick Gorman, who was dead by 1918. William Gorman wasn't that much older than his wife, being 45, she 33. They were living at 195 Drummond Street when they married.

Alice Margaret avoided the problem of her real father, Prince Albert Victor, and listed William Crook, her grandfather, as her father.

She is said to have had two affairs with Walter Sickert, both of which resulted in her giving birth to sons, Charles (1905) and Joseph (1925).

The Sickert story says that Charles was taken from the family and substituted for Prince John. Both children were born in 1905, but John was said to have died when only months old. There is no evidence for the birth of Charles in 1905 - *but, if the story is true, there is no chance of there being any evidence.*

Alice Margaret Gorman died on 20 January 1950 at Whittington Hospital, Highgate Hill, aged 63. Cause of death was stated to be cerebral thrombosis and arteriosclerosis. Alice Margaret and William Gorman were still living at 195 Drummond Street. He was listed as being a fishmonger. Joseph registered his mother's death.

[Whittington Hospital is historically associated with Dick Whittington. Dick - or rather, Sir Richard - Whittington died in 1423, leaving an estate of £5,000 (£3,000,000 now using the Retail Price Index. Using Average Earnings, £29,000,000) to be used for charitable purposes. Almshouses were set up for the poor, and these almshouses were moved to Highgate in the 19th century. The almshouses moved to Felbridge in Sussex in 1966. Amazingly, the Dick Whittington legacy is still helping people today. Dick Whittington's cat is the hospital motif.]

William Gorman's Birth

Details of William Gorman's birth have been conspicuous by their absence. William Gorman, age 8, born London, Middlesex, appears in the census of 1881 in St John's Institute for the Deaf and Dumb in Clifford Cum Boston, Wetherby, Yorkshire, run by the St Vincent de Paul Sisters of Charity. This gives a birth year of 1872-1873. He does not appear on a census after this.

He is listed as being 45 in 1918 when he married Alice Margaret Crook. Again this gives a birth year of 1872-1873. He also states that his father's name is Patrick, and that he is, or was, a Dairyman.

There is no record of a birth of a William Gorman, father Patrick Gorman, 1870-1875 in London - or anywhere else in England.

There is only one birth recorded for a William Gorman in London during the period, 1872-1873, and that is:

William Thomas Gorman, born 1873, St Giles London.

Parents: William Thomas Gorman, Susannah Smith.

[William Thomas Gorman worked as a Cab Driver]

So the birth of *the* William Gorman does not appear where it should, and there are no other census records of him to compare. Although they both agree with each other, could the age listed on the 1881 Census and his marriage certificate be wrong?

Unlikely as it might seem, the age of 8 listed by the census-taker in 1881 is almost certainly wrong. The Institute for the Deaf and Dumb had 98 scholars when this census was taken, and a staff of eight Sisters of Charity. Would one of the Sisters have gone through the 98 scholars' names individually, giving their ages, places of births, etc, to the person asking for details of the inmates?

Most unlikely. She would have simply handed over the school entry-roll to the census-taker for him to copy onto the census. This list would give the age of the scholar when he *entered* the school. So, if a boy was enrolled in the Institute at age 8, and been there for say 18 months, he would still be listed by the census-taker as being 8 years old, although he could be almost 10 years of age.

The age given by William Gorman for his marriage certificate may well have been deliberately false. He obviously would have known all about the Crook family connection to the Jack the Ripper murders, and the treatment meted out to Annie Crook, and of course to Alice Margaret herself. There was also the stolen child, Charles. It was wise to keep as much distance between yourself and the authorities as you could, and misinformation on official documents was about the only means there was. He could do nothing about the troubles already inflicted on the Crook family, and all the horrors which had befallen them, but it would help keep trouble away from members of his own family. Understandably, he was cautious about giving his true age, and careful not to give his father's *real* name. He may have had close relatives living somewhere in London.

It is more than likely that he was named after his father. When William Gorman died in 1951, the age stated on his death certificate is 81. This gives a birth year of c1870. There is a match:

William Gorman born 5 Dec 1870, Kensington, London.
Parents: William Gorman, Mary Daley (sic).

William Gorman, age 4 months, appears on the 1871 Census. His father's occupation is stated to be – *Dairyman*.

[In 1924, William and Alice Margaret Gorman were still careful. On William Alfred's birth certificate, his father's name was listed as - William *Olaf* Gorman.]

[When their daughter Annie Elizabeth married, the family remained cautious. Her father was listed as *Thomas* Gorman.]

Alice Margaret Crook's Other Children

The family story is that as well as having sons Joseph and Charles by the artist Walter Sickert, Alice Margaret Crook had three children by her husband William Gorman. Joseph William Charles was born on 22 October 1925 at 195 Drummond Street, St Pancras. Charles is said to have been born twenty years before in 1905, shortly afterwards being taken from the family after the hushed-up death of Prince John, and substituted for him. Of course, there is no record of Charles' birth. But, once more, the family claims are proven to be correct.

Alice Elizabeth born 10 June 1921, 195 Drummond Street, St Pancras [died 3 Sept 1921, age 3 months, in University College Hospital].
1) Diarrhoea and Vomiting
2) Bronchopneumonia 3 days

William Alfred born 29 January 1924, 19 Drummond Street, St Pancras [died 6 December 1926 age 2 years, in University College Hospital].
1) Bronchopneumonia 3 days

Annie Elizabeth born 8 August 1927, 195 Drummond Street, St Pancras.

Prince John

John was the youngest son of Prince George and Mary of Teck. George was the Duke of Clarence's younger brother, Mary of Teck his former fiancée.

John, born 1905, was Clarence's nephew, Charles (Crook/Sickert), born 1905, his grandson.

John - or Charles, if live baby Charles took the place of dead baby John - suffered from a disease of the nervous system, thought to be epilepsy, and had some kind of neurodevelopment disorder. Of the six royal children, only 'John' had these nervous system afflictions.

It does tend to make one think of the health difficulties Alice Margaret Crook must have suffered after being knocked down by a horse-drawn carriage on two occasions by John Netley.

'John' was hidden away, being consigned to the care of his devoted nanny, Lalla Bill. When he was around the age of 11, his health problems worsened, so he was insulated further from the outside world by being sent to Wood Farm, which was on the Sandringham Estate. He died on 18 January, 1919, after suffering a fit. He was 14 years old.

It was only in 1998, when personal photographs belonging to the late Duke of Windsor were published in newspapers, that his existence was brought to public knowledge. The boy became known as the Lost Prince.

? indicates sufferers of Epilepsy

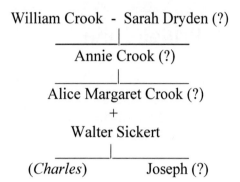

William Crook - Sarah Dryden (?)
_____|_____
Annie Crook (?)
_____|_____
Alice Margaret Crook (?)
+
Walter Sickert
_____|_____
(*Charles*)   Joseph (?)

King George V - Mary of Teck
_____|_____
Edward Albert Mary Henry George John (?)

Appendix IV

John Netley's Twin

John Netley's twin brother, William Henry Netley, died 24th February 1861, at 3 Cambridge Place, Paddington, when he was just nine months old. The cause of his death is listed as 'Convulsions, from Teething'.

William Withey Gull's Middle Name

The children of John and Elizabeth Gull were christened in St Leonard's, Colchester. A contemporary of John Gull was William Withey. Both were Essex barge-masters. William Withey and his wife Elizabeth also had their family christened in the church of St Leonard's, Colchester.

<u>Children of</u>

<u>John Gull - Elizabeth</u>	<u>William Withey - Elizabeth</u>
John	William
Matilda Sarah	Sarah
Mary Ann	Mary Anne
William Withey	Elizabeth

The explanation to the mystery of Gull's middle name seems to be that John Gull simply called him after his friend, William Withey. William Withey Gull's elder brother, John, was the son who followed in his father's footsteps, becoming a barge-master.

Alice Crook

Annie Crook's only surviving sister, Alice, like Annie, worked as a domestic servant. Age 18, she married Alfred Richard Jackson on 9 September 1886 in the Church of St Giles in the Fields. The church was adjacent to New Compton Street, where Alice Crook lived at No 23. Alfred and Alice Jackson lived at 10 Phoenix Street off the Charing Cross Road, later in 4 Wild Court off Kingsway. They had the following children: Alice Elizabeth, Alfred Richard, Charles Henry, Ethel Agnes, Lawrence Edward, Ellen Mary and Florence Edith. Alice lived to the age of 93, dying in St Pancras Hospital on 12th November 1961.

Crossingham's Lodging House

Both Annie Chapman and Elizabeth Stride lived at 35 Dorset Street just prior to their murders. This address has sometimes been regarded as Crossingham's Lodging House. William Crossingham, lodging-house keeper, actually resided at 16-17-18-19 Dorset Street so 35 Dorset Street was not Crossingham's. Obviously the numbers in Dorset Street ran consecutively.

Royal Naval College Osborne

It has been claimed that Prince Albert Victor, Duke of Clarence, could not have been hidden away in Osborne House on the Isle of Wight after his supposed death in 1892 because Osborne House was used as a training college for naval cadets from 1903 to 1921, the building being called the Royal Naval College Osborne. However, the Royal Naval College Osborne was not Osborne House. The college was built in the grounds of Osborne House some distance away - on the site of the old stables.

Inscribed Memorial

HERE STOOD
THE ROYAL NAVAL COLLEGE OSBORNE
WHERE SOME 4000 CADETS
BEGAN THEIR CAREERS IN
THE ROYAL NAVY

251

1903 - 1921
"FEAR GOD HONOUR THE KING"

Erected by surviving former
cadets with the support of
The Department of the Environment
1985

This plaque was unveiled
by
THE COUNTESS MOUNTBATTEN
14th August 1985

The memorial is located by the driveway leading u
to Osborne House.

Appendix V

Robert Cecil, Marquess of Salisbury

[In 1888: Prime Minister of Great Britain]
Robert Cecil, 3rd Marquess of Salisbury - descendant of the notorious anti-Catholic Robert Cecil, 1st Earl of Salisbury, the man infamously connected with the Gunpowder Plot of 1605.

Born: 3 February 1830, Hatfield House, Herts.
Parents: James Brownlow William Cecil, 2nd Marquess of Salisbury. Frances Mary Gascoyne.
Educated: Eton, then Christ Church, Oxford.
1854 Entered the Commons as a Conservative M.P.
1857 Married Lady Georgina Caroline Alderson, 11 July, St Mary Magdalene, Munster Square, Regent's Park.
1865   Made Viscount Cranborne.
1866   Secretary of State for India.
1868   Became Marquess of Salisbury.
1874   Secretary of State for India.
1878   Appointed Foreign Secretary.
1885-86   Prime Minister of Great Britain. [Gladstone was P.M. for part of 1886]
1886-92   Prime Minister of Great Britain. [And also Foreign Secretary from 1887]
1887 The mastermind behind the Jubilee Plot which was arranged to discredit Irish Roman Catholics.

1888   Directed the cover-up of Prince Albert Victor's Roman Catholic marriage which led to the Jack the Ripper murders.

1895-02 Prime Minister of Great Britain. [Relinquished the office of Foreign Secretary in 1900]
Retired in 1902.

1903 Died 22 Aug at Hatfield House - fell, then developed blood poisoning.

Sir Charles Warren

[In 1888: Commissioner of the Metropolitan Police]

Born: 7 February 1840, Bangor, North Wales.
Parents: Major-General Sir Charles Warren KCB, Mary Ann Hughes.
Educated: Bridgnorth, Cheltenham College, Sandhurst, RMA Woolwich.

1857   Commissioned into the Royal Engineers.

1859   Became a Freemason.

1863   Became Past Master. (Someone who has held the office of Master)

1864   Married (1 Sep) Fanny Margaretta Haydon in Guildford, Surrey.

1867-70 (Captain)   Warren   carried   out explorations in Palestine and archaeological excavations on, and under, the Temple Mount in Jerusalem, site of King Solomon's Temple.

1875   Promoted to Major, then brevet Lieutenant-Colonel. (Given rank above that for which he receives pay.)

1877   H.M. Commissioner. Laid down the boundary line of Griqualand West and the Orange Free State. (Griqualand East & Griqualand West were divisions of Cape Province, South Africa.)

Made CMG. [Companion of (the Order of) St Michael and St George]

1878   Became Lieutenant Colonel.

1882   Tracked down the murderers of Professor Palmer's expedition in Egypt. [In 1882, Britain supported the Khédive of Egypt against a rebellion by anti-European Egyptian nationalists. A group entered the Sinai peninsula to gather intelligence about Bedouin tribes. Professor Edward Henry Palmer, speaker of Arabic dialects, and an authority on the Bedouin, was executed (shot) on 11th August along with four others by the Bedouin. A military detachment led by Colonel Warren arrived at the murder site on 24 October. The scattered bones of the victims were found at the bottom of a gully. Those of the three British victims were gathered up and sent back to England. With the help of friendly Bedouin, the perpetrators were tracked down. Five Bedouin were executed for the murders, and eight imprisoned.]

1883   Knighted on 24 May: created KCMG. [Knight Commander of (the Order of) St Michael and St George]

1884   Appointed H.M. Commissioner to Bechuanaland. (Bechuanaland was a district in South Africa between the Zambesi and Orange rivers.)

Created Knight of Justice of (the order of) St John of Jerusalem. Became the founding Master of the lodge of Masonic research: Quatuor Coronati Lodge 2076.

1885   Awarded the GCMG. [Grand Cross of (the order of) St Michael and St George]

1886   Sir Edmund Henderson resigned as Commissioner of the Metropolitan Police on 8th February 1886, and Sir Charles Warren of the Royal Engineers was appointed in his place. [The marriage of Prince Albert Victor and Annie Elizabeth Crook must have taken place shortly before Warren's appointment. The Establishment knew that drastic action would soon have to be taken. A main requirement would be a man at the head of the Metropolitan Police whose loyalty they could totally depend on.]

1887   Involved, together with Salisbury, James Monro, and Robert Anderson, in the Jubilee Plot, which was set up in order to discredit Irish Catholic groups. In command of the police and soldiers during 'Bloody Sunday'.

1888   Created (7 Jan) KCB. [Knight Commander of (the Order of) the Bath] Controlled the police operation into the Jack the Ripper murders having organized the team to commit the murders. Wiped the 'Juwes' message from the wall in Goulston Street. Resigned (8 Nov) as Commissioner of the Metropolitan Police - knowing that the final murder of the series, the Kelly murder, was about to be carried out.

1891   District Grand Master [1891-1895] of the District Grand Lodge of the Eastern Archipelago.

1893   Promoted to Major-General.

1897   Promoted to Lieutenant-General.

1900   Commanded the 5th Division during the British failure at Spion Kop in the Second Boer War.

1904   Promoted to General.

1905   Retired from the army.

1927   Contracted influenza, then developed pneumonia. Died on 21st January.

Robert Anderson

[In 1888:   Assistant Commissioner of the Metropolitan Police and Head of CID]

A staunch Protestant. He described his ancestors as, 'among the Scotch colonists who made Ulster what it is.'

Born: 29 May 1841, Dublin.
Parents: Matthew [Crown Solicitor) and Mary Anderson
Educated: Trinity College, Dublin. BA (1862).

1863   Began his career as a barrister.

1865   Invited into secret-service work.

1868   Joined the Home Office in London. Spymaster. Ran spies in Irish groups, the Fenian Brotherhood and the Clan-na-Gael.

1873   Married Lady Agnes Alexandrina Moore, sister of the Earl of Drogheda.

1877   Appointed Irish Agent at the Home Office.

1884   Edward Jenkinson, head of the 'Secret Department' (anti-terrorist dept) in Whitehall, sacked Anderson, whom he disliked.

1886   Edward Jenkinson sacked.

1887   James Monro made head of the 'Secret Department'. Robert Anderson recalled. Appointed as Monro's assistant. Spymaster: Anderson ran informant inside the Irish group Clan-na-Gael. With Salisbury, Monro, and Warren, involved in the the Jubilee Plot.

1888　　　31st August: James Monro resigned as Assistant Commissioner of the Metropolitan Police supposedly after an argument with Warren. (see James Munro below) Robert Anderson appointed in his place *becoming Sir Charles Warren's right-hand man.* [Sir Charles Warren needed someone who took the same view as himself regarding the solution to the aftermath of the Prince Albert Victor-Annie Crook problem - someone who approved of the series of murders about to commence, the first of which was imminent.]

Anderson also appointed head of the Criminal Investigation Department. The first murder of the series took place on his first day. After the body of the second victim was discovered, Anderson claimed that (having been Assistant Commissioner for nine days) he was suffering from 'exhaustion from overwork' and took extended leave. He went on holiday to Switzerland. On 30th September (after the victims of the double-murder were found) he was sent a letter by the Home Secretary Henry Matthews, requesting that he urgently return to his post. Anderson decided to spend a week in Paris. He did not return until October 6th.

1901　　　Knighted: created KCB. [Knight Commander of (the Order of) the Bath] [Robert Anderson received a knighthood - presumably as reward for services to the Government.]

1918　　　Contracted influenza and died shortly afterwards, on 15th November, at 39 Linden Garden, Notting Hill Gate.

James Monro

[In 1888: Head of the Secret Department]

Born: 25 November 1838, Edinburgh.
Parents: George Munro [Solicitor], Margaret Anderson.
Educated: Edinburgh High School, then Edinburgh and Berlin Universities.

1857   Joined the Bengal Civil Service.
1863   Married Ruth Littlejohn.
1877   Became Inspector-General of the Bengal Police.
1884   Returned to Britain to become Assistant Commissioner of the Metropolitan Police, and head of CID.
1887   Appointed   head   of   the   'Secret Department'   [Special Branch] involved in intelligence operations against Irish terrorists. A major participant in the Jubilee Plot.
1888   Forced out from his position after a so-called argument with Sir Charles Warren, resigning 31st of August (the day of the first Ripper murder) from his posts of Assistant Commissioner and head of CID. Remained as head of the 'Secret Department' Scotland Yard. [The public reason given for the row with Warren was that *grave differences of opinion on questions of police administration had arisen between them.* The real reason, surely, was that he refused to support his superior, Sir Charles Warren, by condoning cold-blooded murder. *Hence, James Monro was moved aside for the period of the Jack the Ripper murders,* and

replaced by Warren's friend, Robert Anderson. Monro could not be sacked - he knew too much - so he was eased aside for a limited period. The truth was later told to his son, when Monro revealed that he had *'refused to do what he had considered to be wrong'*.]

On 24 November, James Monro returned, this time as the Chief Commissioner of the Metropolitan Police, Warren having resigned on the eve of the murder he knew to be the last in the series.

1890   Resigned from the police and returned to Bengal, where he founded and ran the Abode of Mercy Medical Mission, in Ranaghat.

1905   Retired. Returned to England, where he wrote a book called 'Preparing for the Second Coming'.

1920   James Monro died on 28th January.

Appendix VI

Sickert after 1888

Walter Sickert had married Ellen Melicent Cobden, a writer, on 10 June 1885 in Marylebone, London. She was the daughter of the politician, Richard Cobden.

1890-95 Sickert created illustrations and caricatures which were published in magazines.

1896 Ellen Cobden left Walter Sickert because of his many affairs.

1899 Divorced from Ellen Cobden on 27 July. [Sickert was a womaniser. Regarding Ellen Cobden: 'But in those days, when divorce was actually a social slur, they obviously found life together so impossible that they decided to separate. They were eventually divorced in 1899. It was the first of what the lawyers call "constructive desertion," for Sickert was held to have deserted his wife, although it was she who left the house, because he had brought his mistresses to live there.' (Sickert, by Lillian Browse, 1960)

'After his divorce from Ellen Cobden, he left England for six years and made his home in Dieppe.' (Sickert, by Lillian Browse, 1960)

[Further confirmation that Sickert *did not leave London* for Dieppe until *long after* the so-called Jack the Ripper murders.]

1899-1905 Walter Sickert lived in the port of Dieppe, France.

1904-05   He was said to have had an affair with Alice Margaret Crook. [A son named Charles is reputed to have been born in 1905.]

'Twice at least he tried to remarry - at Rowlandson House he proposed to a student who refused him. The second time, so the story goes, his future bride got cold feet at the last moment and did not turn up at the church.' (Sickert, by Lillian Browse, 1960)

[The above event, when his beloved got cold feet, happened in 1911. Sickert proposed to a student from his class at Westminster Technical Institute. He was jilted when his 'intended' failed to turn up at Camden Town Register Office on 3rd June 1911.]

He obviously made a speedy recovery from this emotional trauma, because:

1911   On 29th July, Sickert married Christine Drummond Angus, the daughter of Henry Angus, a Scottish leather merchant, at Paddington Register Office.

1918-22   The Sickerts lived in Envermeu, about 12 miles inland from Dieppe.

1920   Walter Sickert's second wife died of tuberculosis in October. [Christine Drummond Angus was a skilled embroiderer. Proving that Sickert still had royal connections, one of Christine Sickert' creations, a garment of blue damask, known as the Blue Tunicle, was later used at the Coronation of King George VI and Lady Elizabeth Bowes-Lyon in Westminster Abbey in 1937.]

The Blue Tunicle

1925   Sickert began a second affair with Alice Margaret Crook from which Joseph Sickert (registered Joseph Gorman) was born on 22nd Oct 1925.

1926   Walter Sickert married his third wife, Elaine Thérèse Lessore, an artist, on 4th June.

1927   Elected President of the Royal Society of British Artists.

1935   Resigned as President of the Royal Society of British Artists.

1938   The Sickerts moved to Bathampton, less than a mile from Bath.

1942   Walter Sickert died at Bathampton on 22nd January.

Appendix VII

Frederick George Abberline

[In 1888: Inspector investigating the Jack th
Ripper murders]

Born: 8th January 1843, Blandford, Dorset.
Parents: Edward Abberline, a saddler and Sheriff
Officer. Hannah Chinn.

1863   Frederick George Abberline joined th
Metropolitan Police.
1865   Promoted to Sergeant. (seems a ver
quick promotion)
1868   He married Martha Mackness i
Islington. She died of tuberculosis two months later.
1873   Promoted to Inspector.
1876   Abberline married Emma Beamont.
1878   Transferred to H Division (H wa
Whitechapel) where he acquired detailed knowledge c
the East End. [He was stationed at the Police Station i
Commercial Street - amazingly close to streets such a
Dorset Street (Miller's Court), Flower and Dean Stree
and Thrawl Street, where the women involved in th
Ripper murders would be staying in 1888. These stree
branched off Commercial Street. They were only
stone's throw away.]
1887   Transferred to Scotland Yard on 25
July (specifically to CO CID) CO - Commissioner
Office (aka Scotland Yard). [There must have been
reason for this transfer to the Commissioner's Office.

seems certain that the blackmail note had recently arrived from Whitechapel. His local knowledge would be invaluable.]

1888   February 9th, promoted to Inspector 1st Class. Deeply involved in the investigation of the Jack the Ripper murders.

1889   Officer in charge of the police inquiry into the Cleveland Street brothel scandal.

1890   Promoted to Chief Inspector. Despite utter failure in the Jack the Ripper and Cleveland Street cases (looking from the viewpoint that in catching the serial killer, and bringing the main offenders to justice, his investigations were total failures) Abberline is rewarded with promotion. *Of course, from the Government's point of view, his investigations had resulted in complete success.*

1892   Just 49, Abberline retired on 7th February. He received full pension. After his retirement, Frederick George Abberline was employed by the Pinkerton Detective Agency of America, becoming the Pinkerton Agent in Europe.

1893   Wrote in his diary that Annie Chapman's mother, Ruth, died in this year. *This was 5 years after Annie's murder.* Abberline must have kept a check on the surviving adult members of the families of the Ripper victims - *no doubt to make sure that information which (he thought) the murdered women possessed had not been passed on, enabling it to resurface.* There was no group extorting blackmail. Just Mary Jane.

1904   Abberline retired to Bournemouth.

1911   Moved to 195 Holdenhurst Road, Bournemouth, where he opened a guest-house.

1929   Abberline died 10th December, aged 86.

Seventy-two years after the death of Inspector Abberline, and one hundred and thirteen years after the Whitechapel murders, the following ceremony took place:

Saturday, 29th September, 2001: John Grieve, Deputy Assistant Commissioner of the Metropolitan Police, with the Mayor of Bournemouth, unveiled a blue plaque in recognition of Inspector Abberline on his former house at 195 Holdenhurst Road. Details on this plaque include:

"Estcourt" The Final Home of Inspector Frederick George Abberline 1843-1929

Became Well Known for His Work on The Case of Jack The Ripper

The Abberline plaque is said to be the first of its kind to be set up in memory of an ordinary police officer. *Joseph Sickert, son of Walter Richard Sickert was present at the unveiling.* This plaque, celebrating Frederick George Abberline, appears to commemorate total failure, but it is, of course, a silent memorial to absolute success.

However, does the credit not belong to Lieutenant Col. Charles Warren rather than Inspector Abberline? Surely it is Warren who deserves recognition for the success of their mission. He, after all, ran the operation, not Abberline.

Postscript

Sarah Annie Dryden

One of the key points about the marriage of Annie Elizabeth Crook and Prince Albert Victor is that Annie was stated to have been a Roman Catholic like her mother, Sarah Annie Dryden, while her three sisters were Church of England like their father, William Crook. This has always seemed extremely odd, and of course, any evidence of the Catholic connection has long since vanished.

> William Crook   born 1830
> (Church of England)
> Sarah Annie Dryden   born 1838-1841
> (Roman Catholic)

Each census: 1871-1881-1891 suggests she was born between April 1838 - March 1839. Her death details give a birth year of 1840-1841. The censuses are far more likely to be accurate. Would she have said she was 32, 42, 52, when she was 30, 40, 50? Not a chance.

> Annie Elizabeth Crook (Roman Catholic)
> Sarah Mary Crook (Church of England)
> Alice Crook (Church of England)
> Catherine Crook (Church of England)

Although the above situation would seem exceptional amazingly, the Crook family circumstances are actually mirrored in a Scottish family named - *Dryden.*

It is interesting to reflect on her connection to the Dryden family from Edinburgh:

William Dryden - Margaret Revilliod
Born 22 Oct 1810   Bap 10 March 1812
Canongate, Edinburgh.   St Mary's R.C., Edinburgh.

William Dryden   chr 27 Feb 1831 (Church of
                                        Scotland)
Margaret Dryden   chr 9 Jan 1833 (Roman Catholic)
Jane Dryden   chr   2 Apr 1835 (Roman Catholic)
James Dryden   chr 21 Oct 1839 (Roman Catholic)
Ann Dryden   chr   2 Jun 1842 (Roman Catholic)
Williamina Dryden born 11 Oct 1848 (Church of
                                        Scotland)
Martha Dryden   chr 28 Jan 1852 (Church of
                                        Scotland)

The Crook family account stated that Sarah Dryden arrived in London from *Edinburgh* circa 1851.

Her birth could have taken place *right in the middle of the four children baptized as Roman Catholics* between April 1838 – Dec. 1838, during the exact period when the censuses suggest that it *did* take place. This could well be the family of Sarah Annie Dryden. If so, there would not be any surviving record of her Roman Catholic baptism.

On the 1881 Census, her place of birth is listed as Scotland.

On the 1891 Census (after the murders), her place of birth is listed as - Scotland. Berwick.

[Berwick had been part of England since 1482, and was classed as 'a county of itself' since 1836.]
The Berwick entry was probably added to mislead.

Index

274

279

Kelly, William 157
Kensit, John 64
Kent, James 74
Kentwin House 232
Kew Chapel 17-18
Keyler, Mrs Alice 105
Kidney, Michael 78
King George V 225, 242, 248
King George VI, coronation 262
King James I 43-44, 47, 49, 53
King Louis XIV 49
King Solomon's Temple 86, 137, 235, 254
Kirby, Colonel Sir Alfred 117
Knight, Stephen 7, 72, 75, 86, 94, 211, 234
Knysna 23-25

Labouchere, Henry, MP 204
Lalla Bill 247
Langthorne Road Cemetery 116
Langtry, Lillie 125, 127-128
Lawrence, T.E. 125, 129-130
Lazarus Breaks His Fast (Sickert) 153-154
Lees, Robert 211-213
Leman Street Police Station 169
Letchford, Charles 81-83
Lewis and Lewis 224, 226
Lewis, Sarah 105-106
Lightfoot, Hannah 16-22, 27
Lilly, Marjorie 147, 149
Limerick 94, 159-160, 163, 166, 169, 171
Linden Gardens 258
Little Dot Hetherington at the Old Bedford (Sickert) 150
Littlemore Asylum 37-38
Liverpool 156-158, 165, 177
Lloyd, Marie 125
London Fever Hospital 218
Long, (PC) Harry 86

282

288

Bibliography

Books

Jack The Ripper: The Final Solution, Stephen Knight (George G. Harrap, 1976).
The Ripper & The Royals, Melvyn Fairclough (Duckworth, 1991).
The Private World of St John Terrapin, Chapman Pincher (Sidgwick & Jackson, 1982).
The Life and Opinions of Walter Sickert, Robert Emmons (Faber and Faber, 1941).
Sickert, Lillian Browse (Rupert Hart-Davis, 1960).
Victorian Sensation, Michael Diamond (Anthem, 2003).
Fenian Fire, Christy Campbell (Harper Collins, 2002).

Archives

Liverpool Record Office.
City of Westminster Archives Centre, London.
Catholic Family History Society, London.
Catholic Family History Society, Kent.
Berwick-upon-Tweed Record Office.
London Metropolitan Archives, London.
British Newspaper Library, London.
National Archives of Scotland, Edinburgh.
British Library, London.
Cheshire Record Office, Chester.
National Archives, Kew.
Catholic Family History Society, West Midlands.

Family Records Centre, London.
Catholic Children's Society, London.
Catholic Archives Society, Hertfordshire.
County Record Office, Flintshire.
Oxfordshire Health Archives, Oxford.
Westminster Register Office, London.
Camden Archives, London.
Liverpool & SW Lancashire Family History Society,
Liverpool.
Centre for Buckinghamshire Studies.
Buckinghamshire Family History Society.
Argyll and Bute Registration Office, Argyll.
Scottish Catholic Archives, Edinburgh.
Archdiocese of Glasgow.
Religious Society of Friends in Britain, London.
Dumfries and Galloway Archives, Dumfries.
Golden Common Parish Council, Winchester.
Wiltshire & Swindon Record Office, Wiltshire.
Bury St Edmunds Register Office, Suffolk.
Lewisham Archives, London.
Isle of Wight Registration Office.
University of St Andrews.
Admiralty Library, Ministry of Defence, London.
Church of England Record Centre, London.
Dorset Record Office, Dorchester.

Newspapers

Daily News (1888)
Daily Telegraph (1888)
East London Advertiser (1888 & 1973)
Illustrated Police News (1888)
London Morning Advertiser (1888)

Marylebone Mercury & West London Gazette (1903)
Pall Mall Gazette (1888)
Reynold's Newspaper (1888)
The New York Times (1889)
The Star (1888)
The Sun (1987)
The Sunday Times-Herald, Chicago (1895)
The Times (1849 & 1888)

Churches

Our Lady of the Assumption and St Gregory Roman Catholic Church, Golden Square, London.
Our Lady of the Rosary Roman Catholic Church, Old Marylebone Road, London.
Sacred Heart Roman Catholic Church, Lauriston Street, Edinburgh.
St Aloysius Roman Catholic Church, Phoenix Road, London.
St Anne's Roman Catholic Church, Laxton Place, London.
St Anselm and St Cecilia Roman Catholic Church, Lincoln's Inn Fields, London.
St Charles Borromeo Roman Catholic Church, Ogle Street, London.
St Etheldreda's Roman Catholic Church, Holborn Circus, London.
St James's Roman Catholic Church, Spanish Place, London.
St Mary of The Angels Roman Catholic Church, Moorhouse Road, London.
St Mary's Roman Catholic Cathedral, Broughton Street, Edinburgh.

St Mary's Roman Catholic Church, Regent Road, Great Yarmouth.

St Pancras Parish Church, Euston Road, London.

St Patrick's Roman Catholic Church, High Street Edinburgh.

St Patrick's Roman Catholic Church, Soho Square London.

The Faithful Virgin Roman Catholic Church, Central Hill, London.

The Immaculate Conception Roman Catholic Church Farm Street, London.

Lightning Source UK Ltd.
Milton Keynes UK
UKOW042037110313

207488UK00004B/610/P